RED MEN AND WHITE

Specimen Jones

THE BARNES & NOBLE LIBRARY OF ESSENTIAL READING

RED MEN AND WHITE

OWEN WISTER

ILLUSTRATED BY FREDERIC REMINGTON

INTRODUCTION BY ROBERT L. DORMAN

BARNES & NOBLE
NEW YORK

CONTENTS

LIST OF ILLUSTRATIONS

TO

S. B. W. AND O. J. W.

FROM THEIR SON

INTRODUCTION

INDIAN WARS, LYNCH MOBS, DESERT CROSSINGS, MINING CAMPS, AND stagecoach robberies—all are brought vividly to life in Owen Wister's *Red Men and White*, the first book of western stories written by the author of the classic cowboy novel *The Virginian*. Published in 1895, most of the stories are based on actual events as told to Wister during his extensive travels in the Old West. Filled with humor, drama, and tragedy, *Red Men and White* offers a fascinating glimpse of Wister's writing at a time when he was laying the foundations of the modern western.

Owen Wister was born into Philadelphia high society in 1860. His grandmother was the renowned Shakespearean actress Fanny Kemble, and his mother, Sarah Butler Wister, was a respected literary critic and close friend of novelist Henry James. His father, Owen Jones Wister, was a prominent physician from an old Pennsylvania family. After graduating from Harvard, the younger Wister floundered in search of a profession, until a mysterious illness in 1885 sent him on a journey west to recuperate. There he found his purpose in life as a writer seeking to capture the frontier characters and western landscapes that he grew to love. Wister published numerous stories in *Harper's* magazine during the 1890s, many of them illustrated by the artist Frederic Remington. *Red Men and White* solidified Wister's reputation and brought comparisons to Rudyard Kipling. It was followed by a western novel, *Lin McLean* (1897), and another volume of short stories, *The Jimmyjohn Boss* (1900). Wister capped off this most fertile period of his career with *The Virginian* (1902), which became a phenomenal best seller and is credited with transforming the cowboy into a national icon. His later writings included a novel, *Lady Baltimore* (1906), as well as biographies and political commentaries. Wister moved in the most exclusive social circles and was a frequent guest at President Theodore Roosevelt's White House. In the latter years of his life, he encouraged and supported new writers such as Ernest Hemingway and Sinclair Lewis. Wister's last collection of western stories, *When West Was West*, appeared in 1928, ten years before his death.

How a person like Owen Wister became famous for writing stories like those in *Red Men and White* may at first seem puzzling. It was an improbable fate for someone who was raised in the rarefied world of boarding schools and country estates and who once seriously aspired to become a classical composer. Part of the answer lies in the stories themselves: they very much reflect the broader social concerns and anxieties of white educated middle-and upper-class Americans in the late nineteenth century. Three of the stories from *Red Men and White*, "Little Big Horn Medicine," "Specimen Jones," and "The General's Bluff," are episodes from the Indian wars, just ending in 1891. Two other stories, "The Serenade at Siskiyou" and "Salvation Gap," are concerned with vigilante justice—the 1890s witnessed a historically large number of lynchings, particularly in the South (as Wister describes in his preface) but also happening nationwide. Two more of the stories, "The Second Missouri Compromise" and "A Pilgrim on the Gila," which focus on political corruption, were certain to resonate with readers during the decade when a widespread political revolt was challenging both major parties. "La Tinaja Bonita," with its multicultural love triangle, involved questions of ethnic, racial, and gender boundaries in a period when high levels of immigration were remaking life in America's cities also resonated with readers. Seeking to explain the West as a setting for these picturesque tales, Wister in his preface refers to the country's "uneven" historical development, which had resulted in "various centuries . . . jostled together as they are today upon this continent." Yet even if one granted his idea that the West remained a throwback to an earlier time, untouched by progress, the topics of Wister's western stories were as current as the day's headlines.

Above all, *Red Men and White* expressed a desire for *order* in a very disorderly era, a central problem for men of Wister's elite class and background. Such men, exemplified by Theodore Roosevelt, believed that it was up to them to bring order to the nation, with themselves at the top of the social heap. Wister's well-trained ear may have allowed him to convey the speech and dialog of common people, but there is no denying that he was something of a snob. To his credit, he made true friends among the soldiers, cowboys, and wilderness guides that he met on his many trips roughing it in the West, though inevitably some of them borrowed money or were otherwise indebted to him. His attitude toward minorities and others whom he considered his social inferiors was stated all too plainly in an important essay, "The Evolution of the Cow-Puncher," published in September 1895, two months before *Red Men and White* appeared in bookstores. "No rood of modern ground is more debased and mongrel with its hordes of encroaching alien vermin," he wrote, "that turn our cities to Babels and our citizenship into a hybrid farce. . . ." The essay had substantial input from Frederic Remington, who if anything was dimmer in his views of the lower classes. Nevertheless, Wister thought well enough of it to include the essay as a new preface for a later edition of *Red Men and White*. He obviously saw the two works as complementary. The stories dramatized situations of disorder, sometimes set right by characters acting singly or collectively; the essay defined the type of individual who could achieve such mastery: "the Saxon," who throughout history had been "conqueror, invader, navigator, buccaneer, explorer, colonist, tiger-shooter."[1] Such a man became Wister's ideal of the western hero.

This heroic type (or archetype) was eventually personified in Wister's greatest creation, the character known as the Virginian, but it already hovered behind the various plots of *Red Men and White*. In "Specimen Jones," for example, the title character uses his wits in an attempt to avert probable bloodshed with some Apaches, and he does the same for a clique of disgruntled ex-Confederates in "The Second Missouri Compromise." Similarly, the real-life General George Crook in "The General's Bluff" is shown to be every inch the cool customer, seeking to persuade the volatile Indian chief E-egante and his people to yield to federal authority. At times, however, words and stratagems were insufficient, and force became necessary to preserve order, Wister believed. His western men were made of stern stuff, as he depicts with the soldiers confronting the messianic Cheschapah's foolishness in "Little Big Horn Medicine," and with the male citizens in "The Serenade at Siskiyou," who have little patience with the do-gooder meddling of their womenfolk in a matter of crime and punishment. More starkly, his male characters might violently redress offenses against their manhood perpetrated by women, as occurs at the hands of Drylyn in "Salvation Gap" and of Genesmere in "La Tinaja Bonita." And as Wister explores in "A Pilgrim on the Gila," where a classic western holdup is only the most visible sign of a whole web of official corruption, there were also those situations in dire need of a hero, but none appears.

Wister found his ideal of the western hero to be heartening, if not therapeutic, given his general pessimism about turn-of-the-century America and his own prospects within it. He had originally gone west in 1885 suffering from neurasthenia, a diagnostic grab-bag that physicians of the period applied to a wide range of poorly understood physical and psychological problems. Curiously, neurasthenia was never observed among ordinary people; it seemed only to afflict the extra-sensitive natures of the upper crust, who seemed especially susceptible to the pressures and clamor of modern urban-industrial life. Wister's own case occurred after he had abandoned his dream of becoming a composer for a more respectable but humdrum career as a stock-broker, or perhaps a lawyer. He was the only child of demanding and exacting parents, with whom he remained too close; he sent a letter home to his overbearing mother every week well into adulthood. Bored and at loose ends after graduating from college, Wister had lived a rather dissipated life in Boston and co-wrote a risqué novel that was never published. With law school at Harvard looming in the fall of 1885, Wister in June succumbed to some sort of breakdown, and S. Weir Mitchell, the foremost expert on neurasthenia, advised him to take a "rest cure" on a ranch in Wyoming Territory.

Wister had lived and traveled widely in Europe, but prior to this trip had not been more than an hour's train-ride westward from the

East Coast. The ranch was situated at 6,600 feet elevation near the Laramie Mountains, a place completely new to his experience. As Wister's eastern dude narrator in *The Virginian* remarks, looking on the same exotic scene, "'What world am I in?' I said aloud. 'Does this same planet hold Fifth Avenue?'" Wister was quickly rejuvenated by several weeks of "living in the open air, and basking in the perfection of content," camping, hunting, and horseback riding, even helping out at some roundups. His mouthpiece in *The Virginian* summed up the effect on him: "No lotus land ever cast its spell upon a man's heart more than Wyoming had enchanted mine." Yet beyond his sense of personal renewal, this stay and his many subsequent sojourns in the West evoked for Wister, viscerally and powerfully, the myth of the frontier: the notion that a new America—and a new type of American—was being created in the free, pristine, boundless West. It was the "great playground of young men," where their manhood could be tested by nature, savages, and villains, and where their inner Saxon could be unleashed.[2]

The trouble for Wister was that the West was not new, free, pristine, or boundless. Oppression, violence, crime, and corruption occurred there, as did the process of historical change. A number of scholars and critics have noted that Wister in his short stories of the 1890s sought somehow to freeze the passage of time, to achieve with words what Remington seemed to do with paint and sculpture. He wanted to preserve the Wild West and what it stood for as a timeless monument, to depict it as myth rather than as history. Wister's conceit in the preface to *Red Men and White* that the West existed in another century was one hallmark of this attempt, as was the assertion in his "Cow-Puncher" article that the medieval knight and the cowboy were "nothing but the same Saxon of different environments . . . in each shape changelessly untamed."[3] But change had come to the West well before Wister wrote those defiant words. His first arrival in Wyoming virtually coincided with the beginning of the end of the open-range cattle kingdom and the heyday of the cowboy in the West. The terrible winter of 1886–87 decimated herds and drove many operations out of business, including the very ranch where Wister had spent his enchanting summer. The surrender of Apache resistance leader Geronimo in 1886 and the massacre of the Sioux at Wounded Knee in 1890 signaled the conclusion of the Indian wars. In 1893, historian Frederick Jackson Turner gave his famous paper, "The Significance of the Frontier in American History," in which he pronounced the centuries-old frontier closed and saw the country now entering a new and uncertain phase in its historical development. More alarmingly to the conservative Wister, labor strikes and political radicalism were spreading across the West by the mid-1890s, as hard economic times hit the nation. But rather than dwell on all of these developments, he attempted to retreat to the West of his imagination, finding refuge in stories from "ancient surviving centuries" such as those collected in *Red Men and White*.

Wister was only partly successful, as *Red Men and White* reveals—his anxieties still bled through to the story lines. He made his last stand with *The Virginian*, and it could be argued that with this work he did ultimately succeed in creating a timeless Old West, if indirectly. Countless pulp novels as well as western movies and television series, consumed by generation after generation of Americans, can be traced back to the formula concocted in Wister's novel. (*The Virginian* itself was made into no less than five movie versions, the earliest by Cecil B. DeMille in 1914 and the latest produced as recently as 2000.) For Wister personally, however, the mythic vision of the West could not be sustained. He had preserved the West in *Red Men and White* and his two subsequent works of the 1890s. But by the ending of *The Virginian*, it is clear that progress and industry were arriving to close down the "great playground of young men," sealed symbolically by the marriage of the Virginian to the schoolmarm. Certainly, Wister's own marriage and large family may have contributed to his change in mindset. As he put it in *Members of the Family* (1911), one of only two western books that he published after *The Virginian*, "The nomadic, bachelor West is over, the housed, married West is established." He now saw that it had been an "illusion" to think that the "eternal Saturday," the "happy hunting-ground" of his youth, could ever be "permanent."[4]

Wister's later collections of stories, written sporadically over three decades, contrast significantly with *Red Men and White*. Most scholars agree that they are by turns darker and more superficial. Wister was largely done with the West by the time those books appeared in the

1910s and 1920s, reluctant to visit it and instead preferring to vacation in Europe. In one of his last works, though—*Roosevelt: The Story of a Friendship* (1930)—he recalled the fervor that had originally driven him to begin writing of the West in 1891. Wister justly placed himself among the triumvirate who had more or less invented the Old West for modern Americans. He remembered vividly a dinner conversation during which he and a companion talked about the West in literature. They praised Roosevelt, who by that time had already written a book about his experiences as a rancher, and they agreed that Remington's illustrations were capturing the public's imagination. But where was the American Kipling who would enshrine the West in fiction, which as everyone knew, always outlasted fact? That very evening in the autumn of 1891, Wister left the dinner, ran upstairs, and began to write his first western story.

Robert L. Dorman, Ph.D., is monographs librarian and an assistant professor at Oklahoma City University. He is the author of *Revolt of the Provinces: The Regionalist Movement in America, 1920–1945.*

PREFACE

THESE EIGHT STORIES ARE MADE FROM OUR WESTERN FRONTIER AS IT was in a past as near as yesterday and almost as bygone as the Revolution; so swiftly do we proceed. They belong to each other in a kinship of life and manners, and a little through the nearer tie of having here and there a character in common. Thus they resemble faintly the separate parts of a whole, and gain, perhaps, something of the invaluable weight of length; and they have been received by my closest friends with suspicion.

Many sorts of Americans live in America; and the Atlantic American, it is to be feared, often has a cautious and conventional imagination. In his routine he has lived unaware of the violent and romantic era in eruption upon his soil. Only the elk-hunter has at times returned with tales at which the other Atlantic Americans have deported themselves politely; and similarly, but for the assurances of western readers, I should have come to doubt the truth of my own impressions. All this is most natural.

If you will look upon the term "United States" as describing what we are, you must put upon it a strict and Federal construction. We undoubtedly use the city of Washington for our general business office, and in the event of a foreign enemy upon our coasts we should stand bound together more stoutly than we have shown ourselves since 1776. But as we are now, seldom has a great commonwealth been seen less united in its stages of progress, more uneven in its degrees of enlightenment. Never, indeed, it would seem, have such various centuries been jostled together as they are today upon this continent, and within the boundaries of our nation. We have taken the ages out of their processional arrangement and set them marching disorderly abreast in our wide territory, a harlequin platoon. We citizens of the United States date our letters 18—, and speak of ourselves as living in the present era; but the accuracy of that custom depends upon where we happen to be writing. While portions of New York, Chicago, and San Francisco are of this nineteenth century, we have many ancient periods surviving among us. What do you say, for example, to the Kentucky and Tennessee mountaineers, with their vendettas of blood descending from father to son? That was once the prevailing fashion of revenge. Yet even before the day when Columbus sailed had certain communities matured beyond it. This sprout of the Middle Ages flourishes fresh and green some five hundred miles and five hundred years from New York. In the single state of Texas you will find a contrast more violent still. There, not long ago, an African was led upon a platform in a public place for people to see, and tortured slowly to death with knives and fire. To witness this scene young men and women came in crowds. It is said that the railroad ran a special train for spectators from a distance. How might that audience of Paris, Texas, appropriately date its letters? Not Anno Domini, but many years BC. The African deserves no pity. His hideous crime was enough to drive a father to any madness, and too many such monsters have by their acts made Texas justly desperate. But for American citizens to crowd to the retribution, and look on as at a holiday show, reveals the Inquisition, the Pagans, the Stone Age, unreclaimed in our republic. On the other hand, the young men and women who will watch side by side the burning of a negro shrink from using such words as bull or stallion in polite society; many in Texas will say, instead, *male cow* and *caviard horse* (a term spelled as they pronounce it), and consider that delicacy is thus achieved. Yet in this lump Texas holds leaven as sterling as in any state; but it has far to spread.

It were easy to proceed from Maine to California instancing the remote centuries that are daily colliding within our domain, but this is enough to show how little we cohere in opinions. How many states and territories is it that we count united under our Stars and Stripes? I know that there are some forty-five or more, and that though I belong among the original thirteen, it has been my happiness to journey in all the others, in most of them, indeed, many times, for the sake of making my country's acquaintance. With no spread-eagle brag do I gather conviction each year that we Americans, judged not hastily, are sound at heart, kind, courageous, often of the truest delicacy, and always ultimately of excellent good-sense. With such belief, or, rather, knowledge, it is sorrowful to see our fatal complacence, our as yet undisciplined folly, in sending to our state legislatures and to that general business office of ours at Washington a herd of mismanagers that seems each year to grow more inefficient and contemptible, whether branded Republican or Democrat. But I take heart, because often and oftener I hear upon my journey the citizens high and low muttering, "There's too much politics in this country"; and we shake hands.

But all this is growing too serious for a book of short stories. They are about Indians and soldiers and events west of the Missouri. They belong to the past thirty years of our development, but you will find some of those ancient surviving centuries in them if you take my view. In certain ones the incidents, and even some of the names, are left unchanged from their original reality. The visit of Young-man-afraid-of-his-horses to the Little Big Horn and the rise and fall of the young Crow impostor, General Crook's surprise of E-egante, and many other occurrences, noble and ignoble, are told as they were told to me by those who saw them. When our national life, our own soil, is so rich in adventures to record, what need is there for one to call upon his invention save to draw, if he can, characters who shall fit these strange and dramatic scenes? One cannot improve upon such realities. If this fiction is at all faithful to the truth from which it springs, let the thanks be given to the patience and boundless hospitality of the Army friends and other friends across the Missouri who have housed my body and instructed my mind. And if the stories entertain the ignorant without grieving the judicious I am content.

LITTLE BIG HORN MEDICINE

SOMETHING NEW WAS HAPPENING AMONG THE CROW INDIANS. A YOUNG pretender had appeared in the tribe. What this might lead to was unknown alike to white man and to red; but the old Crow chiefs discussed it in their councils, and the soldiers at Fort Custer, and the civilians at the agency twelve miles up the river, and all the white settlers in the valley discussed it also. Lieutenants Stirling and Haines, of the First Cavalry, were speculating upon it as they rode one afternoon.

"Can't tell about Indians," said Stirling. "But I think the Crows are too reasonable to go on the warpath."

"Reasonable!" said Haines. He was young, and new to Indians.

"Just so. Until you come to his superstitions, the Indian can reason as straight as you or I. He's perfectly logical."

"Logical!" echoed Haines again. He held the regulation eastern view that the Indian knows nothing but the three blind appetites.

"You'd know better," remarked Stirling, "if you'd been fighting 'em for fifteen years. They're as shrewd as Æsop's fables."

Just then two Indians appeared round a bluff—one old and shabby, the other young and very gaudy—riding side by side.

"That's Cheschapah," said Stirling. "That's the agitator in all his feathers. His father, you see, dresses more conservatively."

The feathered dandy now did a singular thing. He galloped towards the two officers almost as if to bear them down, and, steering much too close, flashed by yelling, amid a clatter of gravel.

1

"Nice manners," commented Haines. "Seems to have a chip on his shoulder."

But Stirling looked thoughtful. "Yes," he muttered, "he has a chip."

Meanwhile the shabby father was approaching. His face was mild and sad, and he might be seventy. He made a gesture of greeting. "How!" he said, pleasantly, and ambled on his way.

"Now there you have an object lesson," said Stirling. "Old Pounded Meat has no chip. The question is, are the fathers or the sons going to run the Crow Nation?"

"Why did the young chap have a dog on his saddle?" inquired Haines.

"I didn't notice it. For his supper, probably—probably he's getting up a dance. He is scheming to be a chief. Says he is a medicine-man, and can make water boil without fire; but the big men of the tribe take no stock in him—not yet. They've seen soda water before. But I'm told this water-boiling astonishes the young."

"You say the old chiefs take no stock in him *yet?*"

"Ah, that's the puzzle. I told you just now Indians could reason."

"And I was amused."

"Because you're an eastern man. I tell you, Haines, if it wasn't my business to shoot Indians I'd study them."

"You're a crank," said Haines.

But Stirling was not a crank. He knew that so far from being a mere animal, the Indian is of a subtlety more ancient than the Sphinx. In his primal brain—nearer nature than our own—the directness of a child mingles with the profoundest cunning. He believes easily in powers of light and darkness, yet is a skeptic all the while. Stirling knew this; but he could not know just when, if ever, the young charlatan Cheschapah would succeed in cheating the older chiefs; just when, if ever, he would strike the chord of their superstition. Till then they would reason that the white man was more comfortable as a friend than as a foe, that rations and gifts of clothes and farming implements were better than battles and prisons. Once their superstition was set alight, these three thousand Crows might suddenly follow Cheschapah to burn and kill and destroy.

"How does he manage his soda water, do you suppose?" inquired Haines.

"That's mysterious. He has never been known to buy drugs, and he's careful where he does his trick. He's still a little afraid of his father. All Indians are. It's queer where he was going with that dog."

Hard galloping sounded behind them, and a courier from the Indian agency overtook and passed them, hurrying to Fort Custer. The officers hurried too, and, arriving, received news and orders. Forty Sioux were reported up the river coming to visit the Crows. It was peaceable, but untimely. The Sioux agent over at Pine Ridge had given these forty permission to go, without first finding out if it would be convenient to the Crow agent to have them come. It is a rule of the Indian Bureau that if one tribe desire to visit another, the agents of both must consent. Now, most of the Crows were farming and quiet, and it was not wise that a visit from the Sioux and a season of feasting should tempt their hearts and minds away from the tilling of the soil. The visitors must be taken charge of and sent home.

"Very awkward, though," said Stirling to Haines. He had been ordered to take two troops and arrest the unoffending visitors on their way. "The Sioux will be mad, and the Crows will be madder. What a bungle! And how like the way we manage Indian affairs!" And so they started.

Thirty miles away, by a stream towards which Stirling with his command was steadily marching through the night, the visitors were gathered. There was a cook-fire and a pot, and a stewing dog leaped in the froth. Old men in blankets and feathers sat near it, listening to young Cheschapah's talk in the flighty luster of the flames. An old squaw acted as interpreter between Crow and Sioux. Round about, at a certain distance, the figures of the crowd lounged at the edge of the darkness. Two grizzled squaws stirred the pot, spreading a clawed fist to their eyes against the red heat of the coals, while young Cheschapah harangued the older chiefs.

"And more than that, I, Cheschapah, can do," said he, boasting in Indian fashion. "I know how to make the white man's heart soft so he cannot fight." He paused for effect, but his hearers seemed uninterested. "You have come pretty far to see us," resumed the orator, "and I, and my friend Two Whistles, and my father, Pounded Meat, have come a day to meet you and bring you to our place. I have brought you a fat

"Boasting in Indian Fashion"

dog. I say it is good the Crow and the Sioux shall be friends. All the Crow chiefs are glad. Pretty Eagle is a big chief, and he will tell you what I tell you. But I am bigger than Pretty Eagle. I am a medicine-man."

He paused again; but the grim old chiefs were looking at the fire, and not at him. He got a friendly glance from his henchman, Two Whistles, but he heard his father give a grunt.

That enraged him. "I am a medicine-man," he repeated, defiantly. "I have been in the big hole in the mountains where the river goes, and spoken there with the old man who makes the thunder. I talked with him as one chief to another. I am going to kill all the white men."

At this old Pounded Meat looked at his son angrily, but the son was not afraid of his father just then. "I can make medicine to bring the rain," he continued. "I can make water boil when it is cold. With this I can strike the white man blind when he is so far that his eyes do not show his face."

He swept out from his blanket an old cavalry saber painted scarlet. Young Two Whistles made a movement of awe, but Pounded Meat said, "My son's tongue has grown longer than his sword."

Laughter sounded among the old chiefs. Cheschapah turned his impudent yet somewhat visionary face upon his father. "What do you know of medicine?" said he. "Two sorts of Indians are among the Crows today," he continued to the chiefs. "One sort are the fathers, and the sons are the other. The young warriors are not afraid of the white man. The old plant corn with the squaws. Is this the way with the Sioux?"

"With the Sioux," remarked a grim visitor, "no one fears the white man. But the young warriors do not talk much in council."

Pounded Meat put out his hand gently, as if in remonstrance. Other people must not chide his son.

"You say you can make water boil with no fire?" pursued the Sioux, who was named Young-man-afraid-of-his-horses, and had been young once.

Pounded Meat came between. "My son is a good man," said he. "These words of his are not made in the heart, but are head words you need not count. Cheschapah does not like peace. He has heard us sing our wars and the enemies we have killed, and he remembers that he has no deeds, being young. When he thinks of this sometimes he talks words without sense. But my son is a good man."

The father again extended his hand, which trembled a little. The Sioux had listened, looking at him with respect, and forgetful of Cheschapah, who now stood before them with a cup of cold water.

"You shall see," he said, "who it is that talks words without sense."

Two Whistles and the young bucks crowded to watch, but the old men sat where they were. As Cheschapah stood relishing his audience, Pounded Meat stepped up suddenly and upset the cup. He went to the stream and refilled it himself. "Now make it boil," said he.

Cheschapah smiled, and as he spread his hand quickly over the cup, the water foamed up.

"Huh!" said Two Whistles, startled.

The medicine-man quickly seized his moment. "What does Pounded Meat know of my medicine?" said he. "The dog is cooked. Let the dance begin."

The drums set up their dull, blunt beating, and the crowd of young and less important bucks came from the outer circle nearer to the council. Cheschapah set the pot in the midst of the flat camp, to be the center of the dance. None of the old chiefs said more to him, but sat apart with the empty cup, having words among themselves. The flame reared high into the dark, and showed the rock wall towering; close, and at its feet the light lay red on the streaming water. The young Sioux stripped naked of their blankets, hanging them in a screen against the wind from the jaws of the cañon, with more constant shouts as the drumming beat louder, and strokes of echo fell from the black cliffs. The figures twinkled across each other in the glare, drifting and alert, till the dog-dance shaped itself into twelve dancers with a united sway of body and arms, one and another singing his song against the lifted sound of the drums. The twelve sank crouching in simulated hunt for an enemy back and forth over the same space, swinging together.

Presently they sprang with a shout upon their feet, for they had taken the enemy. Cheschapah, leading the line closer to the central pot, began a new figure, dancing the pursuit of the bear. This went faster; and after the bear was taken, followed the elk hunt, and a new sway and crouch of the twelve gesturing bodies. The thudding drums were ceaseless; and as the dance went always faster and always nearer the dog pot, the steady blows of sound inflamed the dancers; their chests heaved, and their arms and bodies swung alike as the excited crew filed and circled closer to the pot, following Cheschapah, and shouting uncontrollably. They came to firing pistols and slashing the air with knives, when suddenly Cheschapah caught up a piece of steaming dog from the pot, gave it to his best friend, and the dance was done. The dripping figures sat quietly, shining and smooth with sweat, eating their dog flesh in the ardent light of the fire and the cool splendor of the moon. By and by they lay in their blankets to sleep at ease.

The elder chiefs had looked with distrust at Cheschapah as he led the dance; now that the entertainment was over, they rose with gravity to go to their beds.

"It is good for the Sioux and the Crows to be friends," said Pounded Meat to Young-man-afraid-of-his-horses. "But we want no war with the white man. It is a few young men who say that war is good now."

"We have not come for war," replied the Sioux. "We have come to eat much meat together, and remember that day when war was good on the Little Horn, and our warriors killed Yellow Hair and all his soldiers."

Pounded Meat came to where he and Cheschapah had their blankets.

"We shall have war," said the confident son to his father. "My medicine is good."

"Peace is also pretty good," said Pounded Meat. "Get new thoughts. My son, do you not care anymore for my words?"

Cheschapah did not reply.

"I have lived a long while. Yet one man may be wrong. But all cannot be. The other chiefs say what I say. The white men are too strong."

"They would not be too strong if the old men were not cowards."

"Have done," said the father, sternly. "If you are a medicine-man, do not talk like a light fool."

The Indian has an "honor thy father" deep in his religion too, and Cheschapah was silent. But after he was asleep, Pounded Meat lay brooding. He felt himself dishonored, and his son to be an evil in the tribe. With these sore notions keeping him awake, he saw the night wane into gray, and then he heard the distant snort of a horse. He looked, and started from his blankets, for the soldiers had come, and he ran to wake the sleeping Indians. Frightened, and ignorant why they should be surrounded, the Sioux leaped to their feet; and Stirling, from where he sat on his horse, saw their rushing, frantic figures.

"Go quick, Kinney," he said to the interpreter, "and tell them it's peace, or they'll be firing on us."

Kinney rode forward alone, with one hand raised; and seeing that sign, they paused, and crept nearer, like crafty rabbits, while the sun rose and turned the place pink. And then came the parley, and the long explanation; and Stirling thanked his stars to see they were going to allow themselves to be peaceably arrested. Bullets you get used to; but after the firing's done, you must justify it to important personages who live comfortably in eastern towns and have never seen an Indian in their lives, and are rancid with philanthropy and ignorance.

Stirling would sooner have faced Sioux than sentimentalists, and he was fervently grateful to these savages for coming with him quietly without obliging him to shoot them. Cheschapah was not behaving so amiably; and recognizing him, Stirling understood about the dog. The medicine-man, with his faithful Two Whistles, was endeavoring to excite the prisoners as they were marched down the river to the Crow Agency.

Stirling sent for Kinney. "Send that rascal away," he said. "I'll not have him bothering here."

The interpreter obeyed, but with a singular smile to himself. When he had ordered Cheschapah away, he rode so as to overhear Stirling and Haines talking. When they speculated about the soda water, Kinney smiled again. He was a quiet sort of man. The people in the valley admired his business head. He supplied grain and steers to Fort Custer, and used to say that business was always slow in time of peace.

By evening Stirling had brought his prisoners to the agency, and there was the lieutenant of Indian police of the Sioux come over from Pine Ridge to bring them home. There was restlessness in the air as night fell round the prisoners and their guard. It was Cheschapah's hour, and the young Crows listened while he declaimed against the white man for thwarting their hospitality. The strong chain of sentinels was kept busy preventing these hosts from breaking through to fraternize with their guests. Cheschapah did not care that the old Crow chiefs would not listen. When Pretty Eagle remarked laconically that peace was good, the agitator laughed; he was gaining a faction, and the faction was feeling its oats. Accordingly, next morning, though the prisoners were meek on being started home by Stirling with twenty soldiers, and the majority of the Crows were meek at seeing them thus started, this was not all. Cheschapah, with a yelling swarm of his young friends, began to buzz about the column as it marched up the river. All had rifles.

"It's an interesting state of affairs," said Stirling to Haines. "There are at least fifty of these devils at our heels now, and more coming. We've got twenty men. Haines, your Indian experiences may begin quite early in your career."

"Yes, especially if our prisoners take to kicking."

"Well, to compensate for spoiling their dinner party, the agent gave them some rations and his parting blessing. It may suffice."

The line of march had been taken up by ten men in advance, followed in the usual straggling fashion by the prisoners, and the rearguard was composed of the other ten soldiers under Stirling and Haines. With them rode the chief of the Crow police and the lieutenant of the Sioux. This little band was, of course, far separated from the advance-guard, and it listened to the young Crow bucks yelling at its heels. They yelled in English. Every Indian knows at least two English words; they are pungent and far from complimentary.

"It's got to stop here," said Stirling, as they came to a ford known as Reno's Crossing. "They've got to be kept on this side."

"Can it be done without gunpowder?" Haines asked.

"If a shot is fired now, my friend, it's war, and a court of inquiry in Washington for you and me, if we're not buried here. Sergeant, you will take five men and see the column is kept moving. The rest remain with me. The prisoners must be got across and away from their friends."

The fording began, and the two officers went over to the east bank to see that the instructions were carried out.

"See that?" observed Stirling. As the last of the rearguard stepped into the stream, the shore they were leaving filled instantly with the Crows. "Every man jack of them is armed. And here's an interesting development," he continued.

It was Cheschapah riding out into the water, and with him Two Whistles. The rear guard passed up the trail, and the little knot of men with the officers stood halted on the bank. There were nine—the two Indian police, the two lieutenants, and five long muscular boys of K troop of the First Cavalry. They remained on the bank, looking at the thick painted swarm that yelled across the ford.

"Bet you there's a hundred," remarked Haines.

"You forget I never gamble," murmured Stirling. Two of the five long boys overheard this, and grinned at each other, which Stirling noted; and he loved them. It was curious to mark the two shores: the feathered multitude and its yells and its fifty yards of rifles that fronted a small spot of white men sitting easily in the saddle, and the clear, pleasant water speeding between. Cheschapah and Two Whistles came tauntingly towards this spot, and the mass of Crows on the other side drew forward a little.

"You tell them," said Stirling to the chief of the Crow police, "that they must go back."

Cheschapah came nearer, by way of obedience.

"Take them over, then," the officer ordered.

The chief of Crow police rode to Cheschapah, speaking and pointing. His horse drew close, shoving the horse of the medicine-man, who now launched an insult that with Indians calls for blood. He struck the man's horse with his whip, and at that a volume of yells chorused from the other bank.

"Looks like the court of inquiry," remarked Stirling. "Don't shoot, boys," he commanded aloud.

The amazed Sioux policeman gasped. "You not shoot?" he said. "But he hit that man's horse—all the same hit your horse, all the same hit you."

"Right. Quite right," growled Stirling. "All the same hit Uncle Sam. But we soldier devils have orders to temporize." His eye rested hard and serious on the party in the water as he went on speaking with jocular unconcern. "Tem-po-rize, Johnny," said he. "You savvy temporize?"

"Ump! Me no savvy."

"Bully for you, Johnny. Too many syllables. Well, now! He's hit that horse again. One more for the court of inquiry. Steady, men! There's Two Whistles switching now. They ought to call that lad Young Dog Tray. And there's a chap in paint fooling with his gun. If any more do that—it's very catching—Yes, we're going to have a circus. Attention! Now what's that, do you suppose?"

An apparition, an old chief, came suddenly on the other bank, pushing through the crowd, grizzled and little and lean, among the smooth, full-limbed young blood. They turned and saw him, and slunk from the tones of his voice and the light in his ancient eye. They swerved and melted among the cottonwoods, so that the ford's edge grew bare of dusky bodies and looked sandy and green again. Cheschapah saw the wrinkled figure coming, and his face sank tame. He stood uncertain in the stream, seeing his banded companions gone and the few white soldiers firm on the bank. The old chief rode to him through the water, his face brightened with a last flare of command.

"Make your medicine!" he said. "Why are the white men not blind? Is the medicine bad today?" And he whipped his son's horse to the right, and to the left he slashed the horse of Two Whistles, and, whirling the leather quirt, drove them cowed before him and out of the stream, with never a look or word to the white men. He crossed the sandy margin, and as a man drives steers to the corral, striking spurs to his horse and following the frightened animals close when they would twist aside, so did old Pounded Meat herd his son down the valley.

"Useful old man," remarked Stirling; "and brings up his children carefully. Let's get these prisoners along."

"How rural the river looks now!" Haines said, as they left the deserted bank.

So the Sioux went home in peace, the lieutenants, with their command of twenty, returned to the post, and all white people felt much obliged to Pounded Meat for his act of timely parental discipline—all except one white person.

Sol Kinney sauntered into the agency store one evening. "I want ten pounds of sugar," said he, "and navy plug as usual. And say, I'll take another bottle of the Seltzer fizz salts. Since I quit whiskey," he explained, "my liver's poorly."

He returned with his purchase to his cabin, and set a lamp in the window. Presently the door opened noiselessly, and Cheschapah came in.

"Maybe you got that now?" he said, in English.

The interpreter fumbled among bottles of liniment and vaseline, and from among these household remedies brought the blue one he had just bought. Cheschapah watched him like a child, following his steps round the cabin. Kinney tore a half page from an old Sunday *World*, and poured a little heap of salts into it. The Indian touched the heap timidly with his ringer. "Maybe no good," he suggested.

"Heap good!" said the interpreter, throwing a pinch into a glass. When Cheschapah saw the water effervesce, he folded his newspaper with the salt into a tight lump, stuck the talisman into his clothes, and departed, leaving Mr. Kinney well content. He was doing his best to nourish the sinews of war, for business in the country was discouragingly slack.

Now the Crows were a tribe that had never warred with us, but only with other tribes; they had been valiant enough to steal our cattle, but sufficiently discreet to stop there; and Kinney realized that he had uphill work before him. His dearest hopes hung upon Cheschapah, in whom he thought he saw a development. From being a mere humbug, the young Indian seemed to be getting a belief in himself as something genuinely out of the common. His success in creating a party had greatly increased his conceit, and he walked with a strut, and his face was more unsettled and visionary than ever. One clear sign of his mental change was that he no longer respected his father at all, though the lonely old man looked at him often with what in one of our race would have been tenderness. Cheschapah had been secretly maturing a plot ever since his humiliation at the crossing, and now he was ready. With his lump of newspaper carefully treasured, he came to Two Whistles.

"Now we go," he said. "We shall fight with the Piegans. I will make big medicine, so that we shall get many of their horses and women. Then Pretty Eagle will be afraid to go against me in the council.

Pounded Meat whipped my horse. Pounded Meat can cut his hay without Cheschapah, since he is so strong."

But little Two Whistles wavered. "I will stay here," he ventured to say to the prophet.

"Does Two Whistles think I cannot do what I say?"

"I think you make good medicine."

"You are afraid of the Piegans."

"No, I am not afraid. I have hay the white man will pay me for. If I go, he will not pay me. If I had a father, I would not leave him." He spoke pleadingly, and his prophet bore him down by ridicule. Two Whistles believed, but he did not want to lose the money the agent was to pay for his hay. And so, not so much because he believed as because he was afraid, he resigned his personal desires.

The next morning the whole band had disappeared with Cheschapah. The agent was taken aback at this marked challenge to his authority—of course they had gone without permission—and even the old Crow chiefs held a council.

Pretty Eagle resorted to sarcasm. "He has taken his friends to the old man who makes the thunder," he said. But others did not feel sarcastic, and one observed, "Cheschapah knows more than we know."

"Let him make rain, then," said Pretty Eagle. "Let him make the white man's heart soft."

The situation was assisted by a step of the careful Kinney. He took a private journey to Junction City, through which place he expected Cheschapah to return, and there he made arrangements to have as much whiskey furnished to the Indian and his friends as they should ask for. It was certainly a good stroke of business. The victorious raiders did return that way, and Junction City was most hospitable to their thirst. The valley of the Big Horn was resonant with their homeward yells. They swept up the river, and the agent heard them coming, and he locked his door immediately. He listened to their descent upon his fold, and he peeped out and saw them ride round the tightly shut buildings in their war paint and the pride of utter success. They had taken booty from the Piegans, and now, knocking at the store, they demanded ammunition, proclaiming at the same time in English that Cheschapah was a big man, and knew a "big heap medicine." The agent told them from inside that they could not have any ammunition. He also informed them that he knew who they were, and that they were under arrest. This touched their primitive sense of the incongruous. On the buoyancy of the whiskey they rode round and round the store containing the agent, and then rushed away, firing shots at the buildings and shots in the air, and so gloriously home among their tribe, while the agent sent a courier packing to Fort Custer.

The young bucks who had not gone on the raid to the Piegans thronged to hear the story, and the warriors told it here and there, walking in their feathers among a knot of friends, who listened with gay exclamations of pleasure and envy. Great was Cheschapah, who had done all this! And one and another told exactly and at length how he had seen the cold water rise into foam beneath the medicine-man's hand; it could not be told too often; not every companion of Cheschapah's had been accorded the privilege of witnessing this miracle, and each narrator in his circle became a wonder himself to the bold boyish faces that surrounded him. And after the miracle he told how the Piegans had been like a flock of birds before the medicine-man. Cheschapah himself passed among the groups, alone and aloof; he spoke to none, and he looked at none, and he noted how their voices fell to whispers as he passed; his ear caught the magic words of praise and awe; he felt the gaze of admiration follow him away, and a mist rose like incense in his brain. He wandered among the scattered tepees, and, turning, came along the same paths again, that he might once more overhear his worshippers. Great was Cheschapah! His heart beat, a throb of power passed through his body, and, "Great is Cheschapah!" said he, aloud; for the fumes of hallucination where-with he had drugged others had begun to make him drunk also. He sought a tepee where the wife of another chief was alone, and at his light call she stood at the entrance and heard him longer than she had ever listened to him before. But she withstood the temptation that was strong in the young chief's looks and words. She did not speak much, but laughed unsteadily, and, shaking her head with averted eyes, left him, and went where several women were together, and sat among them.

Cheschapah told his victory to the council, with many sentences about himself, and how his medicine had fended all hurt from the Crows. The elder chiefs sat cold.

"Ump!" said one, at the close of the oration, and "Heh!" remarked another. The sounds were of assent without surprise.

"It is good," said Pretty Eagle. His voice seemed to enrage Cheschapah.

"Heh! It is always pretty good!" remarked Spotted Horse.

"I have done this too," said Pounded Meat to his son, simply. "Once, twice, three times. The Crows have always been better warriors than the Piegans."

"Have you made water boil like me?" Cheschapah said.

"I am not a medicine-man," replied his father. "But I have taken horses and squaws from the Piegans. You make good medicine, maybe; but a cup of water will not kill many white men. Can you make the river boil? Let Cheschapah make bigger medicine, so the white man shall fear him as well as the Piegans, whose hearts are well known to us."

Cheschapah scowled. "Pounded Meat shall have this," said he. "I will make medicine tomorrow, old fool!"

"Drive him from the council!" said Pretty Eagle.

"Let him stay," said Pounded Meat. "His bad talk was not to the council, but to me, and I do not count it."

But the medicine-man left the presence of the chiefs, and came to the cabin of Kinney.

"Hello!" said the white man. "Sit down."

"You got that?" said the Indian, standing.

"More water medicine? I guess so. Take a seat."

"No, not boil anymore. You got that other?"

"That other, eh? Well, now, you're not going to blind them yet? What's your hurry?"

"Yes. Make blind tomorrow. Me great chief!"

A slight uneasiness passed across the bantering face of Kinney. His Seltzer salts performed what he promised, but he had mentioned another miracle, and he did not want his dupe to find him out until a war was thoroughly set agoing. He looked at the young Indian, noticing his eyes.

"What's the matter with you, anyway, Cheschapah?"

"Me great chief!" the raised voice trembled with unearthly conviction.

"Well, I guess you are. I guess you've got pretty far along," said the frontier cynic. He tilted his chair back and smiled at the child whose primitive brain he had tampered with so easily. The child stood looking at him with intent black eyes. "Better wait, Cheschapah. Come again. Medicine heap better after a while."

The Indian's quick ear caught the insincerity without understanding it. "You give me that quick!" he said, suddenly terrible.

"Oh, all right, Cheschapah. You know more medicine than me."

"Yes, I know more."

The white man brought a pot of scarlet paint, and the Indian's staring eyes contracted. Kinney took the battered cavalry saber in his hand, and set its point in the earth floor of the cabin. "Stand back," he said, in mysterious tones, and Cheschapah shrank from the impending sorcery. Now Kinney had been to school once, in his eastern childhood, and there had committed to memory portions of Shakespeare, Mrs. Hemans, and other poets out of a reader. He had never forgotten a single word of any of them, and it now occurred to him that for the purposes of an incantation it would be both entertaining for himself and impressive to Cheschapah if he should recite "The Battle of Hohenlinden." He was drawing squares and circles with the point of the saber.

"No," he said to himself, "that piece won't do. He knows too much English. Some of them words might strike him as bein' too usual, and he'd start to kill me, and spoil the whole thing. 'Munich' and 'chivalry' are snortin', but 'sun was low' ain't worth a damn. I guess—"

He stopped guessing, for the noon recess at school came in his mind, like a picture, and with it certain old-time preliminaries to the game of tag.

"Eeny, meeny, money, my . . ."

said Kinney, tapping himself, the saber, the paint-pot, and Cheschapah in turn, one for each word. The incantation was begun. He held the saber solemnly upright, while Cheschapah tried to control his excited breathing where he stood flattened against the wall.

> "Butter, leather, boney, stry;
>   Hare-bit, frost-neck,
>   Harrico, barrico, whee, why, whoa, whack!

"You're it, Cheschapah." After that the weapon was given its fresh coat of paint, and Cheschapah went away with his new miracle in the dark.

"He is it," mused Kinney, grave, but inwardly lively. He was one of those sincere artists who need no popular commendation. "And whoever he does catch, it won't be me," he concluded. He felt pretty sure there would be war now.

Dawn showed the summoned troops near the agency at the corral, standing to horse. Cheschapah gathered his hostiles along the brow of the ridge in the rear of the agency buildings, and the two forces watched each other across the intervening four hundred yards.

"There they are," said the agent, jumping about. "Shoot them, colonel; shoot them!"

"You can't do that, you know," said the officer, "without an order from the president, or an overt act from the Indians."

So nothing happened, and Cheschapah told his friends the white men were already afraid of him. He saw more troops arrive, water their horses in the river, form line outside the corral, and dismount. He made ready at this movement, and all Indian onlookers scattered from the expected fight. Yet the white man stayed quiet. It was issue day, but no families remained after drawing their rations. They had had no dance the night before, as was usual, and they did not linger a moment now, but came and departed with their beef and flour at once.

"I have done all this," said Cheschapah to Two Whistles.

"Cheschapah is a great man," assented the friend and follower. He had gone at once to his hay-field on his return from the Piegans, but someone had broken the little Indian's fence, and cattle were wandering in what remained of his crop.

"Our nation knows I will make a war, and therefore they do not stay here," said the medicine-man, caring nothing what Two Whistles might have suffered. "And now they will see that the white soldiers dare not fight with Cheschapah. The sun is high now, but they have not moved because I have stopped them. Do you not see it is my medicine?"

"We see it." It was the voice of the people.

But a chief spoke. "Maybe they wait for us to come."

Cheschapah answered. "Their eyes shall be made sick. I will ride among them, but they will not know it." He galloped away alone, and lifted his red sword as he sped along the ridge of the hills, showing against the sky. Below at the corral the white soldiers waited ready, and heard him chanting his war song through the silence of the day. He turned in a long curve, and came in near the watching troops and through the agency, and then, made bolder by their motionless figures and guns held idle, he turned again and flew, singing, along close to the line, so they saw his eyes; and a few that had been talking low as they stood side by side fell silent at the spectacle. They could not shoot until some Indian should shoot. They watched him and the gray pony pass and return to the hostiles on the hill. Then they saw the hostiles melt away like magic. Their prophet had told them to go to their tepees and wait for the great rain he would now bring. It was noon, and the sky utterly blue over the bright valley. The sun rode a space nearer the west, and the thick black clouds assembled in the mountains and descended; their shadow flooded the valley with a lake of slatish blue, and presently the sudden torrents sluiced down with flashes and the ample thunder of Montana. Thus not alone the law against our soldiers firing the first shot in an Indian excitement, but now also the elements coincided to help the medicine-man's destiny.

Cheschapah sat in a tepee with his father, and as the rain splashed heavily on the earth the old man gazed at the young one.

"Why do you tremble, my son? You have made the white soldier's heart soft," said Pounded Meat. "You are indeed a great man, my son."

Cheschapah rose. "Do not call me your son," said he. "That is a lie." He went out into the fury of the rain, lifting his face against the drops, and exultingly calling out at each glare of the lightning. He went to

Pretty Eagle's young squaw, who held off from him no longer, but got on a horse, and the two rode into the mountains. Before the sun had set, the sky was again utterly blue, and a cool scent rose everywhere in the shining valley.

The Crows came out of their tepees, and there were the white soldiers obeying orders and going away. They watched the column slowly move across the flat land below the bluffs, where the road led down the river twelve miles to the post.

"They are afraid," said new converts. "Cheschapah's rain has made their hearts soft."

"They have not all gone," said Pretty Eagle. "Maybe he did not make enough rain." But even Pretty Eagle began to be shaken, and he heard several of his brother chiefs during the next few days openly declare for the medicine-man. Cheschapah with his woman came from the mountains, and Pretty Eagle did not dare to harm him. Then another coincidence followed that was certainly most reassuring to the war party. Some of them had no meat, and told Cheschapah they were hungry. With consummate audacity he informed them he would give them plenty at once. On the same day another timely electric storm occurred up the river, and six steers were struck by lightning.

When the officers at Fort Custer heard of this they became serious.

"If this was not the nineteenth century," said Haines, "I should begin to think the elements were deliberately against us."

"It's very careless of the weather," said Stirling. "Very inconsiderate, at such a juncture."

Yet nothing more dangerous than red-tape happened for a while. There was an expensive quantity of investigation from Washington, and this gave the hostiles time to increase both in faith and numbers.

Among the excited Crows only a few wise old men held out. As for Cheschapah himself, ambition and success had brought him to the weird enthusiasm of a fanatic. He was still a charlatan, but a charlatan who believed utterly in his star. He moved among his people with growing mystery, and his hapless adjutant. Two Whistles, rode with him, slaved for him, abandoned the plans he had for making himself a farm, and, desiring peace in his heart, weakly cast his lot with war. Then one day there came an order from the agent to all the Indians: they were to come in by a certain fixed day. The department commander had assembled six hundred troops at the post, and these moved up the river and went into camp. The usually empty ridges, and the bottom where the road ran, filled with white and red men. Half a mile to the north of the buildings, on the first rise from the river, lay the cavalry, and some infantry above them with a howitzer, while across the level, three hundred yards opposite, along the riverbank, was the main Indian camp. Even the hostiles had obeyed the agent's order, and came in close to the troops, totally unlike hostiles in general; for Cheschapah had told them he would protect them with his medicine, and they shouted and sang all through this last night. The women joined with harsh cries and shriekings, and a scalp-dance went on, besides lesser commotions and gatherings, with the throbbing of drums everywhere. Through the sleepless din ran the barking of a hundred dogs, that herded and hurried in crowds of twenty at a time, meeting, crossing from fire to fire among the tepees. Their yelps rose to the high bench of land, summoning a horde of coyotes. These cringing nomads gathered from the desert in a tramp army, and, skulking down the bluffs, sat in their outer darkness and ceaselessly howled their long, shrill greeting to the dogs that sat in the circle of light. The general sent scouts to find the nature of the dance and hubbub, and these brought word it was peaceful; and in the morning another scout summoned the elder chiefs to a talk with the friend who had come from the Great Father at Washington to see them and find if their hearts were good.

"Our hearts are good," said Pretty Eagle. "We do not want war. If you want Cheschapah, we will drive him out from the Crows to you."

"There are other young chiefs with bad hearts," said the commissioner, naming the ringleaders that were known. He made a speech, but Pretty Eagle grew sullen. "It is well," said the commissioner; "you will not help me to make things smooth, and now I step aside and the war chief will talk."

"If you want any other chiefs," said Pretty Eagle, "come and take them."

"Pretty Eagle shall have an hour and a half to think on my words," said the general. "I have plenty of men behind me to make my words good. You must send me all those Indians who fired at the agency."

The Crow chiefs returned to the council, which was apart from the war party's camp; and Cheschapah walked in among them, and after him, slowly, old Pounded Meat, to learn how the conference had gone.

"You have made a long talk with the white man," said Cheschapah. "Talk is pretty good for old men. I and the young chiefs will fight now and kill our enemies."

"Cheschapah," said Pounded Meat, "if your medicine is good, it may be the young chiefs will kill our enemies today. But there are other days to come, and after them still others; there are many, many days. My son, the years are a long road. The life of one man is not long, but enough to learn this thing truly: the white man will always return. There was a day on this river when the dead soldiers of Yellow Hair lay in hills, and the squaws of the Sioux warriors climbed among them with their knives. What do the Sioux warriors do now when they meet the white man on this river? Their hearts are on the ground, and they go home like children when the white man says, 'You shall not visit your friends.' My son, I thought war was good once. I have kept you from the arrows of our enemies on many trails when you were so little that my blankets were enough for both. Your mother was not here anymore, and the chiefs laughed because I carried you. Oh, my son, I have seen the hearts of the Sioux broken by the white man, and I do not think war is good."

"The talk of Pounded Meat is very good," said Pretty Eagle. "If Cheschapah were wise like his father, this trouble would not have come to the Crows. But we could not give the white chief so many of our chiefs that he asked for today."

Cheschapah laughed. "Did he ask for so many? He wanted only Cheschapah, who is not wise like Pounded Meat."

"You would have been given to him," said Pretty Eagle.

"Did Pretty Eagle tell the white chief that? Did he say he would give Cheschapah? How would he give me? In one hand, or two? Or would the old warrior take me to the white man's camp on the horse his young squaw left?"

Pretty Eagle raised his rifle, and Pounded Meat, quick as a boy, seized the barrel and pointed it up among the poles of the tepee, where the quiet black fire smoke was oozing out into the air. "Have you lived so long," said Pounded Meat to his ancient comrade, "and do this in the council?" His wrinkled head and hands shook, the sudden strength left him, and the rifle fell free.

"Let Pretty Eagle shoot," said Cheschapah, looking at the council. He stood calm, and the seated chiefs turned their grim eyes upon him. Certainty was in his face, and doubt in theirs. "Let him send his bullet five times—ten times. Then I will go and let the white soldiers shoot at me until they all lie dead."

"It is heavy for me," began Pounded Meat, "that my friend should be the enemy of my son."

"Tell that lie no more," said Cheschapah. "You are not my father. I have made the white man blind, and I have softened his heart with the rain. I will call the rain today." He raised his red sword, and there was a movement among the sitting figures. "The clouds will come from my father's place, where I have talked with him as one chief to another. My mother went into the mountains to gather berries. She was young, and the thunder-maker saw her face. He brought the black clouds, so her feet turned from home, and she walked where the river goes into the great walls of the mountain, and that day she was stricken fruitful by the lightning. You are not the father of Cheschapah." He dealt Pounded Meat a blow, and the old man fell. But the council sat still until the sound of Cheschapah's galloping horse died away. They were ready now to risk everything. Their skepticism was conquered.

The medicine-man galloped to his camp of hostiles, and, seeing him, they yelled and quickly finished plaiting their horses' tails. Cheschapah had accomplished his wish; he had become the prophet of all the Crows, and he led the armies of the faithful. Each man stripped his blanket off and painted his body for the fight. The forms slipped in and out of the brush, buckling their cartridge-belts, bringing their ponies, while many families struck their tepees and moved up nearer the agency. The spare horses were run across the river into the hills, and through the yelling that shifted and swept like flames along the wind the hostiles made ready and gathered, their crowds quivering with motion, and changing place and shape as more mounted Indians appeared.

"Are the holes dug deep as I marked them on the earth?" said Cheschapah to Two Whistles. "That is good. We shall soon have to go into them from the great rain I will bring. Make these strong, to stay as we ride. They are good medicine, and with them the white soldiers will not see you anymore than they saw me when I rode among them that day."

He had strips and capes of red flannel, and he and Two Whistles fastened them to their painted bodies.

"You will let me go with you?" said Two Whistles.

"You are my best friend," said Cheschapah, "and today I will take you. You shall see my great medicine when I make the white man's eyes grow sick."

The two rode forward, and one hundred and fifty followed them, bursting from their tepees like an explosion, and rushing along quickly in skirmish-line. Two Whistles rode beside his speeding prophet, and saw the red sword waving near his face, and the sun in the great still sky, and the swimming, fleeting earth. His superstition and the fierce ride put him in a sort of trance.

"The medicine is beginning!" shouted Cheschapah; and at that Two Whistles saw the day grow large with terrible shining, and heard his own voice calling and could not stop it. They left the hundred and fifty behind, he knew not where or when. He saw the line of troops ahead change to separate waiting shapes of men, and their legs and arms become plain; then all the guns took clear form in lines of steady glitter. He seemed suddenly alone far ahead of the band, but the voice of Cheschapah spoke close by his ear through the singing wind, and he repeated each word without understanding; he was watching the ground rush by, lest it might rise against his face, and all the while he felt his horse's motion under him, smooth and perpetual. Something weighed against his leg, and there was Cheschapah he had forgotten, always there at his side, veering him around somewhere. But there was no red sword waving. Then the white men must be blind already, wherever they were, and Cheschapah, the only thing he could see, sat leaning one hand on his horse's rump firing a pistol. The ground came swimming towards his eyes always, smooth and wide like a gray flood, but Two Whistles knew that Cheschapah would not let it sweep him away. He saw a horse without a rider floated out of blue smoke, and floated in again with a cracking noise; white soldiers moved in a row across his eyes, very small and clear, and broke into a blurred eddy of shapes which the flood swept away clean and empty. Then a dead white man came by on the quick flood. Two Whistles saw the yellow stripe on his sleeve; but he was gone, and there was nothing but sky and blaze, with Cheschapah's headdress in the middle. The horse's even motion continued beneath him, when suddenly the headdress fell out of Two Whistles' sight, and the earth returned. They were in brush, with his horse standing and breathing, and a dead horse on the ground with Cheschapah, and smoke and moving people everywhere outside. He saw Cheschapah run from the dead horse and jump on a gray pony and go. Somehow he was on the ground too, looking at a red sword lying beside his face. He stared at it a long while, then took it in his hand, still staring; all at once he rose and broke it savagely, and fell again. His faith was shivered to pieces like glass. But he got on his horse, and the horse moved away. He was looking at the blood running on his body. The horse moved always, and Two Whistles followed with his eye a little deeper gush of blood along a crease in his painted skin, noticed the flannel, and remembering the lie of his prophet, instantly began tearing the red rags from his body, and flinging them to the ground with cries of scorn. Presently he heard some voices, and soon one voice much nearer, and saw he had come to a new place, where there were white soldiers looking at him quietly. One was riding up and telling him to give up his pistol. Two Whistles got off and stood behind his horse, looking at the pistol. The white soldier came quite near, and at his voice Two Whistles moved slowly out from behind the horse, and listened to the cool words as the soldier repeated his command. The Indian was pointing his pistol uncertainly, and he looked at the soldier's coat and buttons, and the straps on the shoulders, and the bright steel saber, and the white man's blue eyes; then Two Whistles looked at his own naked, clotted body, and, turning the pistol against himself, fired it into his breast.

Far away up the river, on the right of the line, a lieutenant with two men was wading across after some hostiles that had been skirmishing with his troop. The hostiles had fallen back after some hot shooting, and had dispersed among the brush and tepees on the farther shore, picking up their dead, as Indians do. It was interesting work, this

"The Head Lay in the Water"

splashing breast-high through a river into a concealed hornets' nest, and the lieutenant thought a little on his unfinished plans and duties in life; he noted one dead Indian left on the shore, and went steadfastly in among the half-seen tepees, rummaging and beating in the thick brush to be sure no hornets remained. Finding them gone, and their dead spirited away, he came back on the bank to the one dead Indian, who had a fine headdress, and was still ribanded with gay red streamers of flannel, and was worth all the rest of the dead put together, and much more. The head lay in the water, and one hand held the rope of the gray pony, who stood quiet and uninterested over his fallen rider. They began carrying the prize across to the other bank, where many had now collected, among others Kinney and the lieutenant's captain, who subsequently said, "I found the body of Cheschapah"; and, indeed, it was a very good thing to be able to say.

"This busts the war," said Kinney to the captain, as the body was being lifted over the Little Horn. "They know he's killed, and they've all quit. I was up by the tepees near the agency just now, and I could see the hostiles jamming back home for dear life. They was chucking their rifles to the squaws, and jumping in the river—ha! Ha! To wash off their warpaint, and each —— —— would crawl out and sit innercint in the family blanket his squaw had ready. If you was to go there now, cap'n, you'd find just a lot of harmless Injuns eatin' supper like all the year round. Let me help you, boys, with that carcass."

Kinney gave a hand to the lieutenant and men of G troop, First United States Cavalry, and they lifted Cheschapah up the bank. In the tilted position of the body the cartridge-belt slid a little, and a lump of newspaper fell into the stream. Kinney watched it open and float away with a momentary effervescence. The dead medicine-man was laid between the white and red camps, that all might see he could be killed like other people; and this wholesome discovery brought the Crows to terms at once. Pretty Eagle had displayed a flag of truce, and now he surrendered the guilty chiefs whose hearts had been bad. Everyone came where the dead prophet lay to get a look at him. For a space of hours Pretty Eagle and the many other Crows he had deceived rode by in single file, striking him with their whips; after them came a young squaw, and she also lashed the upturned face.

This night was untroubled at the agency, and both camps and the valley lay quiet in the peaceful dark. Only Pounded Meat, alone on the top of a hill, mourned for his son; and his wailing voice sounded through the silence until the new day came. Then the general had him stopped and brought in, for it might be that the old man's noise would unsettle the Crows again.

Specimen Jones

EPHRAIM, THE PROPRIETOR OF TWENTY MILE, HAD WASTED HIS DAY IN burying a man. He did not know the man. He had found him, or what the Apaches had left of him, sprawled among some charred sticks just outside the Cañon del Oro. It was a useful discovery in its way, for otherwise Ephraim might have gone on hunting his strayed horses near the cañon, and ended among charred sticks himself. Very likely the Indians were far away by this time, but he returned to Twenty Mile with the man tied to his saddle, and his pony nervously snorting. And now the day was done, and the man lay in the earth, and they had even built a fence round him; for the hole was pretty shallow, and coyotes have a way of smelling this sort of thing a long way off when they are hungry, and the man was not in a coffin. They were always short of coffins in Arizona.

Day was done at Twenty Mile, and the customary activity prevailed inside that flat-roofed cube of mud. Sounds of singing, shooting, dancing, and Mexican tunes on the concertina came out of the windows hand in hand, to widen and die among the hills. A limber, pretty boy, who might be nineteen, was dancing energetically, while a grave old gentleman, with tobacco running down his beard, pointed a pistol at the boy's heels, and shot a hole in the earth now and then to show that the weapon was really loaded. Everybody was quite used to all of this—excepting the boy. He was an eastern newcomer, passing his first evening at a place of entertainment.

Night in and night out every guest at Twenty Mile was either happy and full of whiskey, or else his friends were making arrangements for his funeral. There was water at Twenty Mile—the only water for twoscore of miles. Consequently it was an important station on the road between the southern country and Old Camp Grant, and the new mines north of the Mescal Range. The stunt, liquor-perfumed adobe cabin lay on the gray floor of the desert like an isolated slab of chocolate. A corral, two desolate stable sheds, and the slowly turning windmill were all else. Here Ephraim and one or two helpers abode, armed against Indians, and selling whiskey. Variety in their vocation of drinking and killing was brought them by the travelers. These passed and passed through the glaring vacant months—some days only one ragged fortune-hunter, riding a pony; again by twos and threes, with high-loaded burros; and sometimes they came in companies, walking beside their clanking freight-wagons. Some were young, and some were old, and all drank whiskey, and wore knives and guns to keep each other civil. Most of them were bound for the mines, and some of them sometimes returned. No man trusted the next man, and their names, when they had any, would be O'Rafferty, Angus, Schwartzmeyer, José Maria, and Smith. All stopped for one night; some longer, remaining drunk and profitable to Ephraim; now and then one stayed permanently, and had a fence built round him. Whoever came, and whatever befell them, Twenty Mile was chronically hilarious after sundown—a dot of riot in the dumb Arizona night.

On this particular evening they had a tenderfoot. The boy, being new in Arizona, still trusted his neighbor. Such people turned up occasionally. This one had paid for everybody's drink several times, because he felt friendly, and never noticed that nobody ever paid for his. They had played cards with him, stolen his spurs, and now they were making him dance. It was an ancient pastime; yet two or three were glad to stand round and watch it, because it was some time since they had been to the opera. Now the tenderfoot had misunderstood these friends at the beginning, supposing himself to be among good fellows, and they therefore naturally set him down as a fool. But even while dancing you may learn much, and suddenly. The boy, besides being limber, had good tough black hair, and it was not in fear, but with a cold blue eye, that he looked at the old gentleman. The trouble had been that his own revolver had somehow hitched, so he could not pull it from the holster at the necessary moment.

"Tried to draw on me, did yer?" said the old gentleman. "Step higher! Step, now, or I'll crack open yer kneepans, ye robin's egg."

"Thinks he's having a bad time," remarked Ephraim. "Wonder how he'd like to have been that man the Injuns had sport with?"

"Weren't his ear funny?" said one who had helped bury the man.

"Ear?" said Ephraim. "You boys ought to been along when I found him, and seen the way they'd fixed up his mouth." Ephraim explained the details simply, and the listeners shivered. But Ephraim was a humorist. "Wonder how it feels," he continued, "to have—"

Here the boy sickened at his comments and the loud laughter. Yet a few hours earlier these same half-drunken jesters had laid the man to rest with decent humanity. The boy was taking his first dose of Arizona. By no means was everybody looking at his jig. They had seen tenderfeet so often. There was a Mexican game of cards; there was the concertina; and over in the corner sat Specimen Jones, with his back to the company, singing to himself. Nothing had been said or done that entertained him in the least. He had seen everything quite often.

"Higher! Skip higher, you elegant calf," remarked the old gentleman to the tenderfoot. "High-yer!" And he placidly fired a fourth shot that scraped the boy's boot at the ankle and threw earth over the clock, so that you could not tell the minute from the hour hand.

"'Drink to me only with thine eyes,'" sang Specimen Jones, softly. They did not care much for his songs in Arizona. These lyrics were all, or nearly all, that he retained of the days when he was twenty, although he was but twenty-six now.

The boy was cutting pigeon-wings, the concertina played "Matamoras," Jones continued his lyric, when two Mexicans leaped at each other, and the concertina stopped with a quack.

"Quit it!" said Ephraim from behind the bar, covering the two with his weapon. "I don't want any greasers scrapping round here tonight. We've just got cleaned up."

It had been cards, but the Mexicans made peace, to the regret of Specimen Jones. He had looked round with some hopes of a crisis, and now for the first time he noticed the boy.

"Blamed if he ain't neat," he said. But interest faded from his eye, and he turned again to the wall. "'*Lieb Vaterland magst ruhig sein,*'" he melodiously observed. His repertory was wide and refined. When he sang he was always grammatical.

"Ye kin stop, kid," said the old gentleman, not unkindly, and he shoved his pistol into his belt.

The boy ceased. He had been thinking matters over. Being lithe and strong, he was not tired nor much out of breath, but he was trembling with the plan and the prospect he had laid out for himself. "Set 'em up," he said to Ephraim. "Set 'em up again all round."

His voice caused Specimen Jones to turn and look once more, while the old gentleman, still benevolent, said, "Yer langwidge means pleasanter than it sounds, kid." He glanced at the boy's holster, and knew he need not keep a very sharp watch as to that. Its owner had bungled over it once already. All the old gentleman did was to place himself next the boy on the off side from the holster; any move the tenderfoot's hand might make for it would be green and unskillful, and easily anticipated. The company lined up along the bar, and the bottle slid from glass to glass. The boy and his tormentor stood together in the middle of the line, and the tormentor, always with half a thought for the holster, handled his drink on the wet counter, waiting till all should be filled and ready to swallow simultaneously, as befits good manners.

"Well, my regards," he said, seeing the boy raise his glass; and as the old gentleman's arm lifted in unison, exposing his waist, the boy reached down a lightning hand, caught the old gentleman's own pistol, and jammed it in his face.

"Now you'll dance," said he.

"Whoop!" exclaimed Specimen Jones, delighted. "*Blamed* if he ain't neat!" And Jones' handsome face lighted keenly.

"Hold on!" the boy sang out, for the amazed old gentleman was mechanically drinking his whiskey out of sheer fright. The rest had forgotten their drinks. "Not one swallow," the boy continued. "No, you'll not put it down either. You'll keep hold of it, and you'll dance all round this place. Around and around. And don't you spill any. And I'll be thinking what you'll do after that."

Specimen Jones eyed the boy with growing esteem. "Why, he ain't bigger than a pint of cider," said he.

"Prance away!" commanded the tenderfoot, and fired a shot between the old gentleman's not widely straddled legs.

"You hev the floor, Mr. Adams," Jones observed, respectfully, at the old gentleman's agile leap. "I'll let no man here interrupt you." So the capering began, and the company stood back to make room. "I've saw juicy things in this territory," continued Specimen Jones, aloud, to himself, "but this combination fills my bill."

He shook his head sagely, following the black-haired boy with his eye. That youth was steering Mr. Adams round the room with the pistol, proud as a ring master. Yet not altogether. He was only nineteen, and though his heart beat stoutly, it was beating alone in a strange country. He had come straight to this from hunting squirrels along the Susquehanna, with his mother keeping supper warm for him in the stone farmhouse among the trees. He had read books in which hardy heroes saw life, and always triumphed with precision on the last page, but he remembered no receipt for this particular situation. Being good game American blood, he did not think now about the Susquehanna, but he did long with all his might to know what he ought to do next to prove himself a man. His buoyant rage, being glutted with the old gentleman's fervent skipping, had cooled, and a stress of reaction was falling hard on his brave young nerves. He imagined everybody against him. He had no notion that there was another American wanderer there, whose reserved and whimsical nature he had touched to the heart.

The fickle audience was with him, of course, for the moment, since he was upper dog and it was a good show; but one in that room was distinctly against him. The old gentleman was dancing with an ugly eye; he had glanced down to see just where his knife hung at his side, and he had made some calculations. He had fired four shots; the boy had fired one. "Four and one hez always made five," the old gentleman told himself with much secret pleasure, and pretended that he was going to stop his double-shuffle. It was an excellent trap, and the boy fell straight into it. He squandered his last precious bullet on the spittoon near which Mr. Adams happened to be at the moment, and the next moment Mr. Adams had him by the throat. They swayed and gulped for breath, rutting the earth with sharp heels; they rolled to the floor and floundered with legs tight tangled, the boy blindly striking at Mr. Adams with the pistol-butt, and the audience drawing closer to lose nothing, when the bright knife flashed suddenly: It poised, and flew across the room, harmless, for a foot had driven into Mr. Adams' arm, and he felt a cold ring grooving his temple. It was the smooth, chilly muzzle of Specimen Jones' six-shooter.

"That's enough," said Jones. "More than enough."

Mr. Adams, being mature in judgment, rose instantly, like a good old sheep, and put his knife back obedient to orders. But in the brain of the overstrained, bewildered boy universal destruction was whirling. With a face stricken lean with ferocity, he staggered to his feet, plucking at his obstinate holster, and glaring for a foe. His eye fell first on his deliverer, leaning easily against the bar watching him, while the more and more curious audience scattered, and held themselves ready to murder the boy if he should point his pistol their way. He was dragging at it clumsily, and at last it came. Specimen Jones sprang like a cat, and held the barrel vertical and gripped the boy's wrist.

"Go easy, son," said he. "I know how you're feelin'."

The boy had been wrenching to get a shot at Jones, and now the quietness of the man's voice reached his brain, and he looked at Specimen Jones. He felt a potent brotherhood in the eyes that were considering him, and he began to fear he had been a fool. There was his dwarf eastern revolver, slack in his inefficient fist, and the singular person still holding its barrel and tapping one derisive finger over the end, careless of the risk to his first joint.

"Why, you little —— ——," said Specimen Jones, caressingly, to the hypnotized youth, "if you was to pop that squirt off at me, I'd turn you up and spank y'u. Set 'em up, Ephraim."

But the commercial Ephraim hesitated, and Jones remembered. His last cent was gone. It was his third day at Ephraim's. He had stopped, having a little money, on his way to Tucson, where a friend

had a job for him, and was waiting. He was far too experienced a character ever to sell his horse or his saddle on these occasions, and go on
drinking. He looked as if he might, but he never did; and this was what
disappointed businessmen like Ephraim in Specimen Jones.

But now, here was this tenderfoot he had undertaken to see through,
and Ephraim reminding him that he had no more of the wherewithal.
"Why, so I haven't," he said, with a short laugh, and his face flushed. "I
guess," he continued, hastily, "this is worth a dollar or two." He drew a
chain up from below his flannel shirt collar and over his head. He drew
it a little slowly. It had not been taken off for a number of years—not,
indeed, since it had been placed there originally. "It ain't brass," he
added, lightly, and strewed it along the counter without looking at it.
Ephraim did look at it, and, being satisfied, began to uncork a new
bottle, while the punctual audience came up for its drink.

"Won't you please let me treat?" said the boy, unsteadily. "I ain't
likely to meet you again, sir." Reaction was giving him trouble inside.

"Where are you bound, kid?"

"Oh, just a ways up the country," answered the boy, keeping a grip
on his voice.

"Well, you *may* get there. Where did you pick up that—that thing?
Your pistol, I mean."

"It's a present from a friend," replied the tenderfoot, with dignity.

"Farewell gift, wasn't it, kid? Yes; I thought so. Now I'd hate to get
an affair like that from a friend. It would start me wondering if he
liked me as well as I'd always thought he did. Put up that money, kid.
You're drinking with me. Say, what's yer name?"

"Cumnor—J. Cumnor."

"Well, J. Cumnor, I'm glad to know y'u. Ephraim, let me make you
acquainted with Mr. Cumnor. Mr. Adams, if you're rested from your
quadrille, you can shake hands with my friend. Step around, you
Miguels and Serapios and Cristobals, whatever y'u claim your names
are. This is Mr. J. Cumnor."

The Mexicans did not understand either the letter or the spirit of
these American words, but they drank their drink, and the concertina
resumed its acrid melody. The boy had taken himself off without
being noticed.

"Say, Spec," said Ephraim to Jones, "I'm no hog. Here's yer chain. You'll be along again."

"Keep it till I'm along again," said the owner.

"Just as you say, Spec," answered Ephraim, smoothly, and he hung the pledge over an advertisement chromo of a nude cream-colored lady with bright straw hair holding out a bottle of somebody's champagne. Specimen Jones sang no more songs, but smoked, and leaned in silence on the bar. The company were talking of bed, and Ephraim plunged his glasses into a bucket to clean them for the morrow.

"Know anything about that kid?" inquired Jones, abruptly.

Ephraim shook his head as he washed.

"Traveling alone, ain't he?"

Ephraim nodded.

"Where did y'u say y'u found that fellow layin' the Injuns got?"

"Mile this side the cañon. 'Mong them sand-humps."

"How long had he been there, do y'u figure?"

"Three days, anyway."

Jones watched Ephraim finish his cleansing. "Your clock needs wiping," he remarked. "A man might suppose it was nine, to see that thing the way the dirt hides the hands. Look again in half an hour and it'll say three. That's the kind of clock gives a man the jams. Sends him crazy."

"Well, that ain't a bad thing to be in this country," said Ephraim, rubbing the glass case and restoring identity to the hands. "If that man had been crazy he'd been livin' right now. Injuns'll never touch lunatics."

"That band have passed here and gone north," Jones said. "I saw a smoke among the foothills as I come along day before yesterday. I guess they're aiming to cross the Santa Catalina. Most likely they're that band from round the San Carlos that were reported as raiding down in Sonora."

"I seen well enough," said Ephraim, "when I found him that they wasn't going to trouble us any, or they'd have been around by then."

He was quite right, but Specimen Jones was thinking of something else. He went out to the corral, feeling disturbed and doubtful. He saw the tall white freight-wagon of the Mexicans, looming and silent, and a little way off the new fence where the man lay. An odd sound startled him, though he knew it was no Indians at this hour, and he looked down into a little dry ditch. It was the boy, hidden away flat on his stomach among the stones, sobbing.

"Oh, snakes!" whispered Specimen Jones, and stepped back. The Latin races embrace and weep, and all goes well; but among Saxons tears are a horrid event. Jones never knew what to do when it was a woman, but this was truly disgusting. He was well seasoned by the frontier, had tried a little of everything: town and country, ranches, saloons, stage-driving, marriage occasionally, and latterly mines. He had sundry claims staked out, and always carried pieces of stone in his pockets, discoursing upon their mineral-bearing capacity, which was apt to be very slight. That is why he was called Specimen Jones. He had exhausted all the important sensations, and did not care much for anything anymore. Perfect health and strength kept him from discovering that he was a saddened, drifting man. He wished to kick the boy for his baby performance, and yet he stepped carefully away from the ditch so the boy should not suspect his presence. He found himself standing still, looking at the dim, broken desert.

"Why, hell," complained Specimen Jones, "he played the little man to start with. He did so. He scared that old horse-thief, Adams, just about dead. Then he went to kill me, that kep' him from bein' buried early tomorrow. I've been wild that way myself, and wantin' to shoot up the whole outfit." Jones looked at the place where his middle finger used to be, before a certain evening in Tombstone. "But I never—" He glanced towards the ditch, perplexed. "What's that mean? Why in the world does he git to cryin' for *now*, do you suppose?" Jones took to singing without knowing it. "'Ye shepherds, tell me, have you seen my Flora pass this way?'" he murmured. Then a thought struck him. "Hello, kid!" he called out. There was no answer. "Of course," said Jones. "Now he's ashamed to hev me see him come out of there." He walked with elaborate slowness round the corral and behind a shed. "Hello, you kid!" he called again.

"I was thinking of going to sleep," said the boy, appearing quite suddenly. "I—I'm not used to riding all day. I'll get used to it, you know," he hastened to add.

"'Ha-ve you seen my Flo'—Say, kid, where y'u bound, anyway?"

"San Carlos."

"San Carlos? Oh. Ah. 'Flora pass this way?'"

"Is it far, sir?"

"Awful far, sometimes. It's always liable to be far through the Arivaypa Cañon."

"I didn't expect to make it between meals," remarked Cumnor.

"No. Sure. What made you come this route?"

"A man told me."

"A man? Oh. Well, it *is* kind o' difficult, I admit, for an Arizonan not to lie to a stranger. But I think I'd have told you to go by Tres Alamos and Point of Mountain. It's the road the man that told you would choose himself every time. Do you like Injuns, kid?"

Cumnor snapped eagerly.

"Of course y'u do. And you've never saw one in the whole minute-and-a-half you've been alive. I know all about it."

"I'm not afraid," said the boy.

"Not afraid? Of course y'u ain't. What's your idea in going to Carlos? Got town lots there?"

"No," said the literal youth, to the huge internal diversion of Jones. "There's a man there I used to know back home. He's in the cavalry. What sort of a town is it for sport?" asked Cumnor, in a gay Lothario tone.

"*Town?*" Specimen Jones caught hold of the top rail of the corral. "*Sport?* Now I'll tell y'u what sort of a town it is. There ain't no streets. There ain't no houses. There ain't any land and water in the usual meaning of them words. There's Mount Turnbull. It's pretty near a usual mountain, but y'u don't want to go there. The Creator didn't make San Carlos. It's a heap older than Him. When He got around to it after slickin' up Paradise and them fruit trees, He just left it to be as He found it, as a sample of the way they done business before He come along. He 'ain't done any work around that spot at all, He 'ain't. Mix up a barrel of sand and ashes and thorns, and jam scorpions and rattlesnakes along in, and dump the outfit on stones, and heat yer stones red-hot, and set the United States army loose over the place chasin' Apaches, and you've got San Carlos."

Cumnor was silent for a moment. "I don't care," he said. "I want to chase Apaches."

"Did you see that man Ephraim found by the cañon?" Jones inquired.

"Didn't get here in time."

"Well, there was a hole in his chest made by an arrow. But there's no harm in that if you die at wunst. That chap didn't, y'u see. You heard Ephraim tell about it. They'd done a number of things to the man before he could die. Roastin' was only one of 'em. Now your road takes you through the mountains where these Injuns hev gone. Kid, come along to Tucson with me," urged Jones, suddenly.

Again Cumnor was silent. "Is my road different from other people's?" he said, finally.

"Not to Grant, it ain't. These Mexicans are hauling freight to Grant. But what's the matter with your coming to Tucson with me?"

"I started to go to San Carlos, and I'm going," said Cumnor.

"You're a poor chuckle-headed fool!" burst out Jones, in a rage. "And y'u can go, for all I care—you and your Christmas tree pistol. Like as not you won't find your cavalry friend at San Carlos. They've killed a lot of them soldiers huntin' Injuns this season. Good night."

Specimen Jones was gone. Cumnor walked to his blanket-roll, where his saddle was slung under the shed. The various doings of the evening had bruised his nerves. He spread his blankets among the dry cattle dung, and sat down, taking off a few clothes slowly. He lumped his coat and overalls under his head for a pillow, and, putting the despised pistol alongside, lay between the blankets. No object showed in the night but the tall freight-wagon. The tenderfoot thought he had made altogether a fool of himself upon the first trial trip of his manhood, alone on the open sea of Arizona. No man, not even Jones now, was his friend. A stranger, who could have had nothing against him but his inexperience, had taken the trouble to direct him on the wrong road. He did not mind definite enemies. He had punched the heads of those in Pennsylvania, and would not object to shooting them here; but this impersonal, surrounding hostility of the unknown was new and bitter: the cruel, assassinating, cowardly Southwest, where prospered those jailbirds whom the vigilantes had driven from California. He thought of the nameless human carcass that lay near, buried that day, and of the jokes about its mutilations.

Cumnor was not an innocent boy, either in principles or in practice, but this laughter about a dead body had burned into his young, unhardened soul. He lay watching with hot, dogged eyes the brilliant stars. A passing wind turned the windmill, which creaked a forlorn minute, and ceased. He must have gone to sleep and slept soundly, for the next he knew it was the cold air of dawn that made him open his eyes. A numb silence lay over all things, and the tenderfoot had that moment of curiosity as to where he was now which comes to those who have journeyed for many days. The Mexicans had already departed with their freight-wagon. It was not entirely light, and the embers where these early starters had cooked their breakfast lay glowing in the sand across the road. The boy remembered seeing a wagon where now he saw only chill, distant peaks, and while he lay quiet and warm, shunning full consciousness, there was a stir in the cabin, and at Ephraim's voice reality broke upon his drowsiness, and he recollected Arizona and the keen stress of shifting for himself. He noted the gray paling round the grave. Indians? He would catch up with the Mexicans, and travel in their company to Grant. Freighters made but fifteen miles in the day, and he could start after breakfast and be with them before they stopped to noon. Six men need not worry about Apaches, Cumnor thought. The voice of Specimen Jones came from the cabin, and sounds of lighting the stove, and the growling conversation of men getting up. Cumnor, lying in his blankets, tried to overhear what Jones was saying, for no better reason than that this was the only man he had met lately who had seemed to care whether he were alive or dead. There was the clink of Ephraim's whiskey bottles, and the cheerful tones of old Mr. Adams, saying, "It's better 'n brushin' yer teeth"; and then further clinking, and an inquiry from Specimen Jones.

"Whose spurs?" said he.

"Mine." This from Mr. Adams.

"How long have they been yourn?"

"Since I got 'em, I guess."

"Well, you've enjoyed them spurs long enough." The voice of Specimen Jones now altered in quality. "And you'll give 'em back to that kid."

Muttering followed that the boy could not catch. "You'll give 'em back," repeated Jones. "I seen y'u lift 'em from under that chair when I was in the corner."

"That's straight, Mr. Adams," said Ephraim. "I noticed it myself, though I had no objections, of course. But Mr. Jones has pointed out—"

"Since when have you growed so honest, Jones?" cackled Mr. Adams, seeing that he must lose his little booty. "And why didn't you raise yer objections when you seen me do it?"

"I didn't know the kid," Jones explained. "And if it don't strike you that game blood deserves respect, why it does strike me."

Hearing this, the tenderfoot, outside in his shed, thought better of mankind and life in general, arose from his nest, and began preening himself. He had all the correct trappings for the frontier, and his toilet in the shed gave him pleasure. The sun came up, and with a stroke struck the world to crystal. The near sand-hills went into rose, the crabbed yucca and the mesquite turned transparent, with lances and pale films of green, like drapery graciously veiling the desert's face, and distant violet peaks and edges framed the vast enchantment beneath the liquid exhalations of the sky. The smell of bacon and coffee from open windows filled the heart with bravery and yearning, and Ephraim, putting his head round the corner, called to Cumnor that he had better come in and eat. Jones, already at table, gave him the briefest nod; but the spurs were there, replaced as Cumnor had left them under a chair in the corner. In Arizona they do not say much at any meal, and at breakfast nothing at all; and as Cumnor swallowed and meditated, he noticed the cream-colored lady and the chain, and he made up his mind he should assert his identity with regard to that business, though how and when was not clear to him. He was in no great haste to take up his journey. The society of the Mexicans whom he must sooner or later overtake did not tempt him. When breakfast was done he idled in the cabin, like the other guests, while Ephraim and his assistant busied about the premises. But the morning grew on, and the guests, after a season of smoking and tilted silence against the wall, shook themselves and their effects together, saddled, and were lost among the waste thorny hills. Twenty Mile became hot and torpid. Jones lay on three consecutive chairs, occasionally singing, and old

Mr. Adams had not gone away either, but watched him, with more tobacco running down his beard.

"Well," said Cumnor, "I'll be going."

"Nobody's stopping y'u," remarked Jones.

"You're going to Tucson?" the boy said, with the chain problem still unsolved in his mind. "Goodbye, Mr. Jones. I hope I'll—we'll—"

"That'll do," said Jones; and the tenderfoot, thrown back by this severity, went to get his saddle-horse and his burro.

Presently Jones remarked to Mr. Adams that he wondered what Ephraim was doing, and went out. The old gentleman was left alone in the room, and he swiftly noticed that the belt and pistol of Specimen Jones were left alone with him. The accoutrement lay by the chair its owner had been lounging in. It is an easy thing to remove cartridges from the chambers of a revolver, and replace the weapon in its holster so that everything looks quite natural. The old gentleman was entertained with the notion that somewhere in Tucson Specimen Jones might have a surprise, and he did not take a minute to prepare this, drop the belt as it lay before, and saunter innocently out of the saloon. Ephraim and Jones were criticizing the tenderfoot's property as he packed his burro.

"Do y'u make it a rule to travel with ice cream?" Jones was inquiring.

"They're for water," Cumnor said. "They told me at Tucson I'd need to carry water for three days on some trails."

It was two good-sized milk-cans that he had, and they bounced about on the little burro's pack, giving him as much amazement as a jackass can feel. Jones and Ephraim were hilarious.

"Don't go without your spurs, Mr. Cumnor," said the voice of old Mr. Adams, as he approached the group. His tone was particularly civil.

The tenderfoot had, indeed, forgotten his spurs, and he ran back to get them. The cream-colored lady still had the chain hanging upon her, and Cumnor's problem was suddenly solved. He put the chain in his pocket, and laid the price of one round of drinks for last night's company on the shelf below the chromo. He returned with his spurs on, and went to his saddle that lay beside that of Specimen Jones under the shed. After a moment he came with his saddle to where the men stood talking by his pony, slung it on, and tightened the cinches:

but the chain was now in the saddlebag of Specimen Jones, mixed up with some tobacco, stale bread, a box of matches, and a hunk of fat bacon. The men at Twenty Mile said good day to the tenderfoot, with monosyllables and indifference, and watched him depart into the heated desert. Wishing for a last look at Jones, he turned once, and saw the three standing, and the chocolate brick of the cabin, and the windmill white and idle in the sun.

"He'll be gutted by night," remarked Mr. Adams.

"I ain't buryin' him, then," said Ephraim.

"Nor I," said Specimen Jones. "Well, it's time I was getting to Tucson."

He went to the saloon, strapped on his pistol, saddled, and rode away. Ephraim and Mr. Adams returned to the cabin; and here is the final conclusion they came to after three hours of discussion as to who took the chain and who had it just then:

Ephraim. Jones, he hadn't no cash.

Mr. Adams. The kid, he hadn't no sense.

Ephraim. The kid, he lent the cash to Jones.

Mr. Adams. Jones, he goes off with his chain.

Both. What damn fools everybody is, anyway!

And they went to dinner. But Mr. Adams did not mention his relations with Jones' pistol. Let it be said, in extenuation of that performance, that Mr. Adams supposed Jones was going to Tucson, where he said he was going, and where a job and a salary were awaiting him. In Tucson an unloaded pistol in the holster of so handy a man on the drop as was Specimen would keep people civil, because they would not know, any more than the owner, that it was unloaded; and the mere possession of it would be sufficient in nine chances out of ten—though it was undoubtedly for the tenth that Mr. Adams had a sneaking hope. But Specimen Jones was not going to Tucson. A contention in his mind as to whether he would do what was good for himself, or what was good for another, had kept him sullen ever since he got up. Now it was settled, and Jones in serene humor again. Of course he had started on the Tucson road, for the benefit of Ephraim and Mr. Adams.

The tenderfoot rode along. The Arizona sun beat down upon the deadly silence, and the world was no longer of crystal, but a mesa, dull and gray and hot. The pony's hoofs grated in the gravel, and after a time the road dived down and up among lumpy hills of stone and cactus, always nearer the fierce glaring Sierra Santa Catalina. It dipped so abruptly in and out of the shallow sudden ravines that, on coming up from one of these into sight of the country again, the tenderfoot's heart jumped at the close apparition of another rider quickly bearing in upon him from gullies where he had been moving unseen. But it was only Specimen Jones.

"Hello!" said he, joining Cumnor. "Hot, ain't it?"

"Where are you going?" inquired Cumnor.

"Up here a ways." And Jones jerked his finger generally towards the Sierra, where they were heading.

"Thought you had a job in Tucson."

"That's what I have."

Specimen Jones had no more to say, and they rode for a while, their ponies' hoofs always grating in the gravel, and the milk-cans lightly clanking on the burro's pack. The bunched blades of the yuccas bristled steel-stiff, and as far as you could see it was a gray waste of mounds and ridges sharp and blunt, up to the forbidding boundary walls of the Tortilita one way and the Santa Catalina the other. Cumnor wondered if Jones had found the chain. Jones was capable of not finding it for several weeks, or of finding it at once and saying nothing.

"You'll excuse my meddling with your business?" the boy hazarded.

Jones looked inquiring.

"Something's wrong with your saddle-pocket."

Specimen saw nothing apparently wrong with it, but perceiving Cumnor was grinning, unbuckled the pouch. He looked at the boy rapidly, and looked away again, and as he rode, still in silence, he put the chain back round his neck below the flannel shirt collar.

"Say, kid," he remarked, after some time, "what does *J* stand for?"

"*J*? Oh, my name! Jock."

"Well, Jock, will y'u explain to me as a friend how y'u ever come to be such a fool as to leave yer home—wherever and whatever it was—in exchange for this here God-forsaken and iniquitous hole?"

"If you'll explain to me," said the boy, greatly heartened, "how you come to be ridin' in the company of a fool, instead of goin' to your job at Tucson."

The explanation was furnished before Specimen Jones had framed his reply. A burning freight-wagon and five dismembered human stumps lay in the road. This was what had happened to the Miguels and Serapios and the concertina. Jones and Cumnor, in their dodging and struggles to exclude all expressions of growing mutual esteem from their speech, had forgotten their journey, and a sudden bend among the rocks where the road had now brought them revealed the blood and fire staring them in the face. The plundered wagon was three parts empty; its splintered, blazing boards slid down as they burned into the fiery heap on the ground; packages of soda and groceries and medicines slid with them, bursting into chemical spots of green and crimson flame; a wheel crushed in and sank, spilling more packages that flickered and hissed; the garbage of combat and murder littered the earth, and in the air hung an odor that Cumnor knew, though he had never smelled it before. Morsels of dropped booty up among the rocks showed where the Indians had gone, and one horse remained, groaning, with an accidental arrow in his belly.

"We'll just kill him," said Jones; and his pistol snapped idly, and snapped again, as his eye caught a motion—a something—two hundred yards up among the bowlders on the hill. He whirled round. The enemy was behind them also. There was no retreat. "Yourn's no good!" yelled Jones, fiercely, for Cumnor was getting out his little, foolish revolver. "Oh, what a trick to play on a man! Drop off yer horse, kid; drop, and do like me. Shootin's no good here, even if I was loaded. *They* shot, and look at them now. God bless them ice cream freezers of yourn, kid! Did y'u ever see a crazy man? If you 'ain't, *make it up as y'u go along!*"

More objects moved up among the bowlders. Specimen Jones ripped off the burro's pack, and the milk-cans rolled on the ground. The burro began grazing quietly, with now and then a step towards new patches of grass. The horses stood where their riders had left them, their reins over their heads, hanging and dragging. From two hundred yards on the hill the ambushed Apaches showed, their dark, scattered figures appearing cautiously one by one, watching with suspicion. Specimen Jones seized up one milk-can, and Cumnor obediently did the same.

"You kin dance, kid, and I kin sing, and we'll go to it," said Jones. He rambled in a wavering loop, and diving eccentrically at Cumnor, clashed the milk-cans together. "'*Es schallt ein Ruf wie Donnerhall,*'" he bawled, beginning the song of "*Die Wacht am Rhein.*" "Why don't you dance?" he shouted, sternly. The boy saw the terrible earnestness of his face, and, clashing his milk-cans in turn, he shuffled a sort of jig. The two went over the sand in loops, toe and heel; the donkey continued his quiet grazing, and the flames rose hot and yellow from the freight-wagon. And all the while the stately German hymn pealed among the rocks, and the Apaches crept down nearer the bowing, scraping men. The sun shone bright, and their bodies poured with sweat. Jones flung off his shirt; his damp, matted hair was half in ridges and half glued to his forehead, and the delicate gold chain swung and struck his broad, naked breast. The Apaches drew nearer again, their bows and arrows held uncertainly. They came down the hill, fifteen or twenty, taking a long time, and stopping every few yards. The milk-cans clashed, and Jones thought he felt the boy's strokes weakening. "*Die Wacht am Rhein*" was finished, and now it was "'Ha-ve you seen my Flora pass this way?'" "Y'u mustn't play out, kid," said Jones, very gently. "Indeed y'u mustn't"; and he at once resumed his song. The silent Apaches had now reached the bottom of the hill. They stood some twenty yards away, and Cumnor had a good chance to see his first Indians. He saw them move, and the color and slim shape of their bodies, their thin arms, and their long, black hair. It went through his mind that if he had no more clothes on than that, dancing would come easier. His boots were growing heavy to lift, and his overalls seemed to wrap his sinews in wet, strangling thongs. He wondered how long he had been keeping this up. The legs of the Apaches were free, with light moccasins only halfway to the thigh, slenderly held up by strings from the waist. Cumnor envied their unencumbered steps as he saw them again walk nearer to where he was dancing. It was long since he had eaten, and he noticed a singing dullness in his brain, and became frightened at his thoughts, which were running and melting into one fixed idea. This idea was to take off his boots, and offer to trade them for a pair of moccasins. It terrified him—this endless, molten rush of thoughts; he could see them coming in different shapes from different places in his head, but they all joined immediately, and always formed the same fixed idea. He ground his teeth to master this encroaching inebriation of his will and judgment. He clashed his can more loudly to wake him to reality, which he still could recognize and appreciate. For a time he found it a good plan to listen to what Specimen Jones was singing, and tell himself the name of the song, if he knew it. At present it was "Yankee Doodle," to which Jones was fitting words of his own. These ran, "Now I'm going to try a bluff, And mind you do what I do"; and then again, over and over. Cumnor waited for the word "bluff"; for it was hard and heavy, and fell into his thoughts, and stopped them for a moment. The dance was so long now he had forgotten about that. A numbness had been spreading through his legs, and he was glad to feel a sharp pain in the sole of his foot. It was a piece of gravel that had somehow worked its way in, and was rubbing through the skin into the flesh. "That's good," he said, aloud. The pebble was eating the numbness away, and Cumnor drove it hard against the raw spot, and relished the tonic of its burning friction. The Apaches had drawn into a circle. Standing at some interval apart, they entirely surrounded the arena. Shrewd, half convinced, and yet with awe, they watched the dancers, who clashed their cans slowly now in rhythm to Jones' hoarse, parched singing. He was quite master of himself, and led the jig round the still blazing wreck of the wagon, and circled in figures of eight between the corpses of the Mexicans, clashing the milk-cans above each one. Then, knowing his strength was coming to an end, he approached an Indian whose splendid fillet and trappings denoted him of consequence; and Jones was near shouting with relief when the Indian shrank backward. Suddenly he saw Cumnor let his can drop, and without stopping to see why, he caught it up, and, slowly rattling both, approached each Indian in turn with tortuous steps. The circle that had never uttered a sound till now receded, chanting almost in a whisper some exorcising song which the man with the fillet had begun. They gathered round him, retreating always, and the strain, with its rapid muttered words, rose and fell softly among them. Jones had supposed the boy was overcome by faintness, and looked to see where he lay. But it was not faintness. Cumnor, with his boots off, came by and walked after the Indians in a trance. They saw him, and quickened their pace, often turning to be sure he was not overtaking them. He called to them unintelligibly, stumbling up the sharp hill, and pointing to the boots. Finally he sat down. They continued ascending the mountain, herding close round the man with the feathers, until the rocks and the filmy tangles screened them from sight; and like a wind that hums uncertainly in grass, their chanting died away.

The sun was half behind the western range when Jones next moved. He called, and, getting no answer, he crawled painfully to where the boy lay on the hill. Cumnor was sleeping heavily; his head was hot, and he moaned. So Jones crawled down, and fetched blankets and the canteen of water. He spread the blankets over the boy, wet a handkerchief and laid it on his forehead; then he lay down himself.

The earth was again magically smitten to crystal. Again the sharp cactus and the sand turned beautiful, and violet floated among the mountains, and rose-colored orange in the sky above them.

"Jock," said Specimen at length.

The boy opened his eyes.

"Your foot is awful, Jock. Can y'u eat?"

"Not with my foot."

"Ah, God bless y'u, Jock! Y'u ain't turruble sick. But *can* y'u eat?"

Cumnor shook his head.

"Eatin's what y'u need, though. Well, here." Specimen poured a judicious mixture of whiskey and water down the boy's throat, and wrapped the awful foot in his own flannel shirt. "They'll fix y'u over to Grant. It's maybe twelve miles through the cañon. It ain't a town any more than Carlos is, but the soldiers'll be good to us. As soon as night comes you and me must somehow git out of this."

Somehow they did, Jones walking and leading his horse and the imperturbable little burro, and also holding Cumnor in the saddle. And when Cumnor was getting well in the military hospital at Grant, he listened to Jones recounting to all that chose to hear how useful a weapon an ice cream freezer can be, and how if you'll only chase Apaches in your stocking feet they are sure to run away. And then Jones and Cumnor both enlisted; and I suppose Jones' friend is still expecting him in Tucson.

The Serenade at Siskiyou

Unskilled at murder and without training in running away, one of the two Healy boys had been caught with ease soon after their crime. What they had done may be best learned in the following extract from a certain official report:

"The stage was within five miles of its destination when it was confronted by the usual apparition of a masked man leveling a double-barreled shotgun at the driver, and the order to 'Pull up, and throw out the express box.' The driver promptly complied. Meanwhile the guard, Buck Montgomery, who occupied a seat inside, from which he caught a glimpse of what was going on, opened fire at the robber, who dropped to his knees at the first shot, but a moment later discharged both barrels of his gun at the stage. The driver dropped from his seat to the footboard with five buckshot in his right leg near the knee, and two in his left leg; a passenger by his side also dropped with three or four buckshot in his legs. Before the guard could reload, two shots came from behind the bushes back of the exposed robber, and Buck fell to the bottom of the stage mortally wounded—shot through the back. The whole murderous sally occupied but a few seconds, and the order came to 'Drive on.' Officers and citizens quickly started in pursuit, and the next day one of the robbers, a well-known young man of that vicinity, son of a respectable farmer in Fresno County, was overtaken and arrested."

Feeling had run high in the streets of Siskiyou when the prisoner was brought into town, and the wretch's life had come near a violent end at the hands of the mob, for Buck Montgomery had many friends. But the steadier citizens preserved the peace, and the murderer was in the prison awaiting his trial by formal law. It was now some weeks since the tragedy, and Judge Campbell sat at breakfast reading his paper.

"Why, that is excellent!" he suddenly exclaimed.

"May I ask what is excellent, judge?" inquired his wife. She had a big nose.

"They've caught the other one, Amanda. Got him last evening in a restaurant at Woodland." The judge read the paragraph to Mrs. Campbell, who listened severely. "And so," he concluded, "when tonight's train gets up, we'll have them both safe in jail."

Mrs. Campbell dallied over her eggs, shaking her head. Presently she sighed. But as Amanda often did this, her husband finished his own eggs and took some more. "Poor boy!" said the lady, pensively. "Only twenty-three last 12th of October. What a cruel fate!"

Now the judge supposed she referred to the murdered man. "Yes," he said. "Vile. You've got him romantically young, my dear. I understood he was thirty-five."

"I know his age perfectly, Judge Campbell. I made it my business to find out. And to think his brother might actually have been lynched!"

"I never knew that either. You seem to have found out all about the family, Amanda. What were they going to lynch the brother for?"

The ample lady folded her fat, middle-aged hands on the edge of the table, and eyed her husband with bland displeasure. "Judge Campbell!" she uttered, and her lips shut wide and firm. She would restrain herself, if possible.

"Well, my dear?"

"You ask me that. You pretend ignorance of that disgraceful scene. Who was it said to me right in the street that he disapproved of lynching? I ask you, judge, who was it right there at the jail—"

"Oh!" said the enlightened judge.

"—Right at the left-hand side of the door of the jail in this town of Siskiyou, who was it got that trembling boy safe inside from those yelling fiends and talked to the crowd on a barrel of number ten nails, and made those wicked men stop and go home?"

"Amanda, I believe I recognize myself."

"I should think you did, Judge Campbell. And now they've caught the other one, and he'll be up with the sheriff on tonight's train, and I suppose they'll lynch *him* now!"

"There's not the slightest danger," said the judge. "The town wants them to have a fair trial. It was natural that immediately after such an atrocious act—"

"Those poor boys had never murdered anybody before in their lives," interrupted Amanda.

"But they did murder Montgomery, you will admit."

"Oh yes!" said Mrs. Campbell, with impatience. "I saw the hole in his back. You needn't tell me all that again. If he'd thrown out the express box quicker they wouldn't have hurt a hair of his head. Wells and Fargo's messengers know that perfectly. It was his own fault. Those boys had no employment, and they only wanted money. They did not seek human blood, and you needn't tell me they did."

"They shed it, however, Amanda. Quite a lot of it. Stage-driver and a passenger too."

"Yes, you keep going back to that as if they'd all been murdered instead of only one, and you don't care about those two poor boys locked in a dungeon, and their gray-haired father down in Fresno County who never did anything wrong at all, and he sixty-one in December."

"The county isn't thinking of hanging the old gentleman," said the judge.

"That will do, Judge Campbell," said his lady, rising. "I shall say no more. Total silence for the present is best for you and best for me. Much best. I will leave you to think of your speech, which was by no means silver. Not even life with you for twenty-five years this coming 10th of July has inured me to insult. I am capable of understanding whom they think of hanging, and your speaking to me as if I did not does you little credit; for it was a mere refuge from a woman's just accusation of heartlessness which you felt, and like a man would not acknowledge; and therefore it is that I say no more but leave you to go down the street to the Ladies' Lyceum where I shall find companions with some spark of humanity in their bosoms and milk of human kindness for those whose hasty youth has plunged them in misery and delivered them to the hands of those who treat them as if they were stones and sticks full of nothing but monstrosity instead of breathing men like themselves to be shielded by brotherhood and hope and not dashed down by cruelty and despair."

It had begun stately as a dome, with symmetry and punctuation, but the climax was untrammeled by a single comma. The orator swept from the room, put on her bonnet and shawl, and the judge, still sitting with his eggs, heard the front door close behind her. She was president of the Ladies' Reform and Literary Lyceum, and she now trod thitherward through Siskiyou.

"I think Amanda will find companions there," mused the judge. "But her notions of sympathy beat me." The judge had a small, wise blue eye, and he liked his wife more than well. She was sincerely good, and had been very courageous in their young days of poverty. She loved their son, and she loved him. Only, when she took to talking, he turned up a mental coat-collar and waited. But if the male sex did not appreciate her powers of eloquence her sister citizens did; and Mrs. Campbell, besides presiding at the Ladies' Reform and Literary Lyceum in Siskiyou, often addressed female meetings in Ashland, Yreka, and even as far away as Tehama and Redding. She found companions this morning.

"To think of it!" they exclaimed, at her news of the capture, for none had read the paper. They had been too busy talking of the next debate, which was upon the question, "Ought we to pray for rain?" But now they instantly forgot the wide spiritual issues raised by this inquiry, and plunged into the fascinations of crime, reciting once more to each other the details of the recent tragedy. The room hired for the Lyceum was in a second story above the apothecary and book shop—a combined enterprise in Siskiyou—and was furnished with fourteen rocking chairs. Pictures of Mount Shasta and Lucretia Mott ornamented the wall, with a photograph from an old master representing Leda and the Swan. This typified the Lyceum's approval of Art, and had been presented by one of the husbands upon returning from a three days' business trip to San Francisco.

"Dear! Dear!" said Mrs. Parsons, after they had all shuddered anew over the shooting and the blood. "With so much suffering in the world, how fulsome seems that gay music!" She referred to the Siskiyou brass-band, which was rehearsing the march from "Fatinitza" in an adjacent room in the building. Mrs. Parsons had large, mournful eyes, a poetic vocabulary, and wanted to be president of the Lyceum herself.

"Melody has its sphere, Gertrude," said Mrs. Campbell, in a whole-some voice. "We must not be morbid. But this I say to you, one and all: Since the men of Siskiyou refuse, it is for the women to vindicate the town's humanity, and show some sympathy for the captive who arrives tonight."

They all thought so too.

"I do not criticize," continued their president, magnanimously, "nor do I complain of anyone. Each in this world has his or her mission, and the most sacred is Woman's own—to console!"

"True, true!" murmured Mrs. Slocum.

"We must do something for the prisoner, to show him we do not desert him in his hour of need," Mrs. Campbell continued.

"We'll go and meet the train!" Mrs. Slocum exclaimed, eagerly. "I've never seen a real murderer."

"A bunch of flowers for him," said Mrs. Parsons, closing her mournful eyes. "Roses." And she smiled faintly.

"Oh, lilies!" cried little Mrs. Day, with rapture. "Lilies would look *real* nice."

"Don't you think," said Miss Sissons, who had not spoken before, and sat a little apart from the close-drawn clump of talkers, "that we might send the widow some flowers too, sometime?" Miss Sissons was a pretty girl, with neat hair. She was engaged to the captain of Siskiyou's baseball nine.

"The widow?" Mrs. Campbell looked vague.

"Mrs. Montgomery, I mean—the murdered man's wife. I—I went to see if I could do anything, for she has some children; but she wouldn't see me," said Miss Sissons. "She said she couldn't talk to anybody."

"Poor thing!" said Mrs. Campbell. "I dare say it was a dreadful shock to her. Yes, dear, we'll attend to her after a while. We'll have her with us right along, you know, whereas these unhappy boys may—may be—may soon meet a cruel death on the scaffold." Mrs. Campbell evaded the phrase "may be hanged" rather skillfully. To her trained oratorical sense it had seemed to lack dignity.

"So young!" said Mrs. Day.

"And both so full of promise, to be cut off!" said Mrs. Parsons.

"Why, they can't hang them both, I should think," said Miss Sissons. "I thought only one killed Mr. Montgomery."

"My dear Louise," said Mrs. Campbell, "they can do anything they want, and they will. Shall I ever forget those ruffians who wanted to lynch the first one? They'll be on the jury!"

The clump returned to their discussion of the flowers, and Miss Sissons presently mentioned she had some errands to do, and departed.

"Would that that girl had more soul!" said Mrs. Parsons.

"She has plenty of soul," replied Mrs. Campbell, "but she's under the influence of a man. Well, as I was saying, roses and lilies are too big."

"Oh, *why?*" said Mrs. Day. "They would *please* him so."

"He couldn't carry them, Mrs. Day. I've thought it all out. He'll be walked to the jail between strong men. We must have some small bokay to pin on his coat, for his hands will be shackled."

"You don't say!" cried Mrs. Slocum. "How awful! I must get to that train. I've never seen a man in shackles in my life."

So violets were selected; Mrs. Campbell brought some in the afternoon from her own borders, and Mrs. Parsons furnished a large pin. She claimed also the right to affix the decoration upon the prisoner's breast because she had suggested the idea of flowers; but the other ladies protested, and the president seemed to think that they all should draw lots. It fell to Mrs. Day.

"Now I declare!" twittered the little matron. "I do believe I'll never dare."

"You must say something to him," said Amanda; "something fitting and choice."

"Oh dear no, Mrs. Campbell. Why, I never—my gracious! Why, if I'd known I was expected—Really, I couldn't think—I'll let *you* do it!"

"We can't hash up the ceremony that way, Mrs. Day," said Amanda, severely. And as they all fell arguing, the whistle blew.

"There!" said Mrs. Slocum. "Now you've made me late, and I'll miss the shackles and everything."

She flew downstairs, and immediately the town of Siskiyou saw twelve members of the Ladies' Reform and Literary Lyceum follow her in a hasty phalanx across the square to the station. The train approached slowly up the grade, and by the time the wide smokestack of the locomotive was puffing its wood smoke in clouds along the platform, Amanda had marshalled her company there.

"Where's the gals all goin', Bill?" inquired a large citizen in boots of the ticket agent.

"Nowheres, I guess, Abe," the agent replied. "Leastways, they 'ain't bought any tickets off me."

"Maybe they're for stealin' a ride," said Abe.

The mail and baggage cars had passed, and the women watched the smoking-car that drew up opposite them. Mrs. Campbell had informed her friends that the sheriff always went in the smoker; but on this occasion, for some reason, he had brought his prisoner in the Pullman sleeper at the rear, some way down the track, and Amanda's vigilant eye suddenly caught the group, already descended and walking away. The platoon of sympathy set off, and rapidly came up with the sheriff, while Bill, Abe, the train conductor, the Pullman conductor, the engineer, and the fireman abandoned their duty, and stared, in company with the brakemen and many passengers. There was perfect silence but for the pumping of the air-brake on the engine. The sheriff, not understanding what was coming, had half drawn his pistol; but now, surrounded by universal petticoats, he pulled off his hat and grinned doubtfully. The friend with him also stood bareheaded and grinning. He was young Jim Hornbrook, the muscular betrothed of Miss Sissons. The prisoner could not remove his hat, or he would have done so. Miss Sissons, who had come to the train to meet her lover, was laughing extremely in the middle of the road.

"Take these violets," faltered Mrs. Day, and held out the bunch, backing away slightly at the same time.

"Nonsense," said Amanda, stepping forward and grasping the flowers. "The women of Siskiyou are with you," she said, "as we are with all the afflicted." Then she pinned the violets firmly to the prisoner's flannel shirt. His face, at first amazed as the sheriff's and Hornbrook's, smoothed into cunning and vanity, while Hornbrook's turned an angry red, and the sheriff stopped grinning.

"Them flowers would look better on Buck Montgomery's grave, madam," said the officer. "Maybe you'll let us pass now." They went on to the jail.

"Waal," said Abe, on the platform, "that's the most disgustin' fool thing I ever did see."

"All aboard!" said the conductor, and the long train continued its way to Portland.

The platoon, well content, dispersed homeward to supper, and Jim Hornbrook walked home with his girl.

"For Lord's sake, Louise," he said, "who started that move?"

She told him the history of the morning.

"Well," he said, "you tell Mrs. Campbell, with my respects, that she's just playing with fire. A good woman like her ought to have more sense. Those men are going to have a fair trial."

"She wouldn't listen to me, Jim, not a bit. And, do you know, she really didn't seem to feel sorry—except just for a minute—about that poor woman."

"Louise, why don't you quit her outfit?"

"Resign from the Lyceum? That's so silly of you, Jim. We're not all crazy there; and that," said Miss Sissons, demurely, "is what makes a girl like me so valuable!"

"Well, I'm not stuck on having you travel with that lot."

"They speak better English than you do, Jim dear. Don't! In the street!"

"Sho! It's dark now," said Jim. "And it's been three whole days since—" But Miss Sissons escaped inside her gate and rang the bell. "Now see here, Louise," he called after her, "when I say they're playing with fire I mean it. That woman will make trouble in this town."

"She's not afraid," said Miss Sissons. "Don't you know enough about us yet to know we can't be threatened?"

"You!" said the young man. "I wasn't thinking of you." And so they separated.

Mrs. Campbell sat opposite the judge at supper, and he saw at once from her complacent reticence that she had achieved some triumph against his principles. She chatted about topics of the day in terms that were ingeniously trite. Then a letter came from their son in Denver, and she forgot her rôle somewhat, and read the letter aloud to the judge, and wondered wistfully who in Denver attended to the boy's buttons and socks; but she made no reference whatever to Siskiyou jail or those inside it. Next morning, however, it was the judge's turn to be angry.

"Amanda," he said, over the paper again, "you had better stick to socks, and leave criminals alone."

Amanda gazed at space with a calm smile.

"And I'll tell you one thing, my dear," her husband said, more incisively, "it don't look well that I should represent the law while my wife figures" (he shook the morning paper) "as a public nuisance. And one thing more: *Look out!* For if I know this community, and I think I do, you may raise something you don't bargain for."

"I can take care of myself, judge," said Amanda, always smiling. These two never were angry both at once, and today it was the judge that sailed out of the house. Amanda pounced instantly upon the paper. The article was headed "Sweet Violets." But the editorial satire only spurred the lady to higher efforts. She proceeded to the Lyceum, and found that "Sweet Violets" had been there before her. Every woman held a copy, and the fourteen rocking chairs were swooping up and down like things in a factory. In the presence of this blizzard, Mount Shasta, Lucretia Mott, and even Leda and the Swan looked singularly serene on their wall, although on the other side of the wall the "Fatinitza" march was booming brilliantly. But Amanda quieted the storm. It was her gift to be calm when others were not, and soon the rocking chairs were merely rippling.

"The way my boys scolded me—" began Mrs. Day.

"For men I care not," said Mrs. Parsons. "But when my own sister upbraids me in a public place—" The lady's voice ceased, and she raised her mournful eyes. It seemed she had encountered her unnatural relative at the post office. Everybody had a tale similar. Siskiyou had denounced their humane act.

"Let them act ugly," said Mrs. Slocum. "We will not swerve."

"I sent roses this morning," said Mrs. Parsons.

"*Did* you, dear?" said Mrs. Day. "My lilies shall go this afternoon."

"Here is a letter from the prisoner," said Amanda, producing the treasure; and they huddled to hear it. It was very affecting. It mentioned the violets blooming beside the hard couch, and spoke of prayer.

"He had lovely hair," said Mrs. Slocum.

"*So* brown!" said Mrs. Day.

"Black, my dear, and curly."

"Light brown. I was a good deal closer, Susan—"

"Never mind about his hair," said Amanda. "We are here not to flinch. We must act. Our course is chosen, and well chosen. The prison fare is a sin, and a beefsteak goes to them both at noon from my house."

"Oh, why didn't we ever think of that before?" cried the ladies, in an ecstasy, and fell to planning a series of lunches in spite of what Siskiyou might say or do. Siskiyou did not say very much; but it looked; and the ladies waxed more enthusiastic, luxuriating in a sense of martyrdom because now the prisoners were stopped writing any more letters to them. This was doubtless a high-handed step, and it set certain pulpits preaching about love. The day set for the trial was approaching; Amanda and her flock were going. Prayer meetings were held, food and flowers for the two in jail increased in volume, and every day saw some of the Lyceum waiting below the prisoners' barred windows till the men inside would thrust a hand through and wave to them; then they would shake a handkerchief in reply, and go away thrilled to talk it over at the Lyceum. And Siskiyou looked on all the while, darker and darker.

Then finally Amanda had a great thought. Listening to "Fatinitza" one morning, she suddenly arose and visited Herr Schwartz, the bandmaster. Herr Schwartz was a wise and well-educated German. They had a lengthy conference.

"I don't pelief dot vill be very goot," said the band-master.

But at that Amanda talked a good deal; and the worthy Teuton was soon bewildered, and at last gave a dubious consent, "since it would blease de ladies."

The president of the Lyceum arranged the coming event after her own heart. The voice of Woman should speak in Siskiyou. The helpless victims of male prejudice and the law of the land were to be flanked with consolation and encouragement upon the eve of their ordeal in court. In their lonely cell they were to feel that there were those outside whose hearts beat with theirs. The floral tribute was to be sumptuous, and Amanda had sent to San Francisco for pound cake. The special quality she desired could not be achieved by the Siskiyou confectioner.

Miss Sissons was not a party to this enterprise, and she told its various details to Jim Hornbrook, half in anger, half in derision. He listened without comment, and his face frightened her a little.

"Jim, what's the matter?" said she.

"Are you going to be at that circus?" he inquired.

"I thought I might just look on, you know," said Miss Sissons. "Mrs. Campbell and a brass-band—"

"You'll stay in the house that night, Louise."

"Why, the ring isn't on my finger yet," laughed the girl, "the fatal promise of obedience—" But she stopped, perceiving her joke was not a good one. "Of course, Jim, if you feel that way," she finished. "Only I'm grown up, and I like reasons."

"Well—that's all right too."

"Ho, ho! All right! Thank you, sir. Dear me!"

"Why, it ain't to please me, Louise; indeed it ain't. I can't swear everything won't be nice and all right and what a woman could be mixed up in, but—well, how should you know what men are, anyway, when they've been a good long time getting mad, and are mad all through? That's what this town is today, Louise."

"I don't know," said Miss Sissons, "and I'm sure I'd rather not know." And so she gave her promise. "But I shouldn't suppose," she added, "that the men of Siskiyou, mad or not, would forget that women are women."

Jim laughed. "Oh no," he said, "they ain't going to forget that."

The appointed day came; and the train came, several hours late, bearing the box of confectionery, addressed to the Ladies' Reform and Literary Lyceum. Bill, the ticket agent, held his lantern over it on the platform.

"That's the cake," said he.

"What cake?" Abe inquired.

Bill told him the rumor.

"Cake?" repeated Abe. "Fer them?" and he tilted his head towards the jail. "Will you say that again, friend? I ain't clear about it. *Cake,* did ye say?"

"Pound cake," said Bill. "Ordered special from San Francisco."

Now pound cake for adults is considered harmless. But it is curious how unwholesome a harmless thing can be if administered at the wrong time. The gaunt, savage-looking Californian went up to the box slowly. Then he kicked it lightly with his big boot, seeming to listen to its reverberation. Then he read the address. Then he sat down on the box to take a think. After a time he began speaking aloud. "They hold up a stage," he said, slowly. "They lay up a passenger fer a month. And they lame Bob Griffiths fer life. And then they do up Buck. Shoot a hole through his spine. And I helped bury him; fer I liked Buck." The speaker paused, and looked at the box. Then he got up. "I hain't attended their prayer-meetin's," said he, "and I hain't smelt their flowers. Such perfume's liable to make me throw up. But I guess I'll hev a look at their cake."

He went to the baggage room and brought an axe. The axe descended, and a splintered slat flew across the platform. "There's a lot of cake," said Abe. The top of the packing-case crashed on the railroad track, and three new men gathered to look on. "It's fresh cake too," remarked the destroyer. The box now fell to pieces, and the tattered paper wrapping was ripped away. "Step up, boys," said Abe, for a little crowd was there now. "Soft, ain't it?" They slung the cake about and tramped it in the grime and oil, and the boards of the box were torn apart and whirled away. There was a singular and growing impulse about all this. No one said anything; they were very quiet; yet the crowd grew quickly, as if called together by something in the air. One voice said, "Don't forgit we're all relyin' on yer serenade, Mark," and this raised a strange united laugh that broke brief and loud, and stopped, leaving the silence deeper than before. Mark and three more left, and walked towards the Lyceum. They were members of the Siskiyou band, and as they went one said that the town would see an interesting trial in the morning. Soon after they had gone the crowd moved from the station, compact and swift.

Meanwhile the Lyceum had been having disappointments. When the train was known to be late, Amanda had abandoned bestowing the cake until morning. But now a horrid thing had happened: the Siskiyou band refused its services! The rocking chairs were plying strenuously; but Amanda strode up and down in front of Mount Shasta and Lucretia Mott.

Herr Schwartz entered. "It's all right, madam," said he. "My trombone haf come back, und—"

"You'll play?" demanded the president.

"We blay for de ladies."

The rocking chairs were abandoned; the Lyceum put on its bonnet and shawl, and marshalled downstairs with the band.

"Ready," said Amanda.

"Ready," said Herr Schwartz to his musicians. "Go a leedle easy mit der Allegro, or we bust 'Fatinitza.'"

The spirited strains were lifted in Siskiyou, and the procession was soon at the jail in excellent order. They came round the corner with the trombone going as well as possible. Two jerking bodies dangled at the end of ropes, above the flare of torches. Amanda and her flock were shrieking.

"So!" exclaimed Herr Schwartz. "Dot was dose Healy boys we haf come to gif serenade." He signed to stop the music.

"No you don't," said two of the masked crowd, closing in with pistols. "You'll play fer them fellers till you're told to quit."

"Cerdainly," said the philosophical Teuton. "Only dey gif brobably very leedle attention to our Allegro."

So "Fatinitza" trumpeted on while the two on the ropes twisted, and grew still by-and-by. Then the masked men let the band go home. The Lyceum had scattered and fled long since, and many days passed before it revived again to civic usefulness, nor did its members find comfort from their men. Herr Schwartz gave a parting look at the bodies of the lynched murderers. "My!" said he, "das Ewigweibliche haf draw them apove sure enough."

Miss Sissons next day was walking and talking off her shock and excitement with her lover. "And oh, Jim," she concluded, after they had said a good many things, "you hadn't anything to do with it, had you?" The young man did not reply, and catching a certain expression on his face, she hastily exclaimed: "Never mind! I don't want to know—ever!"

So James Hornbrook kissed his sweetheart for saying that, and they continued their walk among the pleasant hills.

THE GENERAL'S BLUFF

THE TROOPS THIS DAY HAD GONE INTO WINTER-QUARTERS, AND SAT down to kill the idle time with pleasure until spring. After two hundred and forty days it is a good thing to sit down. The season had been spent in trailing, and sometimes catching, small bands of Indians. These had taken the habit of relieving settlers of their cattle and the tops of their heads. The weather-beaten troops had scouted over some two thousand aimless, veering miles, for the savages were fleet and mostly invisible, and knew the desert well. So, while the year turned, and the heat came, held sway, and went, the ragged troopers on the frontier were led an endless chase by the hostiles, who took them back and forth over flats of lime and ridges of slate, occasionally picking off a packer or a couple of privates, until now the sun was setting at 4:28 and it froze at any time of day. Therefore the rest of the packers and privates were glad to march into Boisé Barracks this morning by eleven, and see a stove.

They rolled for a moment on their bunks to get the feel of a bunk again after two hundred and forty days; they ate their dinner at a table; those who owned any further baggage than that which partially covered their nakedness unpacked it, perhaps nailed up a photograph or two, and found it grateful to sit and do nothing under a roof and listen to the grated snow whip the windows of the gray sandstone quarters. Such comfort, and the prospect of more ahead, of weeks of nothing but post duty and staying in the same place, obliterated Dry Camp, Cow Creek Lake, the blizzard on Meacham's Hill, the horse-killing in the John Day Valley, Saw-Tooth stampede, and all the recent evils of the past; the quarters hummed with cheerfulness. The nearest railroad was some four hundred miles to the southeast, slowly constructing to meet the next nearest, which was some nine hundred to the southeast; but Boisé City was only three-quarters of a mile away, the largest town in the territory, the capital, not a temperance town, a winter resort; and several hundred people lived in it, men and women, few of whom ever died in their beds. The coming days and nights were a luxury to think of.

"Blamed if there ain't a real tree!" exclaimed Private Jones.

"Thet eer ain't no tree, ye plum; thet's the flagpole 'n' th' Merrickin flag," observed a civilian. His name was Jack Long, and he was pack-master.

Sergeant Keyser, listening, smiled. During the winter of '64–65 he had been in command of the first battalion of his regiment, but, on a theory of education, had enlisted after the war. This being known, held the men more shy of him than was his desire.

Jones continued to pick his banjo, while a boyish trooper with tough black hair sat near him and kept time with his heels. "It's a cottonwood-tree I was speakin' of," observed Jones. There was one— a little, shivering white stalk. It stood above the flat where the barracks were, on a bench twenty or thirty feet higher, on which were built the officers' quarters. The air was getting dim with the fine, hard snow that slanted through it. The thermometer was ten above out there. At the mere sight and thought Mr. Long produced a flat bottle, warm from proximity to his flesh. Jones swallowed some drink, and looked at the little tree. "Snakes! But it feels good," said he, "to get something inside y'u and be inside yerself. What's the tax at Mike's dance-house now?"

"Dance 'n' drinks fer two fer one dollar," responded Mr. Long, accurately. He was sixty, but that made no difference.

"You and me'll take that in, Jock," said Jones to his friend, the black-haired boy. "'Sigh no more, ladies,'" he continued, singing. "The blamed banjo won't accompany that," he remarked, and looked out again at the tree. "There's a chap riding into the post now. Shabby-lookin'. Mebbe he's got stuff to sell."

Jack Long looked up on the bench at a rusty figure moving slowly through the storm. "Th' ole man!" he said.

"He ain't specially old," Jones answered. "They're apt to be older, them peddlers."

"Peddlers! Oh, ye-es." A seizure of very remarkable coughing took Jack Long by the throat; but he really had a cough, and, on the fit's leaving him, swallowed a drink, and offered his bottle in a manner so cold and usual that Jones forgot to note anything but the excellence of the whiskey. Mr. Long winked at Sergeant Keyser; he thought it a good plan not to inform his young friends, not just yet at any rate, that their peddler was General Crook. It would be pleasant to hear what else they might have to say.

The general had reached Boisé City that morning by the stage, quietly and unknown, as was his way. He had come to hunt Indians in the district of the Owyhee. Jack Long had discovered this, but only a few had been told the news, for the general wished to ask questions and receive answers, and to find out about all things; and he had noticed that this is not easy when too many people know who you are. He had called upon a friend or two in Boisé, walked about unnoticed, learned a number of facts, and now, true to his habit, entered the post wearing no uniform, none being necessary under the circumstances, and unattended by a single orderly. Jones and the black-haired Cumnor hoped he was a peddler, and innocently sat looking out of the window at him riding along the bench in front of the quarters, and occasionally slouching his wide, dark hat-brim against the stinging of the hard flakes. Jack Long, old and much experienced with the army, had scouted with Crook before, and knew him and his ways well. He also looked out of the window, standing behind Jones and Cumnor, with a huge hairy hand on a shoulder of each, and a huge wink again at Keyser.

"Blamed if he 'ain't stopped in front of the commanding officer's," said Jones.

"Lor'!" said Mr. Long, "there's jest nothin' them peddlers won't do."

"They ain't likely to buy anything off him in there," said Cumnor.

"Mwell, ef he's purvided with any *kind* o' Injun cur'os'tees, the missis she'll fly right on to 'em. Sh' 'ain't been merried out yere only haff'n year, 'n' when she spies feathers 'n' bead truck 'n' buckskin fer sale sh' hollers like a son of a gun. Enthoosiastic, ye know."

"He 'ain't got much of a pack," Jones commented, and at that moment "stables" sounded, and the men ran out to form and march to their grooming. Jack Long stood at the door and watched them file through the snow.

Very few enlisted men of the small command that had come in this morning from its campaign had ever seen General Crook. Jones, though not new to the frontier, had not been long in the army. He and Cumnor had enlisted in a happy-go-lucky manner together at Grant, in Arizona, when the general was elsewhere. Discipline was galling to his vagrant spirit, and after each pay day he had generally slept off the effects in the guard house, going there for other offenses between-whiles; but he was not of the stuff that deserts; also, he was excellent tempered, and his captain liked him for the way in which he could shoot Indians. Jack Long liked him too; and getting always a harmless pleasure from the mistakes of his friends, sincerely trusted there might be more about the peddler. He was startled at hearing his name spoken in his ear.

"*Nah!* Johnny, how you get on?"

"Hello, Sarah! Kla-how-ya, six?" said Long, greeting in Chinook the squaw interpreter who had approached him so noiselessly. "*Hy-as kloshe o-coke sun*" (It is a beautiful day).

The interpreter laughed—she had a broad, sweet, coarse face, and laughed easily—and said in English, "You hear about E-egante?"

Long had heard nothing recently of this Pah-Ute chieftain.

"He heap bad," continued Sarah, laughing broadly. "Come round ranch up here—"

"Anybody killed?" Long interrupted.

"No. All run away quick. Meester Dailey, he old man, he run all same young one. His old woman she run all same man. Get horse. Run away quick. Hu-hu!" and Sarah's rich mockery sounded again. No tragedy had happened this time, and the squaw narrated her story greatly to the relish of Mr. Long. This veteran of trails and mines had seen too much of life's bleakness not to cherish whatever of mirth his days might bring.

"Didn't burn the house?" he said.

"Not burn. Just make heap mess. Cut up featherbed hy-as ten-as [very small] and eat big dinner, hu-hu! Sugar, onions, meat, eat all. Then they find litt' cats walkin' round there."

"Lor'!" said Mr. Long, deeply interested, "they didn't eat *them*?"

"No. Not eat litt' cats. Put 'em two—man-cat and woman-cat—in molasses; put 'em in featherbed; all same bird. Then they hunt for whiskey, break everything, hunt all over, ha-lo whiskey!" Sarah shook her head. "Meester Dailey he good man. Hy-iu temperance. Drink water. They find his medicine; drink all up; make awful sick."

"I guess 'twar th' ole man's liniment," muttered Jack Long.

"Yas, milinut. They can't walk. Stay there long time, then Meester Dailey come back with friends. They think Injuns all gone; make noise, and E-egante he hear him come, and he not very sick. Run away. Some more run. But two Injuns heap sick: can't run. Meester Dailey he come round the corner; see awful mess everywhere; see two litt' cats sittin' in door all same bird, sing very loud. Then he see two Injuns on ground. They dead now."

"Mwell," said Long, "none of eer'll do. We'll hev to ketch E-egante."

"A—h!" drawled Sarah the squaw, in musical derision. "Maybe no catch him. All same jack rabbit."

"Jest ye wait, Sarah; Gray Fox hez come."

"Gen'l Crook!" said the squaw. "He come! Ho! He heap savvy." She stopped, and laughed again, like a pleased child. "Maybe no catch E-egante," she added, rolling her pretty brown eyes at Jack Long.

"You know E-egante?" he demanded.

"Yas, one time. Long time now. I litt' girl then." But Sarah remembered that long time, when she slept in a tent and had not been captured and put to school. And she remembered the tall young boys whom she used to watch shoot arrows, and the tallest, who shot most truly—at least, he certainly did now in her imagination. He had never spoken to her or looked at her. He was a boy of fourteen and she a girl of eight. Now she was twenty-five. Also she was tame and domesticated, with a white husband who was not bad to her, and children for each year of wedlock, who would grow up to speak English better than she could, and her own tongue not at all. And E-egante was not tame, and still lived in a tent. Sarah regarded white people as her friends, but she was proud of being an Indian, and she liked to think that her race could outwit the soldier now and then. She laughed again when she thought of old Mrs. Dailey running from E-egante.

"What's up with ye, Sarah?" said Jack Long, for the squaw's laughter had come suddenly on a spell of silence.

"Hé!" said she. "All same jackrabbit. No catch him." She stood shaking her head at Long, and showing her white, regular teeth. Then abruptly she went away to her tent without any word, not because she was in ill-humor or had thought of something, but because she was an Indian and had thought of nothing, and had no more to say. She met the men returning from the stables; admired Jones and smiled at him, upon which he murmured "Oh fie!" as he passed her. The troop broke ranks and dispersed, to lounge and gossip until mess-call. Cumnor and Jones were puting a little snow down each other's necks with friendly profanity, when Jones saw the peddler standing close and watching them. A high collar of some ragged fur was turned up round his neck, disguising the character of the ancient army overcoat to which it was attached, and spots and long stains extended down the legs of his corduroys to the charred holes at the bottom, where the owner had scorched them warming his heels and calves at many campfires.

"Hello, uncle," said Jones. "What y'u got in your pack?" He and Cumnor left their gambols and eagerly approached, while Mr. Jack Long, seeing the interview, came up also to hear it. "'Ain't y'u got something to sell?" continued Jones. "Y'u haven't gone and dumped yer whole outfit at the commanding officer's, have y'u now?"

"I'm afraid I have." The low voice shook ever so little, and if Jones had looked he would have seen a twinkle come and go in the gray-blue eyes.

"We've been out eight months, yu' know, fairly steady," pursued Jones, "and haven't seen nothing; and we'd buy most anything that ain't too damn bad," he concluded, plaintively.

Mr. Long, in the background, was whining to himself with joy, and he now urgently beckoned Keyser to come and hear this.

"If you've got some cheap poker chips," suggested Cumnor.

"And say, uncle," said Jones, raising his voice, for the peddler was moving away, "decks, and tobacco better than what they keep at the commissary. Me and my friend'll take some off your hands. And if you're comin' with new stock tomorrow, uncle" (Jones was now shouting after him), "why, we're single men, and y'u might fetch along a couple of squaws!"

"Holy smoke!" screeched Mr. Long, dancing on one leg.

"What's up with you, y'u ape?" inquired Specimen Jones. He looked at the departing peddler and saw Sergeant Keyser meet him and salute with stern, soldierly aspect. Then the peddler shook hands with the sergeant, seemed to speak pleasantly, and again Keyser saluted as he passed on. "What's that for?" Jones asked, uneasily. "Who is that hobo?"

But Mr. Long was talking to himself in a highly moralizing strain. "It ain't every young enlisted man," he was saying, "ez hez th' privilege of explainin' his wants at headquarters."

"Jones," said Sergeant Keyser, arriving, "I've a compliment for you. General Crook said you were a fine-looking man."

"General? What's that? Where did y'u see—What? *Him?*" The disgusting truth flashed clear on Jones. Uttering a single disconcerted syllable of rage, he wheeled and went by himself into the barracks, and lay down solitary on his bunk and read a newspaper until mess-call without taking in a word of it. "If they go to put me in the mill fer that," he said, sulkily, to many friends who brought him their congratulations, "I'm going to give 'em what I think about wearin' disguises."

"What do you think, Specimen?" said one.

"Give it to us now, Specimen," said another.

"Against the law, ain't it, Specimen?"

"Begosh!" said Jack Long. "Ef thet's so, don't lose no time warnin' the general, Specimen. Th' ole man 'd hate to be arrested."

And Specimen Jones told them all to shut their heads.

But no thought was more distant from General Crook's busy mind than putting poor Jones in the guard house. The trooper's willingness, after eight months hunting Indians, to buy almost anything brought a

"Ain't y'u got something to Sell?"

smile to his lips, and a certain sympathy in his heart. He knew what those eight months had been like; how monotonous, how well endured, how often dangerous, how invariably plucky, how scant of even the necessities of life, how barren of glory, and unrewarded by public recognition. The American "statesman" does not care about our army until it becomes necessary for his immediate personal protection. General Crook knew all this well; and realizing that these soldiers, who had come into winter-quarters this morning at eleven, had earned a holiday, he was sorry to feel obliged to start them out again tomorrow morning at two; for this was what he had decided upon.

He had received orders to drive on the reservation the various small bands of Indians that were roving through the country of the Snake and its tributaries, a danger to the miners in the Bannock Basin, and to the various ranches in west Idaho and east Oregon. As usual, he had been given an insufficient force to accomplish this, and, as always, he had been instructed by the "statesmen" to do it without violence—that is to say, he must never shoot the poor Indian until after the poor Indian had shot him; he must make him do something he did not want to, pleasantly, by the fascination of argument, in the way a "statesman" would achieve it. The force at the general's disposal was the garrison at Boisé Barracks—one troop of cavalry and one company of infantry. The latter was not adapted to the matter in hand—rapid marching and surprises; all it could be used for was as a reinforcement, and, moreover, somebody must be left at Boisé Barracks. The cavalry had had its full dose of scouting and skirmishing and long exposed marches, the horses were poor, and nobody had any trousers to speak of. Also, the troop was greatly depleted; it numbered forty men. Forty had deserted, and three—a sergeant and three privates—had cooked and eaten a vegetable they had been glad to dig up one day, and had spent the ensuing forty-five minutes in attempting to make their ankles beat the backs of their heads; after that the captain had read over them a sentence beginning, "Man that is born of a woman hath but a short time to live, and is full of misery"; and after that the camp was referred to as Wild Carrot Camp, because the sergeant had said the vegetable was wild carrot, whereas it had really been wild parsnip, which is quite another thing.

General Crook shook his head over what he saw. The men were ill-provided, the commissary and the quartermaster department were ill-provided; but it would have to do; the "statesmen" said our army was an extravagance. The Indians must be impressed and intimidated by the unlimited resources which the general had—not. Having come to this conclusion, he went up to the post commander's, and at supper astonished that officer by casual remarks which revealed a knowledge of the surrounding country, the small streams, the best camps for pasture, spots to avoid on account of bad water, what mules had sore backs, and many other things that the post commander would have liked dearly to ask the general where and when he had learned, only he did not dare. He did not even venture to ask him what he was going to do. Neither did Captain Glynn, who had been asked to meet the general. The general soon told them, however. "It may be a little cold," he concluded.

"Tomorrow, sir?" This from Captain Glynn. He had come in with the forty that morning. He had been enjoying his supper very much.

"I think so," said the general. "This E-egante is likely to make trouble if he is not checked." Then, understanding the thoughts of Captain Glynn, he added, with an invisible smile, "*You* need no preparations. You're in marching order. It's not as if your men had been here a long time and had to get ready for a start."

"Oh no," said Glynn, "it isn't like that." He was silent. "I think, if you'll excuse me, General," he said next, "I'll see my sergeant and give some orders."

"Certainly. And, Captain Glynn, I took the liberty of giving a few directions myself. We'll take an A tent, you know, for you and me. I see Keyser is sergeant in F troop. Glad we have a non-commissioned officer so competent. Haven't seen him since '64, at Winchester. Why, it's cleared off, I declare!"

It had, and the general looked out of the open door as Captain Glynn, departing, was pulling at his cigar. "How beautiful the planets are!" exclaimed Crook. "Look at Jupiter—there, just to the left of that little cottonwood-tree. Haven't you often noticed how much finer the stars shine in this atmosphere than in the East? Oh, Captain! I forgot to speak of extra horseshoes. I want some brought along."

"I'll attend to it, General."

"They shouldn't be too large. These California fourteen-and-a-half horses have smallish hoofs."

"I'll see the blacksmith myself, General."

"Thank you. Good night. And just order fresh stuffing put into the aparejos. I noticed three that had got lumpy." And the general shut the door and went to wipe out the immaculate barrels of his shotgun; for besides Indians there were grouse among the hills where he expected to go.

Captain Glynn, arriving at his own door, stuck his glowing cigar against the thermometer hanging outside: twenty-three below zero. "Oh Lord!" said the captain, briefly. He went in and told his striker to get Sergeant Keyser. Then he sat down and waited. "'Look at Jupiter!'" he muttered, angrily. "What an awful old man!"

It was rather awful. The captain had not supposed generals in the first two hours of their arrival at a post to be in the habit of finding out more about your aparejos than you knew yourself. But old the general was not. At the present day many captains are older than Crook was then.

Down at the barracks there was the same curiosity about what the "Old Man" was going to do as existed at the post commander's during the early part of supper. It pleased the cavalry to tell the infantry that the Old Man proposed to take the infantry to the Columbia River next week; and the infantry replied to the cavalry that they were quite right as to the river and the week, and it was hard luck the general needed only mounted troops on this trip. Others had heard he had come to superintend the building of a line of telegraph to Klamath, which would be a good winter's job for somebody; but nobody supposed that anything would happen yet awhile.

And then a man came in and told them the general had sent his boots to the saddler to have nails hammered in the soles.

"That eer means business," said Jack Long, "'n' I guess I'll nail up mee own cowhides."

"Jock," said Specimen Jones to Cumnor, "you and me 'ain't got any soles to ourn because they're contract boots, y'u see. I'll nail up yer feet if y'u say so. It's liable to be slippery."

Cumnor did not take in the situation at once. "What's your hurry?" he inquired of Jack Long. Therefore it was explained to him that when General Crook ordered his boots fixed you might expect to be on the road shortly. Cumnor swore some resigned, unemphatic oaths, fondly supposing that "shortly" meant some time or other; but hearing in the next five minutes the definite fact that F troop would get up at two, he made use of profound and thorough language, and compared the soldier with the slave.

"Why, y'u talk almost like a man, Jock," said Specimen Jones. "Blamed if y'u don't sound pretty near growed up."

Cumnor invited Jones to mind his business.

"Yer muss-tache has come since Arizona," continued Jones, admiringly, "and yer blue eye is bad-lookin'—worse than when we shot at yer heels and y'u danced fer us."

"I thought they were going to give as a rest," mumbled the youth, flushing. "I thought we'd be let stay here a spell."

"I thought so too, Jock. A little monotony would be fine variety. But a man must take his medicine, y'u know, and not squeal." Jones had lowered his voice, and now spoke without satire to the boy whom he had in a curious manner taken under his protection.

"Look at what they give us for a blanket to sleep in," said Cumnor. "A fellow can see to read the newspaper through it."

"Look at my coat, Cumnor." It was Sergeant Keyser showing the article furnished the soldier by the government. "You can spit through that." He had overheard their talk, and stepped up to show that all were in the same box. At his presence reticence fell upon the privates, and Cumnor hauled his black felt hat down tight in embarrassment, which strain split it open halfway round his head. It was another sample of regulation clothing, and they laughed at it.

"We all know the way it is," said Keyser, "and I've seen it a big sight worse. Cumnor, I've a cap I guess will keep your scalp warm till we get back."

And so at two in the morning F troop left the bunks it had expected to sleep in for some undisturbed weeks, and by four o'clock had eaten its well-known breakfast of bacon and bad coffee, and was following the "awful old man" down the north bank of the Boisé, leaving the silent, dead, wooden town of shanties on the other side half a mile behind in the darkness. The mountains south stood distant, ignoble, plain-featured heights, looming a clean-cut black beneath the piercing stars and the slice of hard, sharp-edged moon, and the surrounding plains of sage and dry-cracking weed slanted up and down to nowhere and nothing with desolate perpetuity. The snowfall was light and dry as sand, and the bare ground jutted through it at every sudden lump or knoll. The column moved through the dead polar silence, scarcely breaking it. Now and then a hoof rang on a stone, here and there a bridle or a saber clinked lightly; but it was too cold and early for talking, and the only steady sound was the flat, can-like tankle of the square bell that hung on the neck of the long-eared leader of the pack-train. They passed the Dailey ranch, and saw the kittens and the liniment-bottle, but could get no information as to what way E-egante had gone. The general did not care for that, however; he had devised his own route for the present, after a talk with the Indian guides. At the second dismounting during march he had word sent back to the pack-train not to fall behind, and the bell was to be taken off if the rest of the mules would follow without the sound of its shallow music. No wind moved the weeds or shook the stiff grass, and the rising sun glittered pink on the patched and motley-shirted men as they blew on their red hands or beat them against their legs. Some were lucky enough to have woollen or fur gloves, but many had only the white cotton affairs furnished by the government. Sarah the squaw laughed at them: the interpreter was warm as she rode in her bright green shawl. While the dismounted troopers stretched their limbs during the halt, she remained on her pony talking to one and another.

"Gray Fox heap savvy," said she to Mr. Long. "He heap get up in the mornin'."

"Thet's what he does, Sarah."

"Yas. No give soldier hy-as Sunday" (a holiday).

"No, no," assented Mr. Long. "Gray Fox go téh-téh" (trot).

"Maybe he catch E-egante, maybe put him in skoo-kum-house [prison]?" suggested Sarah.

"Oh no! Lor'! E-egante good Injun. White Father he feed him. Give him heap clothes," said Mr. Long.

"A—h!" drawled Sarah, dubiously, and rode by herself.

"You'll need watchin'," muttered Jack Long.

The trumpet sounded, the troopers swung into their saddles, and the line of march was taken up as before, Crook at the head of the column, his ragged fur collar turned up, his corduroys stuffed inside a wrinkled pair of boots, the shotgun balanced across his saddle, and nothing to reveal that he was any one in particular, unless you saw his face. As the morning grew bright, and empty, silent Idaho glistened under the clear blue, the general talked a little to Captain Glynn.

"E-egante will have crossed Snake River, I think," said he. "I shall try to do that today; but we must be easy on those horses of yours. We ought to be able to find these Indians in three days."

"If I were a lusty young chief," said Glynn, "I should think it pretty tough to be put on a reservation for dipping a couple of kittens in the molasses."

"So should I, Captain. But next time he might dip Mrs. Dailey. And I'm not sure he didn't have a hand in more serious work. Didn't you run across his tracks anywhere this summer?"

"No, sir. He was over on the Des Chutes."

"Did you hear what he was doing?"

"Having rows about fish and game with those Warm Spring Indians on the west side of the Des Chutes."

"They're always poaching on each other. There's bad blood between E-egante and Uma-Pine."

"Uma-Pine's friendly, sir, isn't he?"

"Well, that's a question," said Crook. "But there's no question about this E-egante and his Pah-Utes. We've got to catch him. I'm sorry for him. He doesn't see why he shouldn't hunt anywhere as his fathers did. I shouldn't see that either."

"How strong is this band reported, sir?"

"I've heard nothing I can set reliance upon," said Crook, instinctively leveling his shotgun at a big bird that rose; then he replaced the piece across his saddle and was silent. Now Captain Glynn had heard there were three hundred Indians with E-egante, which was a larger number than he had been in the habit of attacking with forty men. But he felt discreet about volunteering any information to the general after last night's exhibition of what the general knew. Crook partly answered what was in Glynn's mind. "This is the only available force I have," said he. "We must do what we can with it. You've found out by this time, Captain, that rapidity in following Indians up often works well. They have made up their minds—that is, if I know them— that we're going to loaf inside Boisé Barracks until the hard weather lets up."

Captain Glynn had thought so too, but he did not mention this, and the general continued. "I find that most people entertained this notion," he said, "and I'm glad they did, for it will help my first operations very materially."

The captain agreed that there was nothing like a false impression for assisting the efficacy of military movements, and presently the general asked him to command a halt. It was high noon, and the sun gleamed on the brass trumpet as the long note blew. Again the musical strain sounded on the cold, bright stillness, and the double line of twenty legs swung in a simultaneous arc over the horses' backs as the men dismounted.

"We'll noon here," said the general; and while the cook broke the ice on Boisé River to fill his kettles, Crook went back to the mules to see how the sore backs were standing the march. "How d'ye do, Jack Long?" said he. "Your stock is traveling pretty well, I see. They're loaded with thirty days' rations, but I trust we're not going to need it all."

"Mwell, General, I don't specially kyeer meself 'bout eatin' the hull outfit." Mr. Long showed his respect for the general by never swearing in his presence.

"I see you haven't forgotten how to pack," Crook said to him. "Can we make Snake River today, Jack?"

"That'll be forty miles, General. The days are pretty short."

"What are you feeding to the animals?" Crook inquired.

"Why, General, *you* know jest 's well 's me," said Jack, grinning.

"I suppose I do if you say so, Jack. Ten pounds first ten days, five pounds next ten, and you're out of grain for the next ten. Is that the way still?"

"Thet's the way, General, on these yere thirty-day affairs."

Through all this small-talk Crook had been inspecting the mules and the horses on picket-line, and silently forming his conclusion. He now returned to Captain Glynn and shared his mess-box.

They made Snake River. Crook knew better than Long what the animals could do. And next day they crossed, again by starlight, turned for a little way up the Owyhee, decided that E-egante had not gone that road, trailed up the bluffs and ledges from the Snake Valley on to the barren height of land, and made for the Malheur River, finding the eight hoofs of two deer lying in a melted place where a fire had been. Mr. Dailey had insisted that at least fifty Indians had drunk his liniment and trifled with his cats. Indeed, at times during his talk with General Crook the old gentleman had been sure there were a hundred. If this were their trail which the command had now struck, there may possibly have been eight. It was quite evident that the chief had not taken any three hundred warriors upon that visit, if he had that number anywhere. So the column went up the Malheur main stream through the sagebrush and the gray weather (it was still cold, but no sun any more these last two days), and, coming to the North Fork, turned up towards a spur of the mountains and Castle Rock. The water ran smooth black between its edging of ice, thick, white, and crusted like slabs of cocoanut candy, and there in the hollow of a bend they came suddenly upon what they sought.

Stems of smoke, faint and blue, spindled up from a blurred acre of willow thicket, dense, tall as two men, a netted brown and yellow mesh of twigs and stiff wintry rods. Out from the level of their close, nature-woven tops rose at distances the straight, slight blue smoke-lines, marking each the position of some invisible lodge. The whole acre was a bottom ploughed at some former time by a wash-out, and the troops looked down on it from the edge of the higher ground, silent in the quiet, gray afternoon, the empty sagebrush territory stretching a short way to fluted hills that were white below and blackened with pines above.

The general, taking a rough chance as he often did, sent ground scouts forward and ordered a charge instantly, to catch the savages unready; and the stiff rods snapped and tangled between the beating hoofs. The horses plunged at the elastic edges of this excellent

fortress, sometimes half lifted as a bent willow levered up against
their bellies, and the forward-tilting men fended their faces from the
whipping twigs. They could not wedge a man's length into that pliant labyrinth, and the general called them out. They rallied among
the sagebrush above, Crook's cheeks and many others painted with
purple lines of blood, hardened already and cracking like enamel.
The baffled troopers glared at the thicket. Not a sign nor a sound
came from in there. The willows, with the gentle tints of winter veiling their misty twigs, looked serene and even innocent, fitted to
harbor birds—not birds of prey—and the quiet smoke threaded
upwards through the air. Of course the liniment-drinkers must have
heard the noise.

"What do you suppose they're doing?" inquired Glynn.

"Looking at us," said Crook.

"I wish we could return the compliment," said the captain.

Crook pointed. Had any wind been blowing, what the general saw
would have been less worth watching. Two willow branches shook,
making a vanishing ripple on the smooth surface of the treetops. The
pack-train was just coming in sight over the rise, and Crook immediately sent an orderly with some message. More willow branches
shivered an instant and were still; then, while the general and the
captain sat on their horses and watched, the thicket gave up its secret
to them; for, as little light gusts coming abreast over a lake travel and
touch the water, so in different spots the level maze of twigs was
stirred; and if the eye fastened upon any one of these it could have
been seen to come out from the center towards the edge, successive
twigs moving, as the tops of long grass tremble and mark the progress
of a snake. During a short while this increased greatly, the whole
thicket moving with innumerable tracks. Then everything ceased,
with the blue wands of smoke rising always into the quiet afternoon.

"Can you see 'em?" said Glynn.

"Not a bit. Did you happen to hear anyone give an estimate of
this band?"

Glynn mentioned his tale of the three hundred.

It was not new to the general, but he remarked now that it must
be pretty nearly correct; and his eye turned a moment upon his forty

troopers waiting there, grim and humorous; for they knew that the thicket was looking at them, and it amused their American minds to wonder what the Old Man was going to do about it.

"It's his bet, and he holds poor cards," murmured Specimen Jones; and the neighbors grinned.

And here the Old Man continued the play that he had begun when he sent the orderly to the pack-train. That part of the command had halted in consequence, disposed itself in an easygoing way, half in, half out of sight on the ridge, and men and mules looked entirely careless. Glynn wondered; but no one ever asked the general questions, in spite of his amiable voice and countenance. He now sent for Sarah the squaw.

"You tell E-egante," he said, "that I am not going to fight with his people unless his people make me. I am not going to do them any harm, and I wish to be their friend. The White Father has sent me. Ask E-egante if he has heard of Gray Fox. Tell him Gray Fox wishes E-egante and all his people to be ready to go with him tomorrow at nine o'clock."

And Sarah, standing on the frozen bank, pulled her green shawl closer, and shouted her message faithfully to the willows. Nothing moved or showed, and Crook, riding up to the squaw, held his hand up as a further sign to the flag of peace that had been raised already. "Say that I am Gray Fox," said he.

On that there was a moving in the bushes farther along, and, going opposite that place with the squaw, Crook and Glynn saw a narrow entrance across which some few branches reached that were now spread aside for three figures to stand there.

"E-egante!" said Sarah, eagerly. "See him big man!" she added to Crook, pointing. A tall and splendid buck, gleaming with colors, and rich with fringe and buckskin, watched them. He seemed to look at Sarah, too. She, being ordered, repeated what she had said; but the chief did not answer.

"He is counting our strength," said Glynn.

"He's done that some time ago," said Crook. "Tell E-egante," he continued to the squaw, "that I will not send for more soldiers than he sees here. I do not wish anything but peace unless he wishes otherwise."

Sarah's musical voice sounded again from the bank, and E-egante watched her intently till she was finished. This time he replied at some length. He and his people had not done any harm. He had heard of Gray Fox often. All his people knew Gray Fox was a good man and would not make trouble. There were some flies that stung a man sitting in his house, when he had not hurt them. Gray Fox would not hurt anyone till their hand was raised against him first. E-egante and his people had wondered why the horses made so much noise just now. He and his people would come tomorrow with Gray Fox.

And then he went inside the thicket again, and the willows looked as innocent as ever. Crook and the captain rode away.

"My speech was just a little weak coming on top of a charge of cavalry," the general admitted. "And that fellow put his finger right on the place. I'll give you my notion, Captain. If I had said we had more soldiers behind the hill, like as not this squaw of ours would have told him I lied; she's an uncertain quantity, I find. But I told him the exact truth—that I had no more—and he won't believe it, and that's what I want."

So Glynn understood. The pack-train had been halted in a purposely exposed position, which would look to the Indians as if another force was certainly behind it, and every move was now made to give an impression that the forty were only the advance of a large command. Crook pitched his A tent close to the red men's village, and the troops went into camp regardlessly near. The horses were turned out to graze ostentatiously unprotected, so that the people in the thicket should have every chance to notice how secure the white men felt. The mules pastured comfortably over the shallow snow that crushed as they wandered among the sage-bush, and the square bell hung once more from the neck of the leader and tankled upon the hill. The shelter-tents littered the flat above the wash-out, and besides the cook-fire others were built irregularly far down the Malheur North Fork, shedding an extended glimmer of deceit. It might have been the camp of many hundred. A little blaze shone comfortably on the canvas of Crook's tent, and Sergeant Keyser, being in charge of camp, had adopted the troop cook-fire for his camp guard after the cooks had finished their work. The willow thicket below grew black and mysterious, and quiet fell on the white camp. By eight the troopers had gone to bed. Night had come pretty cold, and a little occasional breeze, that passed like a chill hand laid a moment on the face, and went down into the willows. Now and again the water running through the ice would lap and gurgle at some air-hole. Sergeant Keyser sat by his fire and listened to the lonely bell sounding from the dark. He wished the men would feel more at home with him. With Jack Long, satirical, old, and experienced, they were perfectly familiar, because he was a civilian; but to Keyser, because he had been in command of a battalion, they held the attitude of schoolboys to a master—the instinctive feeling of all privates towards all officers. Jones and Cumnor were members of his camp guard. Being just now off post, they stood at the fire, but away from him.

"How do you like this compared with barracks?" the sergeant asked, conversationally.

"It's all right," said Jones.

"Did you think it was all right that first morning? I didn't enjoy it much myself. Sit down and get warm, won't you?"

The men came and stood awkwardly. "I 'ain't never found any excitement in getting up early," said Jones, and was silent. A burning log shifted, and the bell sounded in a new place as the leader pastured along. Jones kicked the log into better position. "But this affair's gettin' inter-esting," he added.

"Don't you smoke?" Keyser inquired of Cumnor, and tossed him his tobacco-pouch. Presently they were seated, and the conversation going better. Arizona was compared with Idaho. Everybody had gone to bed.

"Arizona's the most outrageous outrage in the United States," declared Jones.

"Why did you stay there six years, then?" said Cumnor.

"Guess I'd been there yet but for you comin' along and us both enlistin' that crazy way. Idaho's better. Only," said Jones, thoughtfully, "coming to an icebox from a hundred thousand in the shade, it's a wonder a man don't just split like a glass chimbly."

The willows crackled, and all laid hands on their pistols.

"How! How!" said a strange, propitiating voice.

It was a man on a horse, and directly they recognized E-egante himself. They would have raised an alarm, but he was alone, and plainly not running away. Nor had he weapons. He rode into the firelight, and "How! How!" he repeated, anxiously. He looked and nodded at the three, who remained seated.

"Good-evening," said the sergeant.

"Christmas is coming," said Jones, amicably.

"How! How!" said E-egante. It was all the English he had. He sat on his horse, looking at the men, the camp, the cook-fire, the A tent, and beyond into the surrounding silence. He started when the bell suddenly jangled near by. The wandering mule had only shifted in towards the camp and shaken his head; but the Indian's nerves were evidently on the sharpest strain.

"Sit down!" said Keyser, making signs, and at these E-egante started suspiciously.

"Warm here!" Jones called to him, and Cumnor showed his pipe.

The chief edged a thought closer. His intent, brilliant eyes seemed almost to listen as well as look, and though he sat his horse with heedless grace and security, there was never a figure more ready for vanishing upon the instant. He came a little nearer still, alert and pretty as an inquisitive buck antelope, watching not the three soldiers only, but everything else at once. He eyed their signs to dismount, looked at their faces, considered, and with the greatest slowness got off and came stalking to the fire. He was a fine tall man, and they smiled and nodded at him, admiring his clean blankets and the magnificence of his buckskin shirt and leggings.

"He's a jim-dandy," said Cumnor.

"You bet the girls think so," said Jones. "He gets his pick. For you're a fighter too, ain't y'u?" he added, to E-egante.

"How! How!" said that personage, looking at them with grave affability from the other side of the fire. Reassured presently, he accepted the sergeant's pipe: but even while he smoked and responded to the gestures, the alertness never left his eye, and his tall body gave no sense of being relaxed. And so they all looked at each other across the waning embers, while the old pack-mule moved about at the edge of camp, crushing the crusted snow and pasturing along. After a time E-egante gave a nod, handed the pipe back, and went into his thicket as he had come. His visit had told him nothing; perhaps he had never supposed it would, and came from curiosity. One person had watched this interview. Sarah the squaw sat out in the night, afraid for her ancient hero; but she was content to look upon his beauty, and go to sleep after he had taken himself from her sight. The soldiers went to bed, and Keyser lay wondering for a while before he took his nap between his surveillances. The little breeze still passed at times, the running water and the ice made sounds together, and he could hear the wandering bell, now distant on the hill, irregularly punctuating the flight of the dark hours.

By nine next day there was the thicket sure enough, and the forty waiting for the three hundred to come out of it. Then it became ten o'clock, but that was the only difference, unless perhaps Sarah the squaw grew more restless. The troopers stood ready to be told what to do, joking together in low voices now and then; Crook sat watching Glynn smoke; and through these stationary people walked Sarah, looking wistfully at the thicket, and then at the faces of the adopted race she served. She hardly knew what was in her own mind. Then it became eleven, and Crook was tired of it, and made the capping move in his bluff. He gave the orders himself.

"Sergeant."

Keyser saluted.

"You will detail eight men to go with you into the Indian camp. The men are to carry pistols under their overcoats, and no other arms. You will tell the Indians to come out. Repeat what I said to them last night. Make it short. I'll give them ten minutes. If they don't come by then a shot will be fired out here. At that signal you will remain in there and blaze away at the Indians."

So Keyser picked his men.

The thirty-one remaining troopers stopped joking, and watched the squad of nine and the interpreter file down the bank to visit the three hundred. The dingy overcoats and the bright green shawl passed into the thicket, and the general looked at his watch. Along the bend of the stream clear noises tinkled from the water and the ice.

"What are they up to?" whispered a teamster to Jack Long. Long's face was stern, but the teamster's was chalky and tight drawn. "Say," he repeated, insistently, "what are we going to do?"

"We're to wait," Long whispered back, "till nothin' happens, and then th' Ole Man'll fire a gun and signal them boys to shoot in there."

"Oh, it's to be waitin'?" said the teamster. He fastened his eyes on the thicket, and his lips grew bloodless. The running river sounded more plainly. "—— ——it!" cried the man, desperately, "let's start the fun, then." He whipped out his pistol, and Jack Long had just time to seize him and stop a false signal.

"Why, you must be skeered," said Long. "I've a mind to beat yer skull in."

"Waitin's so awful," whimpered the man. "I wisht I was along with them in there."

Jack gave him back his revolver. "There," said he; "ye're not skeered, I see. Waitin' ain't nice."

The eight troopers with Keyser were not having anything like so distasteful a time. "Jock," said Specimen Jones to Cumnor, as they followed the sergeant into the willows and began to come among the lodges and striped savages, "you and me has saw Injuns before, Jock."

"And we'll do it again," said Cumnor.

Keyser looked at his watch: Four minutes gone. "Jones," said he, "you patrol this path to the right so you can cover that gang there. There must be four or five lodges down that way. Cumnor, see that dugout with side-thatch and roofing of tule? You attend to that family. It's a big one—all brothers." Thus the sergeant disposed his men quietly and quick through the labyrinth till they became invisible to each other; and all the while flights of Indians passed, half seen, among the tangle, fleeting visions of yellow and red through the quiet-colored twigs. Others squatted stoically, doing nothing. A few had guns, but most used arrows, and had these stacked beside them where they squatted. Keyser singled out a somewhat central figure—Fur Cap was his name—as his starting-point if the signal should sound. It must sound now in a second or two. He would not look at his watch lest it should hamper him. Fur Cap sat by a pile of arrows, with a gun across his knees besides. Keyser calculated that by standing close to him as he was, his boot would catch the Indian under the chin just right, and save one cartridge. Not a red man spoke, but Sarah the squaw dutifully speechified in a central place where paths met near Keyser and Fur Cap. Her voice was persuasive and warning. Some of the savages moved up and felt Keyser's overcoat. They fingered the hard bulge of the pistol underneath, and passed on, laughing, to the next soldier's coat, while Sarah did not cease to harangue. The tall, stately man of last night appeared. His full dark eye met Sarah's, and the woman's voice faltered and her breathing grew troubled as she gazed at him. Once more Keyser looked at his watch: Seven minutes. E-egante noticed Sarah's emotion, and his face showed that her face pleased him. He spoke in a deep voice to Fur Cap, stretching a fringed arm out towards the hill with a royal gesture, at which Fur Cap rose.

"He will come, he will come!" said the squaw, running to Keyser. "They all come now. Do not shoot."

"Let them show outside, then," thundered Keyser, "or it's too late. If that gun goes before I can tell my men—"

He broke off and rushed to the entrance. There were skirmishers deploying from three points, and Crook was raising his hand slowly. There was a pistol in it. "General! General!" Keyser shouted, waving both hands, "No!" Behind him came E-egante, with Sarah, talking in low tones, and Fur Cap came too.

The general saw, and did not give the signal. The sight of the skirmishers hastened E-egante's mind. He spoke in a loud voice, and at once his warriors began to emerge from the willows obediently. Crook's bluff was succeeding. The Indians in waiting after nine were attempting a little bluff of their own; but the unprecedented visit of nine men appeared to them so dauntless that all notion of resistance left them. They were sure Gray Fox had a large army. And they came, and kept coming, and the place became full of them. The troopers had all they could do to form an escort and keep up the delusion, but by degrees order began, and the column was forming. Riding along the edge of the willows came E-egante, gay in his blankets, and saying, "How! How!" to Keyser, the only man at all near him. The pony ambled, and sidled, paused, trotted a little, and Keyser was beginning to wonder, when all at once a woman in a green shawl sprang from the thicket,

"He Hesitated to Kill the Woman"

leaped behind the chief, and the pony flashed by and away, round the curve. Keyser had lifted his carbine, but forbore; for he hesitated to kill the woman. Once more the two appeared, diminutive and scurrying, the green shawl bright against the hillside they climbed. Sarah had been willing to take her chances of death with her hero, and now she vanished with him among his mountains, returning to her kind, and leaving her wedded white man and half-breeds forever.

"I don't feel so mad as I ought," said Specimen Jones.

Crook laughed to Glynn about it. "We've got a big balance of 'em," he said, "if we can get 'em all to Boisé. They'll probably roast me in the East." And they did. Hearing how forty took three hundred, but let one escape (and a few more on the march home), the superannuated cattle of the War Department sat sipping their drink at the club in Washington, and explained to each other how they would have done it.

And so the general's bluff partly failed. E-egante kept his freedom, "all along o' thet yere pizen squaw," as Mr. Long judiciously remarked. It was not until many years after that the chief's destiny overtook him; and concerning that, things both curious and sad could be told.[1]

SALVATION GAP

AFTER CUTTING THE GAZELLE'S THROAT, DRYLYN HAD GONE OUT OF her tent, secure and happy in choosing the skillful moment. They would think it was the other man—the unknown one. There were his boot-prints this fine morning, marking his way from the tent down the hill into the trees. He was not an inhabitant of the camp. This was his first visit, cautiously made, and nobody had seen him come or go except Drylyn.

The woman was proprietor of the dancehall at Salvation Gap, and on account of her beauty and habits had been named the American Beer Gazelle by a traveling naturalist who had education, and was interested in the wild animals of all countries. Drylyn's relations with the Gazelle were colored with sentiment. The sentiment on his part was genuine; so genuine that the shrewd noticing camp joked Drylyn, telling him he had grown to look young again under the elixir of romance. One of the prospectors had remarked fancifully that Drylyn's "rusted mustache had livened up; same ez flow'rs ye've kerried a long ways when yer girl puts 'em in a pitcher o' water." Being the sentiment of a placer miner, the lover's feeling took no offense or wound at any conduct of the Gazelle's that was purely official; it was for him that she personally cared. He never thought of suspecting anything when, after one of her trips to Folsom, she began to send away some of the profits—gold, coined sometimes, sometimes raw dust—that her hall of entertainment earned for her. She mentioned to him that her mother in San Anton' needed it, and simple-minded Drylyn believed. It did not occur to him to ask, or even wonder, how it came that this mother had never needed money until so lately, or why the trips to Folsom became so constant. Counting her middle-aged adorer a fool, the humorous Gazelle had actually, once, on being prevented from taking the journey herself, asked him to carry the package to Folsom for her, and deliver it there to a certain shotgun messenger of the express company, who would see that it went to the right place. A woman's name and an address at San Antonio were certainly scrawled on the parcel. The faithful Drylyn waited till the stage came in, and handed over his treasure to the messenger, who gave him one amazed look that he did not notice. He ought to have seen that young man awhile afterwards, the package torn open, a bag of dust on his knee, laughing almost to tears over a letter he had found with the gold inside the wrapping. But Drylyn was on the road up to Salvation Gap at that time. The shotgun messenger was twenty-three; Drylyn was forty-five. Gazelles are apt to do this sort of thing. After all, though, it was silly, just for the sake of a laugh, to let the old lover learn the face of his secret rival. It was one of those early unimagined nails people sometimes drive in their own coffins. An ancient series of events followed: continued abject faith and passion on the miner's part; continued presents of dust from him to the lady; on her part continued trips to Folsom, a lessened caution, and a brag of manner based upon her very just popularity at the Gap; next, Drylyn's first sickening dawn of doubt, jealousy equipping him with a new and alien slyness; the final accident of his seeing the shotgun messenger on his very first visit to the Gap come out of the Gazelle's tent so early in the morning; the instant blaze of truth and fury that turned Drylyn to a clever, calculating wild beast. So now her throat was cut, and she was good and dead. He had managed well. The whole game had shown instantly like a picture on his brain, complete at a stroke, with every move clear. He had let the man go down the hill—just for the present. The camp had got up, eaten its breakfast, and gone out to the ditches, Drylyn along with the rest. Owing to its situation, neighbors could not see him presently leave his claim and walk back quickly to the Gap at an hour when the dancehall was likely to be lonely. He had ready what to say if the other women should be there; but they were away at the creek below, washing, and the luxurious, unsuspecting Gazelle was in bed in her own tent, not yet disturbed. The quiet wild beast walked through the deserted front entrance of the hall in the most natural manner, and so behind among the empty bottles, and along the plank into the tent; then, after a while, out again. She would never be disturbed now, and the wild beast was back at his claim, knee-deep, and busy among the digging and the wetness, in another pair of overalls just like the ones that were now under some stones at the bottom of a mud-puddle. And then one very bad long scream came up to the ditches, and Drylyn knew the women had returned from their washing.

He raised his head mechanically to listen. He had never been a bad man; had never wished to hurt anybody in his life before that he could remember; but as he pondered upon it in his slow, sure brain, he knew that he was glad he had done this, and was going to do more. He was going to follow those tracks pretty soon, and finish the whole job with his own hand. They had fooled him, and had taken trouble to do it; gone out of their way, made game of him to the quick; and when he remembered, for the twentieth time this morning, that day he had carried the package of gold-dust—some of it very likely his own—to the smooth-faced messenger at Folsom, Drylyn's stolid body trembled from head to foot, and he spoke blind, inarticulate words.

But down below there the screams were sounding. A brother miner came running by. Drylyn realized that he ought to be running too, of course, and so he ran. All the men were running from their various scattered claims, and Salvation Gap grew noisy and full of people at once. There was the sheriff also, come up last evening on the track of some stage-robbers, and quite opportune for this, he thought. He liked things to be done legally. The turmoil of execration and fierce curiosity thrashed about for the right man to pitch on for this crime. The murdered woman had been so good company, so hearty a wit, such a robust songstress, so tireless a dancer, so thoroughly every-body's friend, that it was inconceivable to the mind of Salvation Gap that anybody there had done it. The women were crying and wringing their hands—the Gazelle had been good to them too; the men were talking and cursing, all but Drylyn there among them, serious and strange-looking; so silent that the sheriff eyed him once or twice, though he knew nothing of the miner's infatuation. And then some woman shrieked out the name of Drylyn, and the crowd had him gripped in a second, to let him go the next, laughing at the preposterous idea. Saying nothing? Of course he didn't feel like talking. To be sure he looked dazed. It was hard luck on him. They told the sheriff about him and the Gazelle. They explained that Drylyn was "sort of loony, anyway," and the sheriff said, "Oh!" and began to wonder and surmise in this half-minute they had been now gathered, when suddenly the inevitable boot-prints behind the tent down the hill were found. The shout of discovery startled Drylyn as genuinely as if he had never known, and he joined the wild rush of people to the hill. Nor was this acting. The violence he had set going, and in which he swam like a straw, made him forget, or for the moment drift away from, his arranged thoughts, and the tracks on the hill had gone clean out of his head. He was become a mere blank spectator in the storm, incapable of calculation. His own handiwork had stunned him, for he had not foreseen that consequences were going to rise and burst like this. The next thing he knew he was in a pursuit, with pine-trees passing, and the hurrying sheriff remarking to the band that he proposed to maintain order. Drylyn heard his neighbor, a true Californian, whose words were lightest when his purpose was most serious, telling the sheriff that order was certainly Heaven's first law, and an elegant thing anywhere. But the anxious officer made no retort in kind, and only said that irregularities were damaging to the county's good name, and would keep settlers from moving in. So the neighbor turned to Drylyn and asked him when he was intending to wake up, as sleepwalking was considered to be unhealthy. Drylyn gave a queer, almost wistful, smile, and so they went along; the chatty neighbor spoke low to another man, and said he had never sized up the true state of Drylyn's feeling for the Gazelle, and that the sheriff might persuade some people to keep regular, when they found the man they were hunting, but he doubted if the sheriff would be persuading enough for Drylyn. They came out on a road, and the sleep-walker recognized a rock and knew how far they had gone, and that this was the stage-road between Folsom

and Surprise Springs. They followed the road, and round a bend came
on the man. He had been taking it easily, being in no hurry, He had
come to this point by the stage the night before, and now he was waiting for its return to take him back to Folsom. He had been lunching,
and was seated on a stone by a small creek. He looked up and saw
them, and their gait, and ominous compactness. What he did was not
the thing for him to do. He leaped into cover and drew his revolver.
This attempt at defense and escape was really for the sake of the gold-
dust he had in his pocket. But when he recognized the sheriff's voice,
telling him it would go better with him if he did not try to kill any
more people, he was greatly relieved that it was not highwaymen after
him and his little gold, and he put up his pistol and waited for them,
smiling, secure in his identity; and when they drew nearer he asked
them how many people he had killed already. They came up and
caught him and found the gold in a moment, ripping it from his
pocket, and the yell they gave at that stopped his smiling entirely.
When he found himself in irons and hurried along, he began to
explain that there was some mistake, and was told by the chatty neighbor that maybe killing a woman was always a mistake, certainly one this
time. As they walked him among them they gave small notice to his
growing fright and bewilderment, but when he appealed to the sheriff
on the score of old acquaintanceship, and pitifully begged to know
what they supposed he had done, the miners laughed curiously. That
brought his entreating back to them, and he assured them, looking in
their faces, that he truly did need to be told why they wanted him. So
they held up the gold and asked him whose that had been, and he
made a wretched hesitation in answering. If anything was needed to
clinch their certainty, that did. They could not know that the young
successful lover had recognized Drylyn's strange face, and did not
want to tell the truth before him, and hence was telling an unskillful
lie instead. A rattle of wheels sounded among the pines ahead, and the
stage came up and stopped. Only the driver and a friend were on it,
and both of them knew the shotgun messenger and the sheriff, and
they asked in some astonishment what the trouble was. It had been
stage-robbers the sheriff had started after, the driver thought. And—as
he commented in friendly tones—to turn up with Wells and Fargo's

messenger was the neatest practical joke that had occurred in the county for some time. The always serious and anxious sheriff told the driver the accusation, and it was a genuine cry of horror that the young lover gave at hearing the truth at last, and at feeling the ghastly chain of probability that had wound itself about him.

The sheriff wondered if there were a true ring in the man's voice. It certainly sounded so. He was talking with rapid agony, and it was the whole true story that was coming out now. But the chatty neighbor nudged another neighbor at the new explanation about the gold-dust. That there was no great quantity of it, after all, weighed little against this double accounting for one simple fact; moreover, the new version did not do the messenger credit in the estimation of the miners, but gave them a still worse opinion of him. It is scarcely fair to disbelieve what a man says he did, and at the same time despise him for having done it. Miners, however, are rational rather than logical; while the listening sheriff grew more determined there should be a proper trial, the deputation from the Gap made up its mind more inexorably the other way. It had even been in the miners' heads to finish the business here on the Folsom road, and get home for supper; pine-trees were handy, and there was rope in the stage. They were not much moved by the sheriff's plea that something further might have turned up at the Gap; but at the driver's more forcible suggestion that the Gap would feel disappointed at being left out, they consented to take the man back there. Drylyn never offered any opinion, or spoke at all. It was not necessary that he should, and they forgot about him. It was time to be getting along, they said. What was the good in standing in the road here? They nodded good day to the stage-driver, and took themselves and the prisoner into the pines. Once the sheriff had looked at the driver and his friend perched on the halted stage, but he immediately saw too much risk in his half-formed notion of an alliance with them to gallop off with the prisoner; his part must come later, if at all.

But the driver had perfectly understood the sheriff's glance, and he was on the sheriff's side, though he showed no sign. As he drove along he began thinking about the way the prisoner had cried out just now, and the inconsiderable value of the dust, and it became clear in his mind that this was a matter for a court and twelve quiet men. The friend beside him was also intent upon his own thoughts, and neither said a word to the other upon the lonely road. The horses soon knew that they were not being driven any more, and they slackened their pace, and finding no reproof came for this, they fell to a comfortable walk. Presently several had snatched a branch in passing, and it waved from their mouths as they nibbled. After that they gave up all pretence at being stage-horses, and the driver noticed them. From habit he whipped them up into shape and gait, and the next moment pulled them in short, at the thought that had come to him. The prisoner must be got away from the Gap. The sheriff was too single-handed among such a crowd as that, and the driver put a question to his friend. It could be managed by taking a slight liberty with other people's horses; but Wells and Fargo would not find fault with this when the case was one of their own servants, hitherto so well thought of. The stage, being empty and light, could spare two horses and go on, while those two horses, handled with discretion and timeliness, might be very useful at the Gap. The driver had best not depart from rule so far as to leave his post and duty; one man would be enough. The friend thought well of this plan, and they climbed down into the road from opposite sides and took out the wheelers. To be sure these animals were heavy, and not of the best sort for escaping on, but better than walking; and timeliness and discretion can do a great deal. So in a little while the driver and his stage were gone on their way, the friend with the two horses had disappeared in the wood, and the road was altogether lonely.

The sheriff's brain was hard at work, and he made no protest now as he walked along, passive in the company of the miners and their prisoner. The prisoner had said all that he had to say, and his man's firmness, which the first shock and amazement had wrenched from him, had come to his help again, bringing a certain shame at having let his reserve and bearing fall to pieces, and at having made himself a show; so he spoke no more than his grim captors did, as they took him swiftly through the wood. The sheriff was glad it was some miles they had to go; for though they went very fast, the distance and the time, and even the becoming tired in body, might incline their minds to more deliberation. He could think yet of nothing new to urge. He had seen and heard only the same things that all had, and his present hopes lay upon the Gap and what more might have come to light there since his departure. He looked at Drylyn, but the miner's serious and massive face gave him no suggestion; and the sheriff's reason again destroyed the germ of suspicion that something plainly against reason had several times put in his thoughts. Yet it stuck with him that they had hold of the wrong man.

When they reached the Gap, and he found the people there as he had left them, and things the same way, with nothing new turned up to help his theory, the sheriff once more looked round; but Drylyn was not in the crowd. He had gone, they told him, to look at *her;* he had set a heap of store by her, they repeated.

"A heap of store," said the sheriff, thinking. "Where is she now?"

"On her bed," said a woman, "same as ever, only we've fixed her up some."

"Then I'll take a look at her—and him. You boys won't do anything till I come back, will you?"

"Why, if ye're so anxious to see us do it, sheriff," said the chatty neighbor, "I guess we can wait that long fer ye."

The officer walked to the tent. Drylyn was standing over the body, quiet and dumb. He was safe for the present, the sheriff knew, and so he left him without speaking and returned to the prisoner and his guard in front of the dancehall. He found them duly waiting; the only change was that they had a rope there.

"Once upon a time," said the sheriff, "there was a man in Arkansaw that had no judgment."

"They raise 'em that way in Arkansaw," said the chatty neighbor, as the company made a circle to hear the story—a tight, cautious circle—with the prisoner and the officer beside him standing in the center.

"The man's wife had good judgment," continued the narrator, "but she went and died on him."

"Well, I guess that *was* good judgment," said the neighbor.

"So the man, he had to run the farm alone. Now they raised poultry, which his wife had always attended to. And he knew she had a habit of setting hens on duck eggs. He had never inquired her reasons, being shiftless, but that fact he knew. Well, come to investigate the hen house, there was duck eggs, and hens on 'em, and also a heap of hens' eggs, but no more hens wishing to set. So the man, having no judgment, persuaded a duck to stay with those eggs. Now it's her I'm chiefly interested in. She was a good enough duck, but hasty. When the eggs hatched out, she didn't stop to notice, but up and takes them down to the pond, and gets mad with them, and shoves them in, and they drowns. Next day or two a lot of the young ducks, they hatched out and come down with the hen and got in the water all right, and the duck figured out she'd made some mistake, and she felt distressed. But the chickens were in heaven."

The sheriff studied his audience, and saw that he had lulled their rage a little. "Now," said he, "ain't you boys just a trifle like that duck? I don't know as I can say much to you more than what I have said, and I don't know as I can do anything, fixed as I am. This thing looks bad for him we've got here. Why, I can see that as well as you. But, boys! It's an awful thing to kill an innocent man! I saw that done once, and—God forgive me! I was one of them. I'll tell you how that was. He looked enough like the man we wanted. We were certainly on the right trail. We came on a cabin we'd never known of before, pretty far up in the hills—a strange cabin, you see. That seemed just right; just where a man would hide. We were mad at the crime committed, and took no thought. We knew we had caught him—that's the way we felt. So we got our guns ready, and crept up close through the trees, and surrounded that cabin. We called him to come out, and he came with a book in his hands he'd been reading. He did look like the man, and boys! We gave him no time! He never knew why we fired. He was a harmless old prospector who had got tired of poor luck and knocking around, and over his door he had painted some words: 'Where the wicked cease from troubling.' He had figured that up there by that mountain stream the world would let him alone. And ever since then I have thought my life belonged to him first, and me second. Now this afternoon I'm alone here. You know I can't do much. And I'm going to ask you to help me respect the law. I don't say that in this big country there may not be places, and there may not be times, when the law is too young or else too rotten to take care of itself, and when the

American citizen must go back to bed rock principles. But is that so in our valley? Why, if this prisoner is guilty, you can't name me one man of your acquaintance who would want him to live. And that being so, don't we owe him the chance to clear himself if he can? I can see that prospector now at his door, old, harmless, coming fearless at our call, because he had no guilt upon his conscience—and we shot him down without a word. Boys! He has the call on me now; and if you insist—"

The sheriff paused, satisfied with what he saw on the faces around him. Some of the men knew the story of the prospector—it had been in the papers—but of his part in it they had not known. They understood quite well the sacrifice he stood ready to make now in defending the prisoner. The favorable silence was broken by the sound of horses. Timeliness and discretion were coming up the hill. Drylyn at the same moment came out of the dead woman's tent, and, looking down, realized the intended rescue. With his mind waked suddenly from its dull dream and opened with a human impulse, he ran to help; but the sheriff saw him, and thought he was trying to escape.

"That's the man!" he shouted savagely to the ring.

Some of the Gap ran to the edge of the hill, and, seeing the hurrying Drylyn and the horses below, also realized the rescue. Putting the wrong two and two together, they instantly saw in all this a well-devised scheme of delay and collusion. They came back, running through the dancehall to the front, and the sheriff was pinioned from behind, thrown down, and held.

"So ye were alone, were ye?" said the chatty neighbor. "Well, ye made a good talk. Keep quiet—we don't want to hurt ye."

At this supposed perfidy the Gap's rage was at white-heat again; the men massed together, and fierce and quick as lightning the messenger's fate was wrought. The work of adjusting the rope and noose was complete and death going on in the air when Drylyn, meaning to look the ground over for the rescue, came cautiously back up the hill and saw the body, black against the clear sunset sky. At his outcry they made ready for him, and when he blindly rushed among them they held him, and paid no attention to his ravings. Then, when the rope had finished its work, they let him go, and the sheriff too. The driver's friend had left his horses among the pines, and had come up to see what was going on at the Gap. He how joined the crowd.

"You meant well," the sheriff said to him. "I wish you would tell the boys how you come to be here. They're thinking I lied to them."

"Maybe I can change their minds." It was Drylyn's deep voice. "I am the man you were hunting," he said.

They looked at him seriously, as one looks at a friend whom an illness has seized. The storm of feeling had spent itself, the mood of the Gap was relaxed and torpid, and the serenity of coming dusk began to fill the mountain air.

"You boys think I'm touched in the head," said Drylyn, and paused. "This knife done it," said he. "This one I'm showing you."

They looked at the knife in his hand.

"He come between me and her," Drylyn pursued. "I was aiming to give him his punishment myself. That would have been square." He turned the knife over in his hand, and, glancing up from it, caught the look in their eyes. "You don't believe me!" he exclaimed, savagely. "Well, I'm going to make you. Sheriff, I'll bring you some evidence."

He walked to the creek, and they stood idle and dull till he returned. Then they fell back from him and his evidence, leaving him standing beneath the dead man.

"Does them look like being touched in the head?" inquired Drylyn, and he threw down the overalls, which fell with a damp slap on the ground. "I don't seem to mind telling you," he said. "I feel as quiet—as quiet as them tall pines the sun's just quittin' for the night." He looked at the men expectantly, but none of them stirred. "I'd liked to have it over," said he.

Still no one moved.

"I have a right to ask it shall be quick," he repeated. "You were quick enough with him." And Drylyn lifted his hand towards the messenger.

They followed his gesture, staring up at the wrong man, then down at the right one. The chatty neighbor shook his head. "Seems curious," he said, slowly. "It ought to be done. But I couldn't no more do it— gosh! How *can* a man fire his gun right after it's been discharged?"

The heavy Drylyn looked at his comrades of the Gap. "You won't?" he said.

"You better quit us," suggested the neighbor. "Go somewheres else."

Drylyn's eyes ran painfully over ditch and diggings, the near cabins and the distant hills, then returned to the messenger. "Him and me," he muttered. "It ain't square. Him and me—" Suddenly he broke out, "I don't choose him to think I was that kind of man!"

Before they could catch him he fell, and the wet knife slid from his fingers. "Sheriff," he began, but his tone changed. "I'm overtakin' him!" he said. "He's going to know now. Lay me alongside—"

And so they did.

THE SECOND MISSOURI
COMPROMISE

I

THE LEGISLATURE HAD SAT UP ALL NIGHT, MUCH ABSORBED, HAVING taken off its coat because of the stove. This was the fortieth and final day of its first session under an order of things not new only, but novel. It sat with the retrospect of forty days' duty done, and the prospect of forty days' consequent pay to come. Sleepy it was not, but wide and wider awake over a progressing crisis. Hungry it had been until after a breakfast fetched to it from the Overland at seven, three hours ago. It had taken no intermission to wash its face, nor was there just now any apparatus for this, as the tin pitcher commonly used stood not in the basin in the corner, but on the floor by the governor's chair; so the eyes of the legislature, though earnest, were dilapidated. Last night the pressure of public business had seemed over, and no turning back the hands of the clock likely to be necessary. Besides Governor Ballard, Mr. Hewley, secretary and treasurer, was sitting up too, small, iron-gray, in feature and bearing every inch the capable, dignified official, but his necktie had slipped off during the night. The bearded councilors had the best of it, seeming after their vigil less stale in the face than the member from Silver City, for instance, whose day-old black growth blurred his dingy chin, or the member from Big Camas, whose scantier red crop bristled on his cheeks in sparse wandering arrangements, like spikes on the barrel of a musical box. For comfort, most of the pistols were on the table with the statutes of the United States. Secretary and Treasurer Hewley's lay on his strong-box immediately behind him. The governor's was a light one, and always hung in the armhole of his waistcoat. The graveyard of Boisé City this year had twenty-seven tenants, two brought there by meningitis, and twenty-five by difference of opinion. Many denizens of the territory were miners, and the unsettling element of gold-dust hung in the air, breeding argument. The early, thin, bright morning steadily mellowed against the windows distant from the stove; the panes melted clear until they ran, steamed faintly, and dried, this fresh May day, after the night's untimely cold; while still the legislature sat in its shirt-sleeves, and several statesmen had removed their boots. Even had appearances counted, the session was invisible from the street. Unlike a good number of houses in the town, the State-House (as they called it from old habit) was not all on the ground floor for outsiders to stare into, but up a flight of wood steps to a wood gallery. From this, to be sure, the interior could be watched from several windows on both sides; but the journey up the steps was precisely enough to disincline the idle, and this was counted a sensible thing by the lawmakers. They took the ground that shaping any government for a raw wilderness community needed seclusion, and they set a high value upon unworried privacy.

The sun had set upon a concentrated council, but it rose upon faces that looked momentous. Only the governor's and treasurer's were impassive, and they concealed something even graver than the matter in hand.

"I'll take a hun'red mo', Gove'nuh," said the member from Silver City, softly, his eyes on space. His name was Powhattan Wingo.

The governor counted out the blue, white, and red chips to Wingo, penciled some figures on a thickly ciphered and canceled paper that bore in print the words "Territory of Idaho, Council Chamber," and then filled up his glass from the tin pitcher, adding a little sugar.

"And I'll trouble you fo' the toddy," Wingo added, always softly, and his eyes always on space. "Raise you ten, suh." This was to the treasurer. Only the two were playing at present. The governor was kindly acting as bank; the others were looking on.

"And ten," said the treasurer.

"And ten," said Wingo.

"And twenty," said the treasurer.

"And fifty," said Wingo, gently bestowing his chips in the middle of the table.

The treasurer called.

The member from Silver City showed down five high hearts, and a light rustle went over the legislature when the treasurer displayed three twos and a pair of threes, and gathered in his harvest. He had drawn two cards, Wingo one; and losing to the lowest hand that could have beaten you is under such circumstances truly hard luck. Moreover, it was almost the only sort of luck that had attended Wingo since about half after three that morning. Seven hours of cards just a little lower than your neighbor's is searching to the nerves.

"Gove'nuh, I'll take a hun'red mo'," said Wingo; and once again the legislature rustled lightly, and the new deal began.

Treasurer Hewley's winnings flanked his right, a pillared fortress on the table, built chiefly of Wingo's misfortunes. Hewley had not counted them, and his architecture was for neatness and not ostentation; yet the legislature watched him arrange his gains with sullen eyes. It would have pleased him now to lose; it would have more than pleased him to be able to go to bed quite a long time ago. But winners cannot easily go to bed. The thoughtful treasurer bet his money and deplored this luck. It seemed likely to trap himself and the governor in a predicament they had not foreseen. All had taken a hand at first, and played for several hours, until Fortune's wheel ran into a rut deeper than usual. Wingo slowly became the loser to several, then Hewley had forged ahead, winner from everybody. One by one they had dropped out, each meaning to go home, and all lingering to see the luck turn. It was an extraordinary run, a rare specimen, a breaker of records, something to refer to in the future as a standard of measure and an embellishment of reminiscence; quite enough to keep the Idaho legislature up all night. And then it was their friend who was losing. The only speaking in the room was the brief card talk of the two players.

"Five better," said Hewley, winner again four times in the last five.

"Ten," said Wingo.

"And twenty," said the secretary and treasurer.

"Call you."

"Three kings."

"They are good, suh. Gove'nuh, I'll take a hun'red mo'."

Upon this the wealthy and weary treasurer made a try for liberty and bed. How would it do, he suggested, to have a round of jackpots, say ten—or twenty, if the member from Silver City preferred—and then stop? It would do excellently, the member said, so softly that the governor looked at him. But Wingo's large countenance remained inexpressive, his black eyes still impersonally fixed on space. He sat thus till his chips were counted to him, and then the eyes moved to watch the cards fall. The governor hoped he might win now, under the jackpot system. At noon he should have a disclosure to make; something that would need the most cheerful and contented feelings in Wingo and the legislature to be received with any sort of calm. Wingo was behind the game to the tune of—the governor gave up adding as he ran his eye over the figures of the bank's erased and tormented record, and he shook his head to himself. This was inadvertent.

"May I inquah who yo're shakin' yoh head at, suh?" said Wingo, wheeling upon the surprised governor.

"Certainly," answered that official. "You." He was never surprised for very long. In 1867 it did not do to remain surprised in Idaho.

"And have I done anything which meets yoh disapprobation?" pursued the member from Silver City, enunciating with care.

"You have met my disapprobation."

Wingo's eye was on the governor, and now his friends drew a little together, and as a unit sent a glance of suspicion at the lone bank.

"You will gratify me by being explicit, suh," said Wingo to the bank.

"Well, you've emptied the toddy."

"Ha-ha, Gove'nuh! I rose, suh, to yoh little fly. We'll awduh some mo'."

"Time enough when he comes for the breakfast things," said Governor Ballard, easily.

"As you say, suh. I'll open for five dolluhs." Wingo turned back to his game. He was winning, and as his luck continued his voice ceased to be soft, and became a shade truculent. The governor's ears caught this change, and he also noted the lurking triumph in the faces of Wingo's fellow-statesmen. Cheerfulness and content were scarcely reigning yet in the council chamber of Idaho as Ballard sat watching the friendly game. He was beginning to fear that he must leave the treasurer alone and take some precautions outside. But he would have to be separated for some time from his ally, cut off from giving him any hints. Once the treasurer looked at him, and he immediately winked reassuringly, but the treasurer failed to respond. Hewley might be able to wink after everything was over, but he could not find it in his serious heart to do so now. He was wondering what would happen if this game should last till noon with the company in its present mood. Noon was the time fixed for paying the Legislative Assembly the compensation due for its services during this session; and the governor and the treasurer had put their heads together and arranged a surprise for the Legislative Assembly. They were not going to pay them.

A knock sounded at the door, and on seeing the waiter from the Overland enter, the governor was seized with an idea. Perhaps precaution could be taken from the inside. "Take this pitcher," said he, "and have it refilled with the same. Joseph knows my mixture." But Joseph was night bartender, and now long in his happy bed, with a day successor in the saloon, and this one did not know the mixture. Ballard had foreseen this when he spoke, and that his writing a note of directions would seem quite natural.

"The receipt is as long as the drink," said a legislator, watching the governor's pencil fly.

"He don't know where my private stock is located," explained Ballard. The waiter departed with the breakfast things and the note, and while the jackpots continued the governor's mind went carefully over the situation.

Until lately the western citizen has known one everyday experience that no dweller in our thirteen original colonies has had for two hundred years. In Massachusetts they have not seen it since 1641; in Virginia not since 1628. It is that of belonging to a community of which every adult was born somewhere else. When you come to think of this a little it is dislocating to many of your conventions. Let a citizen of Salem, for instance, or a well-established Philadelphia Quaker, try to imagine his chief-justice fresh from Louisiana, his mayor from Arkansas, his tax-collector from South Carolina, and himself recently arrived in a wagon from a thousand-mile drive. To be governor of such a community Ballard had traveled in a wagon from one quarter of the horizon; from another quarter Wingo had arrived on a mule. People reached Boisé in three ways: by rail to a little west of the Missouri, after which it was wagon, saddle, or walk for the remaining fifteen hundred miles; from California it was shorter; and from Portland, Oregon, only about five hundred miles, and some of these more agreeable, by water up the Columbia. Thus it happened that salt often sold for its weight in gold-dust. A miner in the Bannock Basin would meet a freight teamster coming in with the staples of life, having journeyed perhaps sixty consecutive days through the desert, and valuing his salt highly. The two accordingly bartered in scales, white powder against yellow, and both parties content. Some in Boisé today can remember these bargains. After all, they were struck but thirty years ago. Governor Ballard and Treasurer Hewley did not come from the same place, but they constituted a minority of two in territorial politics because they hailed from north of Mason and Dixon's line. Powhattan Wingo and the rest of the council were from Pike County, Missouri. They had been Secessionists, some of them Knights of the Golden Circle; they had belonged to Price's Left Wing, and they flocked together. They were seven—two lying unwell at the Overland, five now present in the State-House with the governor and treasurer. Wingo, Gascon Claiborne, Gratiot des Pères, Pete Cawthon, and F. Jackson Gilet were their names. Besides this council of seven were thirteen members of the Idaho House of Representatives, mostly of the same political feather with the council, and they too would be present at noon to receive their pay. How Ballard and Hewley came to be a minority of two is a simple matter. Only twenty-five months had gone since Appomattox Courthouse. That surrender was presently followed by Johnston's to Sherman, at Durhams Station, and following this the various Confederate armies in Alabama, or across the Mississippi, or wherever they happened to be, had successively surrendered—but not Price's Left Wing. There was the wide open West under its nose, and no Grant or Sherman infesting that void. Why surrender? Wingos, Claibornes, and all, they melted away.

Price's Left Wing sailed into the prairie and passed below the horizon. To know what it next did you must, like Ballard or Hewley, pass below the horizon yourself, clean out of sight of the dome at Washington to remote, untracked Idaho. There, besides wild red men in quantities, would you find not very tame white ones, gentlemen of the ripest southwestern persuasion, and a legislature to fit. And if, like Ballard or Hewley, you were a Union man, and the president of the United States had appointed you governor or secretary of such a place, your days would be full of awkwardness, though your difference in creed might not hinder you from playing draw-poker with the unreconstructed. These Missourians were whole-souled, ample-natured males in many ways, but born with a habit of hasty shooting. The governor, on setting foot in Idaho, had begun to study pistolship, but acquired thus in middle life it could never be with him that spontaneous art which it was with Price's Left Wing. Not that the weapons now lying loose about the State-House were brought for use there. Everybody always went armed in Boisé, as the gravestones impliedly testified. Still, the thought of the bad quarter of an hour which it might come to at noon did cross Ballard's mind, raising the image of a column in the morrow's paper: "An unfortunate occurrence has ended relations between esteemed gentlemen hitherto the warmest personal friends. . . . They will be laid to rest at 3 PM. . . . As a last token of respect for our lamented governor, the troops from Boisé Barracks. . . ." The governor trusted that if his friends at the post were to do him any service it would not be a funeral one.

The new pitcher of toddy came from the Overland, the jackpots continued, were nearing a finish, and Ballard began to wonder if anything had befallen a part of his note to the bartender, an enclosure addressed to another person.

"Ha, suh!" said Wingo to Hewley. "My pot again, I declah." The chips had been crossing the table his way, and he was now loser but six hundred dollars.

"Ye ain't goin' to whip Mizzooruh all night an' all day, ez a rule," observed Pete Cawthon, councilor from Lost Leg.

"'Tis a long road that has no turnin', Gove'nuh," said F. Jackson Gilet, more urbanely. He had been in public life in Missouri, and was now president of the council in Idaho. He, too, had arrived on a mule, but could at will summon a rhetoric dating from Cicero, and preserved by many luxuriant orators until after the middle of the present century.

"True," said the governor, politely. "But here sits the long-suffering bank, whichever way the road turns. "I'm sleepy."

"You sacrifice yo'self in the good cause," replied Gilet, pointing to the poker game. "On easy lies the head that wahs an office, suh." And Gilet bowed over his compliment.

The governor thought so indeed. He looked at the treasurer's strong-box, where lay the appropriation lately made by Congress to pay the Idaho legislature for its services; and he looked at the treasurer, in whose pocket lay the key of the strong-box. He was accountable to the Treasury at Washington for all money disbursed for territorial expenses.

"Eleven twenty," said Wingo, "and only two hands mo' to play."

The governor slid out his own watch.

"I'll scahsely recoup," said Wingo.

They dealt and played the hand, and the governor strolled to the window.

"Three aces," Wingo announced, winning again handsomely. "I struck my luck too late," he commented to the onlookers. While losing he had been able to sustain a smooth reticence; now he gave his thoughts freely to the company, and continually moved and fingered his increasing chips. The governor was still looking out of the window, where he could see far up the street, when Wingo won the last hand, which was small. "That ends it, suh, I suppose?" he said to Hewley, letting the pack of cards linger in his grasp.

"I wouldn't let him off yet," said Ballard to Wingo from the window, with sudden joviality, and he came back to the players. "I'd make him throw five cold hands with me."

"Ah, Gove'nuh, that's yoh spo'tin' blood! Will you do it, Mistuh Hewley—a hun'red a hand?"

Mr. Hewley did it; and winning the first, he lost the second, third, and fourth in the space of an eager minute, while the councilors drew their chairs close.

"Let me see," said Wingo, calculating, "if I lose this—why still—" He lost. "But I'll not have to ask you to accept my papuh, suh. Wingo liquidates. Fo'ty days at six dolluhs a day makes six times fo' is twenty-fo'—two hun'red an' fo'ty dolluhs spot cash in hand at noon, without computation of mileage to and from Silver City at fo' dolluhs every twenty miles, estimated according to the nearest usually traveled route." He was reciting part of the statute providing mileage for Idaho legislators. He had never served the public before, and he knew all the laws concerning compensation by heart. "You'll not have to wait fo' yoh money, suh," he concluded.

"Well, Mr. Wingo," said Governor Ballard, "it depends on yourself whether your pay comes to you or not." He spoke cheerily. "If you don't see things my way, our treasurer will have to wait for his money." He had not expected to break the news just so, but it made as easy a beginning as any.

"See things yoh way, suh?"

"Yes. As it stands at present I cannot take the responsibility of paying you."

"The United States pays me, suh. My compensation is provided by act of Congress."

"I confess I am unable to discern your responsibility, Gove'nuh," said F. Jackson Gilet. "Mr. Wingo has faithfully attended the session, and is, like every gentleman present, legally entitled to his emoluments."

"You can all readily become entitled—"

"All? Am I—are my friends—included in this new depa'tyuh?"

"The difficulty applies generally, Mr. Gilet."

"Do I understand the Gove'nuh to insinuate—nay, gentlemen, do not rise! Be seated, I beg." For the councilors had leaped to their feet.

"Whar's our money?" said Pete Cawthon. "Our money was put in thet yere box."

Ballard flushed angrily, but a knock at the door stopped him, and he merely said, "Come in."

A trooper, a corporal, stood at the entrance, and the disordered council endeavored to look usual in a stranger's presence. They resumed their seats, but it was not easy to look usual on such short notice.

"Captain Paisley's compliments," said the soldier, mechanically, "and will Governor Ballard take supper with him this evening?"

"Thank Captain Paisley," said the governor (his tone was quite usual), "and say that official business connected with the end of the session makes it imperative for me to be at the State-House. Imperative."

The trooper withdrew. He was a heavy-built, handsome fellow, with black mustache and black eyes that watched through two straight, narrow slits beneath straight black brows. His expression in the council chamber had been of the regulation military indifference, and as he went down the steps he irrelevantly sang an old English tune:

> "Since first I saw your face I resolved
>   To honor and re—

"I guess," he interrupted himself as he unhitched his horse, "parrot and monkey hev broke loose."

The legislature, always in its shirt-sleeves, the cards on the table, and the toddy on the floor, sat calm a moment, cooled by this brief pause from the first heat of its surprise, while the clatter of Corporal Jones' galloping shrank quickly into silence.

II

Captain Paisley walked slowly from the adjutant's office at Boisé Barracks to his quarters, and his orderly walked behind him. The captain carried a letter in his hand, and the orderly, though distant a respectful ten paces, could hear him swearing plain as day. When he reached his front door Mrs. Paisley met him.

"Jim," cried she, "two more chickens froze in the night." And the delighted orderly heard the captain so plainly that he had to blow his nose or burst.

The lady, merely remarking "My goodness, Jim," retired immediately to the kitchen, where she had a soldier cook baking, and feared he was not quite sober enough to do it alone. The captain had paid eighty dollars for forty hens this year at Boisé, and twenty-nine had now passed away, victims to the climate. His wise wife perceived his extreme language not to have been all on account of hens, however;

but he never allowed her to share in his professional worries, so she stayed safe with the baking, and he sat in the front room with a cigar in his mouth.

Boisé was a two-company post without a major, and Paisley, being senior captain, was in command, an office to which he did not object. But his duties so far this month of May had not pleased him in the least. Theoretically, you can have at a two-company post the following responsible people: one major, two captains, four lieutenants, a doctor, and a chaplain. The major has been spoken of; it is almost needless to say that the chaplain was on leave, and had never been seen at Boisé by any of the present garrison; two of the lieutenants were also on leave, and two on surveying details—they had influence at Washington; the other captain was on a scout with General Crook somewhere near the Malheur Agency, and the doctor had only arrived this week. There had resulted a period when Captain Paisley was his own adjutant, quartermaster, and post surgeon, with not even an efficient sergeant to rely upon; and during this period his wife had stayed a good deal in the kitchen. Happily the doctor's coming had given relief to the hospital steward and several patients, and to the captain not only an equal, but an old friend, with whom to pour out his disgust; and together every evening they freely expressed their opinion of the War Department and its treatment of the western army.

There were steps at the door, and Paisley hurried out. "Only you!" he exclaimed, with such frank vexation that the doctor laughed loudly. "Come in, man, come in," Paisley continued, leading him strongly by the arm, sitting him down, and giving him a cigar. "Here's a pretty how de do!"

"More Indians?" inquired Dr. Tuck.

"Bother! They're nothing. It's senators—councilors—whatever the territorial devils call themselves."

"Gone on the warpath?" the doctor said, quite ignorant how nearly he had touched the council.

"Precisely, man. Warpath. Here's the governor writing me they'll be scalping him in the State-House at twelve o'clock. It's past 11:30. They'll be whetting knives about now." And the captain roared.

"I know you haven't gone crazy," said the doctor, "but who has?"

"The lot of them. Ballard's a good man, and—what's his name? The little secretary. The balance are just mad dogs—mad dogs. Look here: 'Dear Captain'—that's Ballard to me. I just got it—'I find myself unexpectedly hampered this morning. The South shows signs of being too solid. Unless I am supported, my plan for bringing our legislature to terms will have to be postponed. Hewley and I are more likely to be brought to terms ourselves—a bad precedent to establish in Idaho. Noon is the hour for drawing salaries. Ask me to supper as quick as you can, and act on my reply.' I've asked him," continued Paisley, "but I haven't told Mrs. Paisley to cook anything extra yet." The captain paused to roar again, shaking Tuck's shoulder for sympathy. Then he explained the situation in Idaho to the justly bewildered doctor. Ballard had confided many of his difficulties lately to Paisley.

"He means you're to send troops?" Tuck inquired.

"What else should the poor man mean?"

"Are you sure it's constitutional?"

"Hang constitutional! What do I know about their legal quibbles at Washington?"

"But, Paisley—"

"They're unsurrendered rebels, I tell you. Never signed a parole."

"But the general amnesty—"

"Bother general amnesty! Ballard represents the Federal government in this territory, and Uncle Sam's army is here to protect the Federal government. If Ballard calls on the army it's our business to obey, and if there's any mistake in judgment it's Ballard's, not mine." Which was sound soldier common sense, and happened to be equally good law. This is not always the case.

"You haven't got any force to send," said Tuck.

This was true. General Crook had taken with him both Captain Sinclair's infantry and the troop (or company, as cavalry was also then called) of the First.

"A detail of five or six with a reliable non-commissioned officer will do to remind them it's the United States they're bucking against," said Paisley. "There's a deal in the moral of these things. Crook—" Paisley broke off and ran to the door. "Hold his horse!" he called out to the orderly; for he had heard the hoofs, and was out of the house before Corporal Jones had fairly arrived. So Jones sprang off and hurried up, saluting. He delivered his message.

"Urn—umpra—what's that? Is it *imperative* you mean?" suggested Paisley.

"Yes, sir," said Jones, reforming his pronunciation of that unaccustomed word. "He said it twiced."

"What were they doing?"

"Blamed if I—beg the captain's pardon—they looked like they was waitin' fer me to git out."

"Go on—go on. How many were there?"

"Seven, sir. There was Governor Ballard and Mr. Hewley and—well, them's all the names I know. But," Jones hastened on with eagerness, "I've saw them five other fellows before at a—at—" The corporal's voice failed, and he stood looking at the captain.

"Well? Where?"

"At a cockfight, sir," murmured Jones, casting his eyes down.

A slight sound came from the room where Tuck was seated, listening, and Paisley's round gray eyes rolled once, then steadied themselves fiercely upon Jones.

"Did you notice anything further unusual, Corporal?"

"No, sir, except they was excited in there. Looked like they might be goin' to hev considerable rough house—a fuss, I mean, sir. Two was in their socks. I counted four guns on a table."

"Take five men and go at once to the State-House. If the governor needs assistance you will give it, but do nothing hasty. Stop trouble, and make none. You've got twenty minutes."

"Captain—if anybody needs arrestin'—"

"You must be judge of that." Paisley went into the house. There was no time for particulars.

"Snakes!" remarked Jones. He jumped on his horse and dashed down the slope to the men's quarters.

"Crook may be here any day or any hour," said Paisley, returning to the doctor. "With two companies in the background, I think Price's Left Wing will subside this morning."

"Supposing they don't?"

"I'll go myself; and when it gets to Washington that the commanding officer at Boisé personally interfered with the legislature of Idaho, it'll shock 'em to that extent that the government will have to pay for a special commission of investigation and two tons of red tape. I've got to trust to that corporal's good sense. I haven't another man at the post."

Corporal Jones had three-quarters of a mile to go, and it was ten minutes before noon, so he started his five men at a run. His plan was to walk and look quiet as soon as he reached the town, and thus excite no curiosity. The citizens were accustomed to the sight of passing soldiers. Jones had thought out several things, and he was not going to order bayonets fixed until the final necessary moment. "Stop trouble and make none" was firm in his mind. He had not long been a corporal. It was still his first enlistment. His habits were by no means exemplary; and his frontier personality, strongly developed by six years of vagabonding before he enlisted, was scarcely yet disciplined into the military machine of the regulation pattern that it should and must become before he could be counted a model soldier. His captain had promoted him to steady him, if that could be, and to give his better qualities a chance. Since then he had never been drunk at the wrong time. Two years ago it would not have entered his freelance heart to be reticent with any man, high or low, about any pleasure in which he saw fit to indulge; today he had been shy over confessing to the commanding officer his leaning to cockfights—a sign of his approach to the correct mental attitude of the enlisted man. Being corporal had wakened in him a new instinct, and this State-House affair was the first chance he had had to show himself. He gave the order to proceed at a walk in such a tone that one of the troopers whispered to another, "Specimen ain't going to forget he's wearing a chevron."

III

The brief silence that Jones and his invitation to supper had caused among the councilors was first broken by F. Jackson Gilet.

"Gentlemen," he said, "as president of the council I rejoice in an interruption that has given pause to our haste and saved us from

"His Plan Was to Walk and Keep Quiet"

ill-considered expressions of opinion. The Gove'nuh has, I confess, surprised me. Befo' examining the legal aspect of our case I will ask the Gove'nuh if he is familiar with the sundry statutes applicable."

"I think so," Ballard replied, pleasantly.

"I had supposed," continued the president of the council—"nay, I had congratulated myself that our weightiuh tasks of lawmaking and so fo'th were consummated yesterday, our thirty-ninth day, and that our friendly game of last night would be, as it were, the finis that crowned with pleashuh the work of a session memorable for its harmony."

This was not wholly accurate, but near enough. The governor had vetoed several bills, but Price's Left Wing had had much more than the required two-thirds vote of both Houses to make these bills laws over the governor's head. This may be called harmony in a manner. Gilet now went on to say that any doubts which the governor entertained concerning the legality of his paying any salaries could easily be settled without entering upon discussion. Discussion at such a juncture could not but tend towards informality. The president of the council could well remember most unfortunate discussions in Missouri between the years 1856 and 1860, in some of which he had had the honor to take part—*minima pars,* gentlemen! Here he digressed elegantly upon civil dissensions, and Ballard, listening to him and marking the slow, sure progress of the hour, told himself that never before had Gilet's oratory seemed more welcome or less lengthy. A plan had come to him, the orator next announced, a way out of the present dilemma, simple and regular in every aspect. Let some gentleman present now kindly draft a bill setting forth in its preamble the acts of Congress providing for the legislature's compensation, and let this bill in conclusion provide that all members immediately receive the full amount due for their services. At noon both Houses would convene; they would push back the clock, and pass this bill before the term of their session should expire.

"Then, Gove'nuh," said Gilet, "you can amply vindicate yo'self by a veto, which, together with our votes on reconsideration of yoh objections, will be reco'ded in the journal of our proceedings, and copies transmitted to Washington within thirty days as required by law. Thus, suh, will you become absolved from all responsibility."

The orator's face, while he explained this simple and regular way out of the dilemma, beamed with acumen and statesmanship. Here they would make a law, and the governor must obey the law!

Nothing could have been more to Ballard's mind as he calculated the fleeting minutes than this peaceful, pompous farce. "Draw your bill, gentlemen," he said. "I would not object if I could."

The statutes of the United States were procured from among the pistols and opened at the proper page. Gascon Claiborne, upon another sheet of paper headed "Territory of Idaho, Council Chamber," set about formulating some phrases which began "Whereas," and Gratiot des Pères read aloud to him from the statutes. Ballard conversed apart with Hewley; in fact, there was much conversing aside.

"'Third March 1863, c. 117, s. 8, v. 12, p. 811,'" dictated Des Pères.

"Skip the chaptuhs and sections," said Claiborne. "We only require the date."

"'Third March 1863. The sessions of the Legislative Assemblies of the several Territories of the United States shall be limited to forty days' duration.'"

"Wise provision that," whispered Ballard. "No telling how long a poker game might last."

But Hewley could not take anything in this spirit. "Genuine business was not got through till yesterday," he said.

"'The members of each branch of the legislature,'" read Des Pères, "'shall receive a compensation of six dollars per day during the sessions herein provided for, and they shall receive such mileage as now provided by law: *Provided,* That the president of the council and the Speaker of the House of Representatives shall each receive a compensation of ten dollars a day.'"

At this the president of the council waved a deprecatory hand to signify that it was a principle, not profit, for which he battled. They had completed their *Whereases,* incorporating the language of the several sections as to how the appropriation should be made, who disbursed such money, mileage, and, in short, all things pertinent to their bill, when Pete Cawthon made a suggestion.

"Ain't there anything 'bout how much the Gove'nuh gits?" he asks.

"And the secretary?" added Wingo.

"Oh, you can leave us out," said Ballard.

"Pardon me, Gove'nuh," said Gilet. "You stated that yoh difficulty was not confined to Mr. Wingo or any individual gentleman, but was general. Does it not apply to yo'self, suh? Do you not need any bill?"

"Oh no," said Ballard, laughing. "I don't need any bill."

"And why not?" said Cawthon. "You've jist ez much earned yoh money ez us fellers."

"Quite as much," said Ballard. "But we're not alike—at present."

Gilet grew very stately. "Except certain differences in political opinions, suh, I am not awah of how we differ in merit as public servants of this territory."

"The difference is of your own making, Mr. Gilet, and no bill you could frame would cure it or destroy my responsibility. You cannot make any law contrary to a law of the United States."

"Contrary to a law of the United States? And what, suh, has the United States to say about my pay I have earned in Idaho?"

"Mr. Gilet, there has been but one government in this country since April 1865, and as friends you and I have often agreed to differ as to how many there were before then. That government has a law compelling people like you and me to go through a formality, which I have done, and you and your friends have refused to do each time it has been suggested to you. I have raised no point until now, having my reasons, which were mainly that it would make less trouble now for the territory of which I have been appointed governor. I am held accountable to the secretary of the treasury semiannually for the manner in which the appropriation has been expended. If you will kindly hand me that book—"

Gilet, more and more stately, handed Ballard the statutes, which he had taken from Des Pères. The others were watching Ballard with gathering sullenness, as they had watched Hewley while he was winning Wingo's money, only now the sullenness was of a more decided complexion.

Ballard turned the pages. "'Second July 1862. Every person elected or appointed to any office of honor or profit, either in the civil, military, or naval service, . . . shall, before entering upon the duties of such office, and before being entitled to any salary or other emoluments thereof, take and subscribe the following oath: I—'"

"What does this mean, suh?" said Gilet.

"It means there is no difference in our positions as to what preliminaries the law requires of us, no matter how we may vary in convictions. I as governor have taken the oath of allegiance to the United States, and you as councilor must do the same before you can get your pay. Look at the book."

"I decline, suh. I repudiate yoh proposition. There is a wide difference in our positions."

"What do you understand it to be, Mr. Gilet?" Ballard's temper was rising.

"If you have chosen to take an oath that did not go against yoh convictions—"

"Oh, Mr. Gilet!" said Ballard, smiling. "Look at the book." He would not risk losing his temper through further discussion. He would stick to the law as it lay open before them.

But the Northern smile sent Missouri logic to the winds. "In what are you superior to me, suh, that I cannot choose? Who are you that I and these gentlemen must take oaths befo' you?"

"Not before me. Look at the book."

"I'll look at no book, suh. Do you mean to tell me you have seen me day aftuh day and meditated this treacherous attempt?"

"There is no attempt and no treachery, Mr. Gilet. You could have taken the oath long ago, like other officials. You can take it today—or take the consequences."

"What? You threaten me, suh? Do I understand you to threaten me? Gentlemen of the council, it seems Idaho will be less free than Missouri unless we look to it." The president of the council had risen in his indignant oratorical might, and his more and more restless friends glared admiration at him. "When was the time that Price's Left Wing surrendered?" asked the orator. "Nevuh! Others have, be it said to their shame. We have not toiled these thousand miles fo' that! Others have crooked the pliant hinges of the knee that thrift might follow fawning. As fo' myself, two grandfathers who fought fo' our libuhties rest in the soil of Virginia, and two uncles who fought in the Revolution sleep in the land of the Dark and Bloody Ground. With such blood in my veins I will nevuh, nevuh, nevuh submit to Northern rule and dictation. I will risk all to be with the Southern people, and if defeated I can, with a patriot of old, exclaim,

> "More true joy an exile feels
> Than Cæssuh with a Senate at his heels.

"Aye, gentlemen! And we will not be defeated! Our rights are here and are ours." He stretched his arm towards the treasurer's strong-box, and his enthusiastic audience rose at the rhetoric. "Contain yo'selves, gentlemen," said the orator. "Twelve o'clock and our bill!"

"I've said my say," said Ballard, remaining seated.

"An' what'll ye do?" inquired Pete Cawthon from the agitated group.

"I forbid you to touch that!" shouted Ballard. He saw Wingo moving towards the box.

"Gentlemen, do not resort—" began Gilet.

But small, iron-gray Hewley snatched his pistol from the box, and sat down astraddle of it, guarding his charge. At this hostile movement the others precipitated themselves towards the table where lay their weapons, and Governor Ballard, whipping his own from his armhole, said, as he covered the table: "Go easy, gentlemen! Don't hurt our treasurer!"

"Don't nobody hurt anybody," said Specimen Jones, opening the door.

This prudent corporal had been looking in at a window and hearing plainly for the past two minutes, and he had his men posted. Each member of the council stopped as he stood, his pistol not quite yet attained; Ballard restored his own to its armhole and sat in his chair; little Hewley sat on his box; and F. Jackson Gilet towered haughtily, gazing at the intruding blue uniform of the United States.

"I'll hev to take you to the commanding officer," said Jones, briefly, to Hewley. "You and yer box."

"Oh, my stars and stripes, but that's a keen move!" rejoiced Ballard to himself. "He's arresting *us*."

In Jones' judgment, after he had taken in the situation, this had seemed the only possible way to stop trouble without making any, and therefore, even now, bayonets were not fixed. Best not ruffle Price's Left Wing just now, if you could avoid it. For a new corporal it was well thought and done. But it was high noon, the clock not pushed back, and punctual representatives strolling innocently towards their expected pay. There must be no time for a gathering and possible reaction. "I'll hev to clear this State-House out," Jones decided. "We're makin' an arrest," he said, aloud, "and we want a little room." The outside bystanders stood back obediently, but the councilors delayed. Their pistols were, with Ballard's and Hewley's, of course in custody. "Here," said Jones, restoring them. "Go home now. The commanding officer's waitin' fer the prisoner. Put yer boots on, sir, and leave," he added to Pete Cawthon, who still stood in his stockings. "I don't want to hev to disperse anybody more'n what I've done."

Disconcerted Price's Left Wing now saw file out between armed soldiers the treasurer and his strongbox; and thus guarded they were brought to Boisé Barracks, whence they did not reappear. The governor also went to the post.

After delivering Hewley and his treasure to the commanding officer, Jones with his five troopers went to the sutler's store and took a drink at Jones' expense. Then one of them asked the corporal to have another. But Jones refused. "If a man drinks much of that," said he (and the whiskey certainly was of a livid, unlikely flavor), "he's liable to go home and steal his own pants." He walked away to his quarters, and as he went they heard him thoughtfully humming his most inveterate song, "Ye shepherds tell me have you seen my Flora pass this way."

But poisonous whiskey was not the inner reason for his moderation. He felt very much like a responsible corporal today, and the troopers knew it. "Jones has done himself a good turn in this fuss," they said. "He'll be changing his chevron."

That afternoon the legislature sat in the State-House and read to itself in the statutes all about oaths. It is not believed that any of them sat up another night; sleeping on a problem is often much better. Next morning the commanding officer and Governor Ballard were called upon by F. Jackson Gilet and the Speaker of the House. Everyone was civil and hearty as possible. Gilet pronounced the captain's whiskey "equal to any at the Southern, Saint Louey," and conversed for some time about the cold season, General Crook's remarkable astuteness in dealing with Indians, and other topics of public interest. "And concernin' yoh difficulty yesterday, Gove'nuh," said he, "I've been consulting the laws, suh, and I perceive yoh construction is entahley correct."

And so the legislature signed that form of oath prescribed for participants in the late Rebellion, and Hewley did not have to wait for his poker money. He and Wingo played many subsequent games; for, as they all said in referring to the matter, "A little thing like that should nevuh stand between friends."

Thus was accomplished by Ballard, Paisley—and Jones—the Second Missouri Compromise, at Boisé City, Idaho, 1867—an eccentric moment in the eccentric years of our development westward, and historic also. That it has gone unrecorded until now is because of Ballard's modesty, Paisley's preference for the sword, and Jones' hatred of the pen. He was never known to write except, later, in the pages of his company roster and such unavoidable official places; for the troopers were prophetic. In not many months there was no longer a Corporal Jones, but a person widely known as Sergeant Jones of Company A; called also the "Singing Sergeant"; but still familiar to his intimate friends as "Specimen."

LA TINAJA BONITA

And it came to pass after a while that the brook dried up,
because there had been no rain in the land.

—I KINGS XVII. 7

A PRETTY GIRL WAS KNEELING ON THE ROOF OF A FLAT MUD CABIN, A
harvest of red peppers round her knees. On the ground below her
stood a swarthy young man, the bloom on his Mexican cheeks rich
and dusky, like her own. His face was irresponsible and winning, and
his watching eyes shone upon her with admiration and desire. She
on the roof was entertained by her visitor's attention, but unfavorable to it. Through the livelong sunny day she had parried his
love-talk with light and complete skill, enjoying herself, and liking
him very well, as she had done since they were two children playing
together in the Arizona desert. She was quite mistress of the situation, because she was a woman, and he as yet merely a boy; he was
only twenty-two; she was almost sixteen. The Mexican man at twenty-
two may be as experienced as his Northern brother of thirty, but at
sixteen the Mexican woman is also mature, and can competently
deal with the man. So this girl had relished the thoughtless morning
and noon as they passed; but twice lately she had glanced across the
low treetops of her garden down the trail, where the cañon descended
to the silent plain below.

"I think I must go back now," said the young man, not thinking so.
He had a guitar from the cabin.

122

"Oh!" said she, diverted by his youthful feint. "Well, if you think it is so late." She busied herself with the harvest. Her red handkerchief and strands of her black hair had fallen loosely together from her head to her shoulders. The red peppers were heaped thick, hiding the whole roof, and she stooped among them, leveling them to a ripening layer with buckskin gloves (for peppers sting sharper than mustard), sorting and turning them in the bright sun. The boy looked at her most wistfully.

"It is not precisely late—yet," said he.

"To be sure not," she assented, consulting the sky. "We have still three hours of day."

He brightened as he lounged against a water-barrel. "But after night it is so very dark on the trail to camp," he insincerely objected.

"I never could have believed you were afraid of the dark."

"It is for the horse's legs, Lolita. Of course I fear nothing."

"Bueno! I was sure of it. Do you know, Luis, you have become a man quite suddenly? That mustache will be beautiful in a few years. And you have a good figure."

"I am much heavier than last year," said he. "My arm—"

"I can see, I can see. I am not sure I shall let you kiss me anymore. You didn't offer to when you came this morning—and that shows you men perceive things more quickly than we can. But don't go yet. You can lead your horse. His legs will come to no harm, eased of your weight. I should have been lonely today, and you have made it pass so quickly. You have talked so much that my peppers are not half spread."

"We could finish them in five minutes together," said the youth, taking a step.

"Two up here among all these peppers! Oh no, Luis. We should tread on them, and our ankles would burn all night. If you want to help me, go bring some fresh water. The barrel is almost empty."

But Luis stood ardently gazing up at the roof.

"Very well, then," said Lolita. "If you like this better, finish the peppers, and I'll go for the water."

"Why do you look down the trail so often?" said the baffled love-maker, petulantly.

"Because Uncle Ramon said the American would be coming today," the girl replied, softly.

"Was it Uncle Ramon said that? He told you that?"

"Why not?" She shaded her eyes, and looked where the cañon's widening slit gave view of a slant of sand merging fan-spread into a changeless waste of plain. Many watercourses, crooked and straight, came out of the gaps, creasing the sudden Sierra, descending to the flat through bushes and leaning margin trees; but in these empty shapes not a rill tinkled to refresh the silence, nor did a drop slide over the glaring rocks, or even dampen the heated, cheating sand. Lolita strained her gaze at the dry distance, and stooped again to her harvest.

"What does he come here for?" demanded Luis.

"The American? We buy white flour of him sometimes."

"Sometimes! That must be worth his while! He will get rich!" Luis lounged back against his water-barrel, and was silent. As he watched Lolita, serenely working, his silver crescent earrings swung a little with the slight tilting of his head, and his fingers, forgotten and unguided by his thoughts, ruffled the strings of the guitar, drawing from it gay, purposeless tendrils of sound. Occasionally, when Lolita knew the song, she would hum it on the roof, inattentively, busy rolling her peppers:

> Soy purita mejicana;
> Nada tengo español.

(I am a pure Mexican. I have nothing Spanish about me.) And this melodious inattention of Lolita's Luis felt to be the extreme of slight.

"Have you seen him lately?" he asked, sourly.

"Not very. Not since the last time he came to the mines from Maricopa."

"I heard a man at Gun Sight say he was dead," snapped Luis.

But she made no sign. "That would be a pity," she said, humming gayly.

"Very sad. Uncle Ramon would have to go himself to Maricopa for that white flour."

Pleased with this remark, the youth took to song himself; and there they were like two mischievous birds. Only the bird on the ground was cross with a sense of failure. He sang:

> "*El telele se murió.*
> The hunchback is dead.
> Ay! Ay! Ay!
> And no one could be found to bury him except—"

"Luis, aren't you going to get my water for me?"

"*Poco tiempo*: I'll bring it directly."

"You have to go to the Tinaja Bonita for it."

The Pretty Spring—or waterhole, or tank—was half a mile from the cabin.

"Well, it's not nice out there in the sun. I like it better in here, where it is pleasant."

> "And no one could be found to bury him except
> Five dragoons and a corporal
> And the sacristan's cat."

Singing resentfully, young Luis stayed in here, where it was pleasant. Bright green branches of fruit trees and small cottonwoods and a fenced irrigated square of green growing garden hid the tiny adobe home like a nut, smooth and hard and dry in their clustered midst. The lightest air that could blow among these limber, ready leaves set going at once their varnished twinkling round the house. Their white and dark sides gleamed and went out with chasing lights that quickened the torpid place into a holiday of motion. Closed in by this cool green, you did not have to see or think of Arizona, just outside.

"Where is Uncle Ramon today?" inquired Luis, dropping his music.

She sighed. "He has gone to drive our cattle to a new spring. There is no pasture at the Tinaja Bonita. Our streams and ditches went dry last week. They have never done so in all the years before. I don't know what is going to happen to us." The anxiety in the girl's face seemed to come outward more plainly for a moment, and then recede to its permanent abiding-place.

"There cannot be much water to keep flour-sellers alive on the trail to Maricopa," chirped the bird on the ground.

She made no answer to this. "What are you doing nowadays?" she asked.

"I have been working very hard on the wood contract for the American soldiers," he replied, promptly.

"By Tucson?"

"No. Huachuca."

"Away over there again? I thought you had cut all they wanted last May."

"It is of that enterprise of which I speak, Lolita."

"But it's October now!" Lolita lifted her face, ruddy with stooping, and broke into laughter.

"I do not see why you mock me. No one has asked me to work since."

"Have you asked anyone for work?"

"It is not my way to beg."

"Luis, I don't believe you're quite a man yet, in spite of your mustache. You complain there's no money for Mexicans in Arizona because the Americans get it all. Why don't you go back to Sonora, then, and be rich in five minutes? It would sound finely: 'Luis Romero, Merchant, Hermosillo.' Or perhaps gold would fall more quickly into your lap at Guaymas. You would live in a big house, perhaps with two stories, and I would come and visit you at Easter—if your wife would allow it." Here Lolita threw a pepper at him.

The guitar grated a few pretty notes; otherwise there was silence.

"And it was Uncle Ramon persuaded them to hire you in May. He told the American contractor you owned a strong burro good for heavy loads. He didn't say much about you," added the little lady.

"Much good it did me! The American contractor-pig retained my wages to pay for the food he supplied us. They charge you extra for starvation, those gringos. They are all pigs. Ah, Lolita, a man needs a wife, so he may strive to win a home for her."

"I have heard men say that they needed a home before they could strive to win a wife for it. But you go about it the other way."

"I am not an American pig, I thank the Virgin! I have none of their gringo customs."

"You speak truly indeed," murmured Lolita.

"It is you who know about them," the boy said, angry like a child. He had seen her eye drawn to the trail again as by a magnet. "They say you prefer gringos to your own people."

"Who dares say that?"

The elated Luis played loudly on the guitar. He had touched her that time.

But Lolita's eye softened at the instant of speaking, and she broke into her sweet laugh. "There!" she said, recapturing the situation; "is it not like old times for you and me to be fighting."

"Me? I am not fighting."

"You relieve me."

"I do not consider a gringo worth my notice."

"Sensible boy! You speak as wisely as one who has been to school in a large city. Luis, do you remember the day Uncle Ramon locked me up for riding on the kicking burro, and you came and unlocked me when uncle was gone? You took me walking, and lost us both in the mountains. We were really only a little, little way from home, but I thought we had got into another country where they eat children. I was six, and I beat you for losing me, and cried, and you were big, and you kissed me till I stopped crying. Do you remember?"

"No."

"Don't you remember?"

"I don't remember child's tricks."

"Luis, I have come to a conclusion. You are still young enough for me to kiss quite safely. Every time you fight with me—I shall kiss you. Won't you get me some fresh water now?"

He lounged, sulky, against his barrel.

"Come, querido! Must I go all that way myself? Well, then, if you intend to stand and glare at me till the moon rises—Ah! He moves!"

Luis laid the guitar gradually down, and gradually lifting a pail in which the dipper rattled with emptiness, he proceeded to crawl on his journey.

"You know that is not the one we use, muchacho," (little boy), remarked Lolita.

"Keep your kisses for your gringo," the water-carrier growled, with his back to her.

"I shall always save some for my little cousin."

The pail clattered on the stones, and the child stopped crawling. She on the roof stared at this performance for an open-mouthed moment, gloves idle among the spicy peppers. Then, laughing, she sprang to her feet, descended, and, catching up the water-jar (the olla de agua), overtook him, and shook it in his face with the sweetest derision. "Now we'll go together," said she, and started gayly through the green trees and the garden. He followed her, two paces behind, half ashamed, and gazing at her red handkerchief, and the black hair blowing a little; thus did they cross the tiny cool home acre through the twinkling pleasantness of the leaves, and pass at once outside the magic circle of irrigation into Arizona's domain, among a prone herd of carcasses upon the ground—dead cattle, two seasons dead now, hunted to this sanctuary by the drought, killed in the sanctuary by cold water.

A wise, quiet man, with a man's will, may sometimes after three days of thirst still hold grip enough upon his slipping mind to know, when he has found the water, that he must not drink it, must only dampen his lips and tongue in a drop-by-drop fashion until he has endured the passing of many slow, insidious hours. Even a wise man had best have a friend by his side then, who shall fight and tear him from the perilous excesses that he craves, knock him senseless if he cannot pin him down; but cattle know nothing of drop by drop, and you cannot pin down a hundred head that have found water after three days. So these hundred had drunk themselves swollen, and died. Cracked hide and white bone they lay, brown, dry, gaping humps straddled stiff askew in the last convulsion; and over them presided Arizona—silent, vast, all sunshine everlasting.

Luis saw these corpses that had stumbled to their fate, and he remembered; with Lolita in those trees all day, he had forgotten for a while. He pointed to the wide-strewn sight, familiar, monotonous as misfortune. "There will be many more," he said. "Another rainy season is gone without doing anything for the country. It cannot rain now for another year, Lolita."

"God help us and our cattle, and travelers!" she whispered.

Luis musingly repeated a saying of the country about the Tinaja Bonita,

"When you see the Black Cross dry,
    Fill the wagon cisterns high"

—a doggerel in homely Spanish meter, unwritten mouth-to-mouth wisdom, stable as a proverb, enduring through generations of unrecorded wanderers, that repeated it for a few years, and passed beneath the desert.

"But the Black Cross has never been dry yet," Luis said.

"You have not seen it lately," said Lolita.

"Lolita! Do you mean—" He looked in her troubled eyes, and they went on in silence together. They left behind them the bones and the bald level on which they lay, and came to where the cañon's broader descent quickened until they sank below that sight of the cattle, and for a time below the home and trees. They went down steeply by cactus and dry rock to a meeting of several cañons opening from side rifts in the Sierra, furrowing the main valley's mesa with deep watercourses that brought no water. Finding their way in this lumpy meeting-ground, they came upon the lurking-place of the Tinaja Bonita. They stood above it at the edge of a pitch of rock, watching the motionless crystal of the pool.

"How well it hides down there in its own cañon!" said Luis. "How pretty and clear! But there's plenty of water, Lolita."

"Can you see the Black Cross?"

"Not from here."

They began descending around the sides of the crumbled slate-rock face that tilted too steep for foothold.

"The other well is dry, of course," said Lolita. In the slaty, many-ledged formation a little lower down the cañon, towards the peep of outlying open country which the cloven hills let in, was a second round hole, twin of the first. Except after storms, water was never in this place, and it lay dry as a kiln nine-tenths of the year. But in size and depth and color, and the circular fashion of its shaft, which seemed man's rather than nature's design, it might have been the real Tinaja's reflection, conjured in some evil mirror where everything was faithfully represented except the water.

"It must have been a real well once," said Luis.

"Once, yes."

"And what made it go dry?"

"Who knows?"

"How strange it should be the lower well that failed, Lolita!"

The boy and girl were climbing down slowly, drawing near each other as they reached the bottom of the hollow. The peep of open country was blocked, and the tall tops of the mountains were all of the outer world to be seen down here below the mesa's level. The silence was like something older than this world, like the silence of space before any worlds were made.

"Do you believe it ever can go dry?" asked Luis. They were now on the edge of the Tinaja.

"Father Rafael says that it is miraculous," said the girl, believingly.

Opposite, and everywhere except where they were, the walls went sheer down, not slate-colored, but white, with a sudden up-cropping formation of brick-shaped stones. These also were many-layered and crumbling, cracking off into the pool if the hand hung or the foot weighed on them. No safe way went to the water but at this lower side, where the riven, tumbled white blocks shelved easily to the bottom; and Luis and Lolita looked down these natural stairs at the portent in the well. In that white formation shot up from the earth's bowels, arbitrary and irrelevant amid the surrounding alien layers of slate, four black stones were lodged as if built into the wall by some hand—four small stones shaping a cross, back against the white, symmetrical and plain.

"It has come farther—more uncovered since yesterday," Lolita whispered.

"Can the Tinaja sink altogether?" repeated Luis. The arms of the cross were a measurable space above the water-line, and he had always seen it entirely submerged.

"How could it sink?" said Lolita, simply. "It will stop when the black stones are wholly dry."

"You believe Father Rafael," Luis said, always in a low voice; "but it was only Indians, after all, who told the mission fathers at the first."

"That was very long ago," said she, "and there has always been water in the Tinaja Bonita."

Boy and girl had set the jar down, and forgotten it and why they had come. Luis looked uneasily at the circular pool, and up from this creviced middle of the cañon to the small high tops of the mountains rising in the free sky.

"This is an evil place," he said. "As for the water—no one, no three, can live long enough to be sure."

But it was part of Lolita's religion. "I am sure," said she.

The young Mexican's eyes rested on the face of the girl beside him, more beautiful just then with some wave of secret fear and faith.

"Come away with me, Lolita!" he pleaded, suddenly. "I can work. I can be a man. It is fearful for you to live here alone."

"Alone, Luis?" His voice had called her from her reverie back to her gay, alert self. "Do you consider Uncle Ramon nobody to live with?"

"Yes. Nobody—for you."

"Promise me never to tell that to uncle. He is so considerate that he might make me marry somebody for company. And then, you know, my husband would be certain to be stupid about your coming to see me, querido."

"Why do you always mock me, Lolita?"

"Mock you? What a fancy! Oh, see how the sun's going! If we do not get our water, your terrible Tinaja will go dry before supper. Come, Luis, I carried the olla. Must I do everything?"

He looked at her disconsolate. "Ah!" he vibrated, reveling in deep imaginary passion.

"Go! Go!" she cried, pushing him. "Take your olla."

Upon the lightest passing puff of sentiment the Southern breast can heave with every genuine symptom of storm, except wreck. Of course she stirred his gregarious heart. Was she not lovely and he twenty-two? He went down the natural stairs and came slowly up with the water, stopping a step below her. "Lolita," he said, "don't you love me at all? Not a very little?"

"You are my dearest, oldest friend, Luis," she said, looking at him with such full sweetness that his eyes fell. "But why do you pretend five beans make ten?"

"Of course they only make ten with gringos."

She held up a warning finger.

"Oh yes, oh yes! Strangers make fine lovers!" With this he swelled to a fond, dangerous appearance, and muttered, "It is not difficult to kill a man, Lolita."

"Fighting! After what I told you!" Lolita stooped and kissed her cousin Luis, and he instantly made the most of that chance.

"As often as you please," he said, as she released herself angrily, and then a stroke of sound struck their two hearts still. They jumped apart, trembling. Some of the rock slide had rattled down and plunged into the Tinaja with a gulping resonance. Loitering strings of sand strewed after it, and the boy's and girl's superstitious eyes looked up from the ringed, waving water to the ledge. Lolita's single shriek of terror turned to joy as she uttered it.

"I thought—I thought you would not come!" she cried out.

The dismounted horseman above made no sign of understanding her words. He stepped carefully away from the ledge his foot had crumbled, and they saw him using his rifle like a staff, steadying its stock in successive niches, and so working back to his horse. There he slid the rifle into its leather sling along the left side of his saddle.

"So he is not dead," murmured Luis, "and we need not live alone."

"Come down!" the girl called, and waved her hand. But the new-comer stood by his horse like an apparition.

"Perhaps he is dead, after all," Luis said. "You might say some of the Mass, only he was a heretic. But his horse is Mexican, and a believer."

Lolita had no eyes or ears for Luis anymore. He prattled away on the stone stairs of the Tinaja, flippant after a piercing shock of fear. To him, unstrung by the silence and the Black Cross and the presence of the sinking pool, the stone had crashed like a clap of sorcery, and he had started and stared to see—not a spirit, but a man, dismounted from his horse, with a rifle. At that his heart clutched him like talons, and in the flashing spasm of his mind came a picture—smoke from the rifle, and himself bleeding in the dust. Costly lovemaking! For Luis did not believe the rifle to have been brought to the ledge there as a staff, and he thanked the Virgin for the stone that fell and frightened him, and made him move suddenly. He had chattered himself cool now, and ready. Lolita was smiling at the man on the hill, glowing without concealment of her heart's desire.

"Come down!" she repeated. "Come round the side." And, lifting the olla, she tapped it, and signed the way to him.

"He has probably brought too much white flour for Uncle Ramon to care to climb more than he must," said Luis. But the man had stirred at last from his sentinel stillness, and began leading his horse down. Presently he was near enough for Luis to read his face. "Your gringo is a handsome fellow, certainly," he commented. "But he does not like me today."

"Like you! He doesn't think about you," said Lolita.

"Ha! That's your opinion?"

"It is also his opinion—if you'll ask him."

"He is afraid of Cousin Luis," stated the youth.

"Cousin grasshopper! He could eat you—if he could see you."

"There are other things in this world besides brute muscle, Lolita. Your gringo thinks I am worth notice, if you do not."

"How little he knows you!"

"It is you he does not know very well," the boy said, with a pang.

The scornful girl stared.

"Oh, the innocent one!" sneered Luis. "Grasshopper, indeed! Well, one man can always recognize another, and the women don't know much."

But Lolita had run off to meet her chosen lover. She did not stop to read his face. He was here; and as she hurried towards him she had no thought except that he was come at last. She saw his eyes and lips, and to her they were only the eyes and lips that she had longed for. "You have come just in time," she called out to him. At the voice, he looked at her one instant, and looked away; but the nearer sight of her sent a tide of scarlet across his face. His actions he could control, his bearing, and the steadiness of his speech, but not the coursing of his blood. It must have been a minute he had stood on the ledge above, getting a grip of himself. "Luis was becoming really afraid that he might have to do some work," continued Lolita, coming up the stony hill. "You know Luis?"

"I know him."

"You can fill your two canteens and carry the olla for us," she pursued, arriving eagerly beside him, her face lifted to her strong, tall lover.

"I can."

At this second chill of his voice, and his way of meeting her when she had come running, she looked at him bewildered, and the smile fluttered on her lips and left them. She walked beside him, talking no more; nor could she see his furtive other hand mutely open and shut, helping him keep his grip.

Luis also looked at the man who had taken Lolita's thoughts away from him and all other men. "No, indeed, he does not understand her very well," he repeated, bitter in knowing the man's suspicion and its needlessness. Something—disappointment, it may be—had wrought more reality in the young Mexican's easygoing love. "And she likes this gringo because—because he is light-colored!" he said, watching the American's bronzed Saxon face, almost as young as his own, but of sterner stuff. Its look left him no further doubt, and he held himself forewarned. The American came to the bottom, powerful, blue-eyed, his mustache golden, his cheek clean-cut, and beaten to shining health by the weather. He swung his blue-overalled leg over his saddle and rode to the Tinaja, with a short greeting to the watcher, while the pale Lolita unclasped the canteen straps and brought the water herself, brushing coldly by Luis to hook the canteens to the saddle again. This slighting touch changed the Mexican boy's temper to diversion and malice. Here were mountains from molehills! Here were five beans making ten with a vengeance!

"Give me that," said the American; and Luis handed up the water-jar to him with such feline politeness that the American's blue eyes filled with fire and rested on him for a doubtful second. But Luis was quite ready, and more diverted than ever over the suppressed violence of his Saxon friend. The horseman wheeled at once, and took a smooth trail out to the top of the mesa, the girl and boy following.

As the three went silent up the cañon, Luis caught sight of Lolita's eyes shining with the hurt of her lover's rebuff, and his face sparkled with further mischief. "She has been despising me all day," he said to himself. "Very well, very well. Señor Don Ruz," he began aloud, elaborately, "we are having a bad drought."

The American rode on, inspecting the country.

"I know at least four sorts of kisses," reflected the Mexican trifler. "But there! Very likely to me also they would appear alike from the top of a rock." He looked the American over, the rifle under his leg, his pistol, and his knife. "How clumsy these gringos are when it's about a girl!" thought Luis. "Any fool could fool them. Now I should take much care to be friendly if ever I did want to kill a man in earnest. Comical gringo! Yes, very dry weather, Don Ruz. And the rainy season gone!"

The American continued to inspect the country, his supple, flannel-shirted back hinting no interest in the talk.

"Water is getting scarce, Don Ruz," persisted the gadfly, lighting again. "Don Ramon's spring does not run now, and so we must come to the Tinaja Bonita, you see. Don Ramon removed the cattle yesterday. Everybody absent from home, except Lolita." Luis thought he could see his Don Ruz listening to that last piece of gossip, and his smile over himself and his skill grew more engaging. "Lolita has been telling me all today that even the Tinaja will go dry."

"It was you said that!" exclaimed the brooding, helpless Lolita.

"So I did. And it was you said no. Well, we found something to disagree about." The man in the flannel shirt was plainly attending to his tormentor. "*No sabe cuantos son cinco,*" Luis whispered, stepping close to Lolita. "Your gringo could not say boo to a goose just now." Lolita drew away from her cousin, and her lover happened to turn his head slightly, so that he caught sight of her drawing away. "But what do you say yourself, Don Ruz?" inquired Luis, pleased at this slight coincidence. "Will the Tinaja go dry, do you think?"

"I expect guessing won't interfere with the water's movements much," finally remarked Don Ruz—Russ Genesmere. His drawl and the body in his voice were not much like the Mexican's light fluency. They were music to Lolita, and her gaze went to him once more, but he got no answer. The bitter Luis relished this too.

"You are right, Don Ruz. Guessing is idle. Yet how can we help wondering about this mysterious Tinaja? I am sure that you can never have seen so much of the cross out of water. Lolita says—"

"So that's that place," said Genesmere, roughly.

Luis looked inquiring.

"Down there," Genesmere explained, with a jerk of his head back along the road they had come.

Luis was surprised that Don Ruz, who knew this country so well, should never have seen the Tinaja Bonita until today.

"I'd have seen it if I'd had any use for it," said Genesmere.

"To be sure, it lay off the róad of travel," Luis assented. And of course Don Ruz knew all that was needful—how to find it. He knew what people said—did he not? Father Rafael, Don Ramon, everybody? Lolita perhaps had told him? And that if the cross ever rose entirely above the water, that was a sign all other waterholes in the region were empty. Therefore it was a good warning for travelers, since by it they could judge how much water to carry on a journey. But certainly he and Lolita were surprised to see how low the Tinaja had fallen today. No doubt what the Indians said about the great underground snake that came and sucked all the wells dry in the lower country, and in consequence was nearly satisfied before he reached the Tinaja, was untrue.

To this tale of Jesuits and peons the American listened with unexpressed contempt, caring too little to mention that he had heard some of it before, or even to say that in the last few days he had crossed the desert from Tucson and found water on the trail as usual where he expected. He rode on, leading the way slowly up the cañon, suffering the glib Mexican to talk unanswered. His own suppressed feelings still smoldered in his eye, still now and then knotted the muscles in his cheeks; but of Luis' chatter he said his whole opinion in one word, a single English syllable, which he uttered quietly for his own benefit. It also benefited Luis. He was familiar with that order of English, and, overhearing, he understood. It consoled the Mexican to feel how easily he could play this simple, unskillful American.

They passed through the hundred corpses to the home and the green trees, where the sun was setting against the little shaking leaves.

"So you will camp here tonight, Don Ruz?" said Luis, perceiving the American's pack-mules. Genesmere had come over from the mines at Gun Sight, found the cabin empty, and followed Lolita's and her cousin's trail, until he had suddenly seen the two from that ledge above the Tinaja. "You are always welcome to what we have at our camp, you know, Don Ruz. All that is mine is yours also. Tonight it is probably frijoles. But no doubt you have white flour here." He was giving his pony water from the barrel, and next he threw the saddle on and mounted. "I must be going back, or they will decide I am not coming till tomorrow, and quickly eat my supper." He spoke jauntily from his horse, arm akimbo, natty short jacket put on for today's courting, gray steeple-hat silver-embroidered, a spruce, pretty boy, not likely to toil severely at wood contracts so long as he could hold soul and body together and otherwise be merry, and the hand of that careless arm soft on his pistol, lest Don Ruz should abruptly dislike him too much; for Luis contrived atone for his small-talk that would have disconcerted the most sluggish, sweet to his own mischievous ears, healing to his galled self-esteem. "Good night, Don Ruz. Good night, Lolita. Perhaps I shall come tomorrow, mañana en la mañana."

"Good night," said Lolita, harshly, which increased his joy; "I cannot stop you from passing my house."

Genesmere said nothing, but sat still on his white horse, hands folded upon the horns of his saddle, and Luis, always engaging and at ease, ambled away with his song about the hunchback. He knew that the American was not the man to wait until his enemy's back was turned.

> "*El telele se murió*
> *A enterrar ya le llevan—*"

The tin-pan Mexican voice was empty of melody and full of rhythm.

> "Ay! Ay! Ay!"

Lolita and Genesmere stood as they had stood, not very near each other, looking after him and his gayety that the sun shone bright upon. The minstrel truly sparkled. His clothes were more elegant than the American's shirt and overalls, and his face luxuriant with thoughtlessness. Like most of his basking Southern breed, he had no visible means of support, and nothing could worry him for longer than three minutes. Frijoles do not come high, out-of-doors is good enough to sleep in if you or your friend have no roof, and it is not a hard thing to sell some other man's horses over the border and get a fine coat and hat.

"Cinco dragones y un cabo,
Oh, no no no no no!
Y un gato de sacristan."

Coat and hat were getting up the cañon's side among the cactus, the little horse climbing the trail shrewdly with his light-weight rider; and dusty, unmusical Genesmere and sullen Lolita watched them till they went behind a bend, and nothing remained but the tin-pan song singing in Genesmere's brain. The gadfly had stung more poisonously than he knew, and still Lolita and Genesmere stood watching nothing, while the sun—the sun of Arizona at the day's transfigured immortal passing—became a crimson coal in a lake of saffron, burning and beating like a heart, till the desert seemed no longer dead, but only asleep, and breathing out wide rays of rainbow color that rose expanded over earth and sky.

Then Genesmere spoke his first volunteered word to Lolita. "I didn't shoot because I was afraid of hitting you," he said.

So now she too realized clearly. He had got off his horse above the Tinaja to kill Luis during that kiss. Complete innocence had made her stupid and slow.

"Are you going to eat?" she inquired.

"Oh yes. I guess I'll eat."

She set about the routine of fire-lighting and supper as if it had been Uncle Ramon, and this evening like all evenings. He, not so easily, and with small blunderings that he cursed, attended to his horse and mules, coming in at length to sit against the wall where she was cooking.

"It is getting dark," said Lolita. So he found the lamp and lighted it, and sat down again.

"I've never hurt a woman," he said, presently, the vision of his rifle's white front sight held steady on the two below the ledge once more flooding his brain. He spoke slowly.

"Then you have a good chance now," said Lolita, quickly, busy over her cooking. In her Southern ears such words sounded a threat. It was not in her blood to comprehend this Northern way of speaking and walking and sitting, and being one thing outside and another inside.

"And I wouldn't hurt a woman"—he was hardly talking to her—"not if I could think in time."

"Men do it," she said, with the same defiance. "But it makes talk."

"Talk's nothing to me," said Genesmere, flaming to fierceness. "Do I care for opinions? Only my own." The fierceness passed from his face, and he was remote from her again. Again he fell to musing aloud, changing from Mexican to his mother-tongue. "I wouldn't want to have to remember a thing like that." He stretched himself, and leaned his elbows on his knees and his head in his hands, the yellow hair hiding his fingers. She had often seen him do this when he felt lazy; it was not a sign by which she could read a spiritual standstill, a quivering wreck of faith and passion. "I have to live a heap of my life alone," the lounger went on. "Journey alone. Camp alone. Me and my mules. And I don't propose to have thoughts a man should be ashamed of." Lolita was throwing a cloth over the table and straightening it. "I'm twenty-five, and I've laid by no such thoughts yet. Church folks might say different."

"It is ready," said Lolita, finishing her preparations.

He looked up, and, seeing the cloth and the places set, pulled his chair to the table, and passively took the food she brought him. She moved about the room between shelves and fire, and, when she had served him, seated herself at leisure to begin her own supper. Uncle Ramon was a peon of some substance, doing business in towns and living comparatively well. Besides the shredded spiced stew of meat, there were several dishes for supper. Genesmere ate the meal deliberately, attending to his plate and cup, and Lolita was as silent as himself, only occasionally looking at him; and in time his thoughts came to the surface again in words. He turned and addressed Lolita in Mexican: "So, you see, you saved his life down there."

She laid her fork down and gave a laugh, hard and harsh; and she said nothing, but waited for what next.

"You don't believe that. You don't know that. He knows that."

She laughed again, more briefly.

"You can tell him so. From me."

Replies seemed to struggle together on Lolita's lips and hinder each other's escaping.

"And you can tell him another thing. He wouldn't have stopped. He'd have shot. Say that. From me. He'd have shot, because he's a Spaniard, like you."

"You lie!" This side issue in some manner set free the girl's tongue, "I am not Spanish. I care nothing for Spaniards or what they may do. I am Mexican, and I waited to see you kill him. I wanted to watch his blood. But you! You listened to his false talk, and believed him, and let him go. I save his life? Go after him now! Do it with this knife, and tell him it is Lolita's. But do not sit there and talk anymore. I have had enough of men's talk today. Enough, enough, enough!"

Genesmere remained in his chair, while she had risen to her feet. "I suppose," he said, very slowly, "that folks like you folks can't understand about love—not about the kind I mean."

Lolita's two hands clinched the edge of the table, and she called upon her gods. "Believe it, then! Believe it! And kill me, if that will make you contented. But do not talk anymore. Yes, he told me that he loved me. Yes, I kissed him; I have kissed him hundreds of times, always, since before I can remember. And I had been laughing at him today, having nothing in my heart but you. All day it had rejoiced me to hear his folly and think of you, and think how little he knew, and how you would come soon. But your folly is worse. Kill me in this house tonight, and I will tell you, dying, that I love you, and that it is you who are the fool."

She looked at her lover, and seeing his face and eyes she had sought to bring before her in the days that she had waited for him, she rushed to him.

"Lolita!" he whispered. "Lolita!"

But she could only sob as she felt his arms and his lips. And when presently he heard her voice again murmuring brokenly to him in the way that he knew and had said over in his mind and dwelt upon through the desert stages he had ridden, he trembled, and with savage triumph drew her close, and let his doubt and the thoughts that had chilled and changed him sink deep beneath the flood of this present rapture. "My life!" she said. "*Toda mi vida!* All my life!" Through the open door the air of the cañon blew cool into the little room over-heated by the fire and the lamp, and in time they grew aware of the endless rustling of the trees, and went out and stood in the darkness together, until it ceased to be darkness, and their eyes could discern the near and distant shapes of their world. The sky was black and splendid, with four or five planets too bright for lesser stars to show, and the promontories of the keen mountains shone almost as in moonlight. A certain hill down towards the Tinaja and its slate ledge caught Genesmere's eye, and Lolita felt him shudder, and she wound her arm more tightly about him.

"What is it?" she said.

"Nothing." He was staring at the hill. "Nothing," he replied to himself.

"Dreamer, come!" said Lolita, pulling him. "It is cold here in the night—and if you choose to forget, I choose you shall remember."

"What does this girl want now?"

"The cards! Our cards!"

"Why, to be sure!" He ran after her, and joy beat in her heart at the fleet kiss he tried for and half missed. She escaped into the room, laughing for delight at her lover's being himself again—his own right self that she talked with always in the long days she waited alone.

"Take it!" she cried out, putting the guitar at him so he should keep his distance. "There! Now you have broken it, songless Americano! You shall buy me another." She flung the light instrument, that fell in a corner with a loud complaint of all the strings together, collapsing to a blurred hollow humming, and silence.

"Now you have done it!" said Genesmere, mock serious.

"I don't care. I am glad. He played on that today. He can have it, and you shall give me a new one.

> *"Yo soy purita mejicana;*
> *Nada tengo español."*

sang the excited, breathless Lolita to her American, and seated herself at the table, beginning a brisk shuffle of a dim, dog-eared pack. "You sit there!" She nodded to the opposite side of the table. "Very well, move the lamp then." Genesmere had moved it because it hid her face from him. "He thinks I cheat! Now, Señor Don Ruz, it shall be for the guitar. Do you hear?"

"Too many pesos, señorita."

"Oh, oh! The miser!"

"I'm not going broke on any señoritas—not even my own girl!"

"Have you no newer thing than poverty to tell me? Now if you look at me like that I cannot shuffle properly."

"How am I to look, please?" He held his glance on her.

"Not foolish like a boy. There, take them, then!" She threw the cards at him, blushing and perturbed by his eyes, while he scrambled to punish her across the table.

"Generous one!" she said. "Ardent pretender! He won't let me shuffle because he fears to lose."

"You shall have a silk handkerchief with flowers on it," said he, shuffling.

"I have two already. I can see you arranging those cards, miser!"

It was the custom of their meetings, whether at the cabin or whether she stole out to his camp, to play for the token he should bring for her when he next came from town. She named one thing, he some other, and the cards judged between them. And to see Genesmere in these hours, his oldest friend could not have known him any more than he knew himself. Never had a woman been for him like Lolita, conjuring the Saxon to forget himself and bask openly in that Southern joy and laughter of the moment.

"Say my name!" he ordered; and at the child effort she made over "Russ" he smiled with delight. "Again!" he exclaimed, bending to catch her _R_ and the whole odd little word she made. "More!"

"No," pouted the girl, and beat at him, blushing again.

"Make your bet!" he said, laying out the Mexican cards before him. "Quick! Which shall it be?"

"The caballo. Oh, my dear, I wanted to die this afternoon, and now I am so happy!"

It brought the tears to her eyes, and almost to his, till he suddenly declared she had stolen a card, and with that they came to soft blows and laughing again. So did the two sit and wrangle, seizing the pack out of turn, feigning rage at being cheated, until he juggled to make her win three times out of five; and when chance had thus settled for the guitar, they played for kisses, and so forgot the cards at last. And at last Genesmere began to speak of the next time, and Lolita to forbid such talk as that so soon. She laid her hand over his lips, at which he yielded for a little, and she improvised questions of moment to ask him, without time for stopping, until she saw that this would avail no longer. Then she sighed, and let him leave her to see to his animals, while she lighted the fire again to make breakfast for him. At that parting meal an anxiety slowly came in her face, and it was she that broke their silence after a while.

"Which road do you go this time, querido?" she asked.

"Tucson, Maricopa, and then straight here to you."

"From Maricopa? That is longer across the desert."

"Shorter to my girl."

"I—I wish you would not come that way."

"Why?"

"That—that desert!"

"There's desert both ways—all ways. The other road puts an extra week between you and me."

"Yes, yes. I have counted."

"What is all this, Lolita?"

Once more she hesitated, smiling uneasily beneath his scrutiny. "*Yo no sé*" (I don't know). "You will laugh. You do not believe the things that I believe. The Tinaja Bonita—"

"That again!"

"Yes," she half whispered. "I am afraid."

He looked at her steadily.

"Return the same road by Tucson," she urged. "That way is only half so much desert, and you can carry water from Poso Blanco. Do not trust the Coyote Wells. They are little and shallow, and if the Black Cross—Oh, my darling, if you do not believe, do this for me because you love me, love me!"

He did not speak at once. The two had risen, and stood by the open door, where the dawn was entering and mixing with the lamp. "Because I love you," he repeated at length, slowly, out of his uncertain thoughts.

She implored him, and he studied her in silence.

Suddenly hardness stamped his face. "I'll come by Tucson, then—since I love you!" And he walked at once out of the door. She followed him to his horse, and there reached up and pulled him round to her, locking her fingers behind his neck. Again his passion swept him, and burned the doubt from his eyes. "I believe you love me!" he broke out.

"Ah, why need you say that?"

"*Adiòs, chiquita.*" He was smiling, and she looked at his white teeth and golden mustache. She felt his hands begin to unlock her own.

"Not yet—not yet!"

"*Adios, chiquita.*"

"*O mi querido!*" she murmured; "with you I forget day and night!"

"Bastante!" He kissed her once for all.

"Goodbye! Goodbye! *Mis labios van estar frios hasta que tu los toques otra vez.*" (My lips will be cold until you touch them again).

He caught her two hands, as if to cling to something. "Say that once more. Tell me that once more."

She told him with all her heart and soul, and he sprang into his saddle. She went beside him through the cold, pale-lighted trees to the garden's edge, and there stood while he took his way across the barren ground among the carcasses. She watched the tip of his mustache that came beyond the line of his cheek, and when he was farther, his whole strong figure, while the clack of the hoofs on the dead ground grew fainter. When the steeper fall of the cañon hid him from her she ran to the house, and from its roof among her peppers she saw him come into sight again below, the wide, foreshortened slant of ground between them, the white horse and dark rider and the mules, until they became a mere line of something moving, and so vanished into the increasing day.

Genesmere rode, and took presently to smoking. Coming to a sandy place, he saw prints of feet and of a shod horse in the trail heading the other way. That was his own horse, and the feet were Lolita's and Luis'—the record and the memory of yesterday afternoon. He looked up from the trail to the hills, now lambent with violet and shifting orange, and their shapes as they moved out into his approaching

view were the shapes of yesterday afternoon. He came soon to the
forking of the trails, one for Tucson and the other leading down into
the lumpy country, and here again were the prints in the sand, the
shod horse, the man and the woman, coming in from the lumpy
country that lay to the left; and Genesmere found himself stock-still
by the forking trails, looking at his watch. His many-journeyed mules
knew which was the Tucson trail, and, not understanding why he
turned them from their routine, walked asunder, puzzled at being
thus driven in the wrong direction. They went along a strange up-and-
down path, loose with sliding stones, and came to an end at a ledge
of slate, and stood about on the tricky footing looking at their master
and leaning their heads together. The master sat quiet on his horse,
staring down where a circular pool lay below; and the sun rose everywhere, except in his mind. So far had he come yesterday with that
mind easy over his garnered prosperity, free and soaring on its daily
flight among the towers of his hopes—those constructions that are
common with men who grow fond: the air-castle rises and reaches,
possessing the architect, who cherishes its slow creation with hourly
changes and additions to the plan. A house was part of Genesmere's
castle, a home with a wife inside, and no more camping alone. Thus
far, to this exact ledge, the edifice had gone forward fortunately, and
then a blast had crumbled house and days to come into indistinguish-
able dust. The heavy echo jarred in Genesmere, now that he had
been lured to look again upon the site of the disaster, and a lightning
violence crossed his face. He saw the two down there as they had
stood, the man with his arms holding the woman, before the falling
stone had startled them. Were the Mexican present now in the flesh,
he would destroy him just for what he had tried to do. If she were
true—She was true—that was no thanks to the Mexican. Genesmere
was sorry second thoughts had spared that fellow yesterday, and he
looked at his watch again. It was time to be starting on the Tucson
trail, and the mules alertly turned their steps from the Tinaja Bonita.
They could see no good in having come here. Evidently it was not to
get water. Why, then? What use was there in looking down a place
into a hole? The mules gave it up. Genesmere himself thought the
Tinaja poorly named. It was not pretty. In his experience of trail and

cañon he knew no other such hole. He was not aware of the twin, dried up, thirty yards below, and therefore only half knew the wonders of the spot.

He rode back to the forks across the rolling steepness, rebuilding the castle; then, discovering something too distant to be sure about, used his glass quickly. It was another rider, also moving slowly among the knolls and gullies of the mesa, and Genesmere could not make him out. He was going towards the cabin, but it was not the same horse that Luis had ridden yesterday. This proved nothing, and it would be easy to circle and see the man closer—only not worth the trouble. Let the Mexican go to the cabin. Let him go every day. He probably would, if she permitted. Most likely she would tell him to keep away from her. She ought to. She might hurt him if he annoyed her. She was a good shot with a pistol. But women work differently from men— and then she was Mexican. She might hide her feelings and make herself pleasant for three weeks. She would tell him when he returned, and they would laugh together over how she had fooled this Luis. After all, shooting would have been too much punishment. A man with a girl like Lolita must expect to find other men after her. It depends on your girl. You find that out when you go after other men's girls. When a woman surely loves some other man she will not look at you. And Lolita's love was a sure thing. A woman can say love and a man will believe her—until he has experienced the genuine article once; after that he can always tell. And to have a house, with her inside waiting for you! Such a turn was strange luck for a man, not to be accounted for. If anybody had said last year—why, as late as the 20th of last March—that settling down was what you were coming to—and now—Genesmere wondered how he could ever have seen anything in riding a horse up and down the earth and caring nothing for what next. "No longer alone!" he said aloud, suddenly, and surprised the white horse.

The song about the hunchback and the sacristan's cat stirred its rhythm in his mind. He was not a singer, but he could think the tune, trace it, naked of melody, in the dry realm of the brain. And it was a diversion to piece out the gait of the phantom notes, low after high, quick after slow, until they went of themselves. Lolita would never kiss

Luis again; would never want to—not even as a joke. Genesmere turned his head back to take another look at the rider, and there stood the whole mountains like a picture, and himself far out in the flat country, and the bare sun in the sky. He had come six miles on the road since he had last noticed. Six miles, and the air-castle was rebuilt and perfect, with no difference from the old one except its foundation, which was upon sand. To see the unexpected plain around him, and the islands of blue, sharp peaks lying in it, drove the tune from his head, and he considered the well-known country, reflecting that man could not be meant to live here. The small mountain-islands lay at all distances, blue in a dozen ways, amid the dead calm of this sand archipelago. They rose singly from it, sheer and sudden, toothed and triangled like icebergs, hot as stoves. The channels to the north, Santa Rosa way, opened broad and yellow, and ended without shore upon the clean horizon, and to the south narrowed with lagoons into Sonora. Genesmere could just see one top of the Sierra de la Quitabac jutting up from below the earth-line, splitting the main channel, the faintest blue of all. They could be having no trouble over their water down there, with the Laguna Esperanca and the Poso de Mazis. Genesmere killed some more of the way rehearsing the trails and waterholes of this country, known to him like his pocket; and by-and-by food-cooking and mule-feeding and the small machine repetitions of a camp and a journey brought the Quijotoa Mountains behind him to replace Gun Sight and the Sierra de la Naril; and later still the Cababi hid the Quijotoa, and Genesmere counted days and nights to the good, and was at the Coyote Wells.

These were holes in rocks, but shallow, as Lolita said. No shallower than ordinary, however; he would see on the way back if they gave signs of failing. No wonder if they did, with this spell of drought—but why mix up a plain thing with a lot of nonsense about a black cross down a hole? Genesmere was critically struck with the words of the tune he now noticed steadily running in his head again, beneath the random surface of his thoughts:

Cinco dragones y un cabo,
Y un gato de sacristan.

That made no sense either; but Mexicans found something in it. Liked it. Now American songs had some sense:

> They bathed his head in vinegar
>   To fetch him up to time,
> And now he drives a mule team on
>   The Denver City line.

A man could understand that. A proud stage-driver makes a mistake about a female passenger. Thinks he has got an heiress, and she turns out to peddle sarsaparilla. "So he's naturally used up," commented Genesmere. "You estimate a girl as one thing, and she—" Here the undercurrent welled up, breaking the surface. "Did she mean that? Was that her genuine reason?" In memory he took a look at his girl's face, and repeated her words when she besought him to come the longer way and hesitated over why. Was that shame at owning she believed such stuff? True, after asking him once about his religion and hearing what he said, she had never spoken of these things again. That must be a woman's way when she loved you first—to hide her notions that differed from yours, and not ruffle happy days. "Return the same road by Tucson!" He unwrapped a clean, many-crumpled handkerchief, and held Lolita's photograph for a while. Then he burst into an unhappy oath, and folded the picture up again. What if her priest did tell her? He had heard the minister tell about eternal punishment when he was a boy, and just as soon as he started thinking it over he knew it was a lie. And this quack Tinaja was worse foolishness, and had nothing to do with religion. Lolita afraid of his coming to grief in a country he had traveled hundreds, thousands of miles in! Perhaps she had never started thinking for herself yet. But she had. She was smarter than any girl of her age he had ever seen. She did not want him back so soon. That was what it was. Yet she had looked true; her voice had sounded that way. Again he dwelt upon her words and caresses; and harboring these various thoughts, he killed still more of the long road, until, passing after a while Poso Blanco, and later Marsh's ranch well at the forks where the Sonora road comes in, he reached Tucson a man divided against himself. Divided beyond his will into two selves—one of faith besieged, and one of besieging inimical reason—the inextricable error!

Business and pleasure were waiting in Tucson, and friends whose ways and company had not been of late for him; but he frequented them this time, tasting no pleasure, yet finding the ways and company better than his own. After the desert's changeless, unfathomed silence, in which nothing new came day or night to break the fettering spell his mind was falling under, the clink and knocking of bottles was good to hear, and he listened for more, craving any sound that might liven or distract his haunted spirit. Instead of the sun and stars, here was a roof; instead of the pitiless clear air, here was tobacco smoke; and beneath his boot-heels a wooden floor wet with spilled liquids instead of the unwatered crumbling sand. Without drinking, he moved his chair near the noisiest drinkers, and thus among the tobacco smoke sought to hide from his own looming doubt. Later the purring tinkle of guitars reminded him of that promised present, and the next morning he was the owner of the best instrument that he could buy. Leaving it with a friend to keep until he should come through again from Maricopa, he departed that way with his mules, finding in the new place the same sort of friends and business, and by night looking upon the same untasted pleasures. He went about town with some cattlemen— carousing bankrupts, who remembered their ruin in the middle of whiskey, and broke off to curse it and the times and climate, and their starved herds that none would buy at any price. Genesmere touched nothing, yet still drew his chair among these drinkers.

"Aren't you feeling good tonight, Russ?" asked one at length.

And Genesmere's eyes roused from seeing visions, and his ears became aware of the loud company. In Tucson he had been able to sit in the smoke, and compass a cheerful deceit of appearance even to himself. Choosing and buying the guitar had lent reality to his imitated peace of mind; he had been careful over its strings, selecting such as Lolita preferred, wrapt in carrying out this spiritual forgery of another Genesmere. But here they had noticed him; appearances had slipped from him. He listened to a piece of late Arizona news someone was in the middle of telling—the trial of several Mormons for robbing a paymaster near Cedar Springs. This was the fourth time he had heard the story, because it was new; but the present narrator dwelt upon the dodgings of a witness, a negress, who had seen everything and told nothing, outwitting the government, furnishing no proofs. This brought Genesmere quite back.

"No proofs!" he muttered. "No proofs!" He laughed and became alert. "She lied to them good, did she?"

They looked at him, because he had not spoken for so long; and he was told that she had certainly lied good.

"Fooled them clean through, did she? On oath! Tell about her."

The flattered narrator, who had been in court, gave all he knew, and Genesmere received each morsel of perjury gravely with a nod. He sat still when the story was done.

"Yes," he said, after a time. "Yes." And again, "Yes." Then he briefly bade the boys good night, and went out from the lamps and whiskey into the dark.

He walked up and down alone, round the corral where his mules stood, round the stable where his bed-blankets were; and one or two carousers came by, who suggested further enjoyments to him. He went to the edge of the town and walked where passers would not meet him, turning now and then to look in the direction of Tucson, where the guitar was waiting. When he felt the change of dawn he went to the stable, and by the first early gray had his mules packed. He looked once again towards Tucson, and took the road he had promised not to take, leaving the guitar behind him altogether. His faith protested a little, but the other self invented a quibble, the mockery that he had already "come by Tucson," according to his literal word; and this device answered. It is a comfort to be divided no longer against one's self. Genesmere was at ease in his thraldom to the demon with whom he had wrestled through the dark hours. As the day brightened he wondered how he had come to fool a night away over a promise such as that. He took out the face in the handkerchief, and gave it a curious, defiant smile. She had said waiting would be long. She should have him quickly. And he was going to know about that visitor at the cabin, the steeple-hatted man he saw in his visions. So Maricopa drew behind him, small, clear-grouped in the unheated morning, and the sun found the united man and his mules moving into the desert.

By the well in the bottom of the Santa Cruz River he met with cattle and little late-born calves trying to trot. Their mothers, the foreman explained, had not milk enough for them, nor the cursed country food or water for the mothers. They could not chew cactus. These animals had been driven here to feed and fatten inexpensively, and get quick money for the owner. But, instead, half of them had died, and the men were driving the rest to new pastures—as many, that is, as could still walk. Genesmere knew, the foreman supposed, that this well was the last for more than a hundred miles? Funny to call a thing like that Santa Cruz a river! Well, it was an Arizona river; all right enough, no doubt, somewhere a thousand feet or so underground. Pity you weren't a prairie dog that eats sand when he gets a thirst on him. Got any tobacco? Goodbye.

Think of any valleys that you know between high mountains. Such was southern Arizona once—before we came. Then fill up your valleys with sand until the mountains show no feet or shoulders, but become as men buried to the neck. That is what makes separate islands of their protruding peaks, and that is why water slinks from the surface whenever it can and flows useless underneath, entombed in the original valley. This is Arizona now—since the pterodactyls have gone. In such a place the traveler turns mariner, only, instead of the stars, he studies the water-wells, shaping his course by these. Not seagulls, but ravens, fly over this waste, seeking their meal. Some were in front of Genesmere now, settled black in the recent trail of the cattle. He did not much care that the last well was gone by, for he was broken in by long travel to the water of the 'dobe-holes that people rely upon through this journey. These 'dobe-holes are occasional wallows in clayey spots, and men and cattle know each one. The cattle, of course, roll in them, and they become worn into circular hollows, their edges tramped into muck, and surrounded by a thicket belt of mesquite. The water is not good, but will save life. The first one lay two stages from the well, and Genesmere accordingly made an expected dry camp the first night, carrying water from the well in the Santa Cruz, and dribbling all of it but a cupful among his animals, and the second night reached his calculated 'dobe-hole. The animals rolled luxuriously in the brown, dungy mixture, and

Genesmere made his coffee strong. He had had no shade at the first camp, and here it was good under the tangle of the mesquite, and he slept sound. He was early awakened by the ravens, whose loose, dislocated croaking came from where they sat at breakfast on the other side of the wallow. They had not suspected his presence among the mesquite, and when he stepped to the mud-hole and dipped its gummy fluid in his coffeepot they rose hoarse and hovering, and flapped twenty yards away, and sat watching until he was gone into the desert, when they clouded back again round their carrion.

This day was over ground yellow and hard with dearth, until afternoon brought a footing of sifting sand heavy to travel in. He had plenty of time for thinking. His ease after the first snapping from his promise had changed to an eagerness to come unawares and catch the man in the steeple-hat. Till that there could be no proofs. Genesmere had along the road nearly emptied his second canteen of its brown-amber drink, wetting the beasts' tongues more than his own. The neighborhood of the next 'dobe-hole might be known by the three miles of cactus you went through before coming on it, a wide-set plantation of the yucca. The posted plants deployed over the plain in strange extended order like legions and legions of figures, each shock-head of spears bunched bristling at the top of its lank, scaly stalk, and out of that stuck the blossom-pole, a pigtail on end, with its knot of bell-flowers seeded to pods ten feet in the air. Genesmere's horse started and nearly threw him, but it was only a young calf lying for shade by a yucca. Genesmere could tell from its unlicked hide that the mother had gone to hunt water, and been away for some time. This unseasonable waif made a try at running away, but fell in a heap, and lay as man and mules passed on. Presently he passed a sentinel cow. She stood among the thorns guarding the calves of her sisters till they should return from getting their water. The desert cattle learn this shift, and the sentinel now, at the stranger's approach, lowered her head, and with a feeble but hostile sound made ready to protect her charge, keeping her face to the passing enemy. Farther along gaunt cows stood or lay under the perpetual yuccas, an animal to every plant. They stared at Genesmere passing on; some rose to look after him; some lifted their heads from the ground, and seeing, laid them down again. He came upon a calf watching its mother, who had fallen in such a position that the calf could not suck. The cow's foreleg was caught over her own head, and so she held herself from rising. The sand was rolled and grooved into a wheel by her circlings; her body heaved and fell with breathing, and the sand was wet where her pivot nostrils had ground it. While Genesmere untangled her and gave her tongue the last of his canteen the calf walked round and round. He placed the cow upon her feet, and as soon as he moved away to his horse the calf came to its mother, who began to lick it. He presently marked ahead the position of the coming 'dobe-hole by the ravens assembled in the air, continually rising and lighting. The white horse and mules quickened their step, and the trail became obliterated by hundreds of hoof-marks leading to the water. As a spider looks in the center of an empty web, so did the round wallow sit in the middle of the plain, with threaded feet conducting from everywhere to it. Mules and white horse scraped through the scratching mesquite, and the ravens flapped up. To Genesmere their croaking seemed suddenly to fill all space with loud total clamor, for no water was left, only mud. He eased the animals of their loads and saddles, and they rolled in the stiff mud, squeezing from it a faint ooze, and getting a sort of refreshment. Genesmere chewed the mud, and felt sorry for the beasts. He turned both canteens upsidedown and licked the bungs. A cow had had his last drink. Well, that would keep her alive several hours more. Hardly worth while; but spilled milk decidedly. Milk! That was an idea. He caught animal after animal, and got a few sickly drops. There was no gain in camping at this spot, no water for coffee; so Genesmere moved several hundred yards away to be rid of the ravens and their all-day-long meal and the smell. He lay thinking what to do. Go back? At the rate he could push the animals now that last hole might be used up by the cattle before he got there—and then it was two stages more to the Santa Cruz well. And the man would be gaining just so many more days unhindered at the cabin. Out of the question. Forward, it was one shortish drive to the next hole. If that were dry, he could forsake the trail and make a try by a shortcut for that Tinaja place. And he must start soon, too, as soon as the animals could stand it, and travel by night and rest when the sun got bad.

What business had October to be hot like this? So in the darkness he mounted again, and noon found him with eyes shut under a yucca. It was here that he held a talk with Lolita. They were married, and sitting in a room with curtains that let you see flowers growing outside by the window, as he had always intended. Lolita said to him that there was no fool like an old fool, and he was telling her that love could make a man more a fool than age, when she threw the door open, letting in bright light, and said, "No proofs." The bright light was the real sun coming round the yucca on his face, and he sat up and saw the desert. No cows were here, but he noticed the roughened hides and sunk eyes of his own beasts, and spoke to them.

"Cheer up, Jeff! Stonewall!" He stopped at the pain. It was in his lips and mouth. He put up his hand, and the feel of his tongue frightened him. He looked round to see what country he was in, and noted the signs that it was not so very far now. The blue crags of the islands were showing, and the blue sterile sky spread over them and the ceaseless sunlight like a plague. Man and horse and mules were the only life in the naked bottom of this caldron. The mirage had caught the nearest island, and blunted and dissolved its points and frayed its base away to a transparent fringe.

"Like a lump of sugar melts in hot tod," remarked Genesmere, aloud, and remembered his thickened mouth again. "I can stand it off for a while yet, though—if they can travel." His mules looked at him when he came—looked when he tightened their cinches. "I know, Jeff," he said, and inspected the sky. "No heaven's up there. Nothing's back of that thing, unless it's hell."

He got the animals going, and the next 'dobe-hole was like the last, and busy with the black flapping of the birds. "You didn't fool me," said Genesmere, addressing the mud. "I knew you'd be dry." His eye ran over the cattle, that lay in various conditions. "That foreman was not too soon getting his livestock out of your country," he continued to the hole, his tongue clacking as it made his words. "This livestock here's not enjoying itself like its owners in town. This live-stock was intended for eastern folks' dinner. But you've got ahead of 'em this trip," he said to the ravens. He laughed loudly, and, hearing himself, stopped, and his face became stern. "You don't want to talk this way,

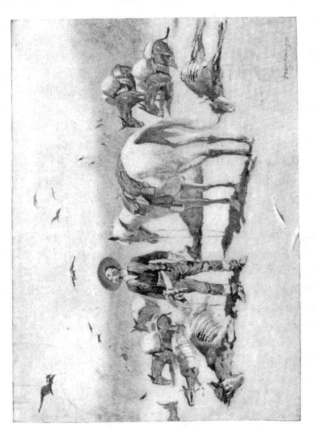

"You don't want to Talk this Way. You're Alone"

Russ Genesmere. Shut your head. You're alone. I wish I'd never known!" he suddenly cried out.

He went to his animals and sat down by them, clasping and unclasping his hands. The mules were lying down on the baked mud of the wallow with their loads on, and he loosed them. He stroked his white horse for some little while, thinking; and it was in his heart that he had brought these beasts into this scrape. It was sunset and cool. Against the divine fires of the west the peaks towered clear in splendor impassive, and forever aloof, and the universe seemed to fill with infinite sadness. "If she'll tell me it's not so," he said, "I'll believe her. I will believe her now. I'll make myself. She'll help me to." He took what rest he dared, and started up from it much later than he had intended, having had the talk with Lolita again in the room with the curtains. It was nine when he set out for the shortcut under the moon, dazed by his increasing torture. The brilliant disk, blurring to the eye, showed the mountains unearthly plain, beautiful, and tall in the night. By-and-by a mule fell and could not rise, and Genesmere decided it was as well for all to rest again. The next he knew it was blazing sunshine, and the sky at the same time bedded invisible in black clouds. And when his hand reached for a cloud that came bellying down to him, it changed into a pretzel, and salt burned in his mouth at the sight of it. He turned away and saw the hot, unshaded mountains wrinkled in the sun, glazed and shrunk, gullied like the parchment of an old man's throat; and then he saw a man in a steeple-hat. He could no more lay the spectre that wasted his mind than the thirst-demon which raged in his body. He shut his eyes, and then his arm was beating at something to keep it away. Pillowed on his saddle, he beat until he forgot. A blow at the corner of his eye brought him up sitting, and a raven jumped from his chest.

"You're not experienced," said Genesmere. "I'm not dead yet. But I'm obliged to you for being so enterprising. You've cleared my head. Quit that talk, Russ Genesmere." He went to the mule that had given out during the night. "Poor Jeff! We must lighten your pack. Now if that hunchback had died here, the birds would have done his business for him without help from any of your cats. Am I saying that, now, or only thinking it? I know I'm alone. I've traveled that way in this world.

Why?" He turned his face, expecting someone to answer, and the answer came in a fierce voice: "Because you're a man, and can stand this world off by yourself. You look to no one." He suddenly took out the handkerchief and tore the photograph to scraps. "That's lightened my pack all it needs. Now for these boys, or they'll never make camp." He took what the mules carried, his merchandise, and hid it carefully between stones—for they had come near the mountain country—and, looking at the plain he was leaving, he saw a river. "Ha, ha!" he said, slyly. "You're not there, though. And I'll prove it to you." He chose another direction, and saw another flowing river. "I was expecting you," he stated, quietly. "Don't bother me. I'm thirsty."

But presently as he journeyed he saw lying to his right a wide, fertile place, with fruit trees and water everywhere. "Peaches too!" he sang out, and sprang off to run, but checked himself in five steps. "I don't seem able to stop your foolish talking," he said, "but you shall not chase around like that. You'll stay with me. I tell you that's a sham. Look at it." Obedient, he looked hard at it, and the cactus and rocks thrust through the watery image of the lake like two photographs on the same plate. He shouted with strangling triumph, and continued shouting until brier roses along a brook and a farmhouse unrolled to his left, and he ran halfway there, calling his mother's name. "Why, you fool, she's dead!" He looked slowly at his cut hands, for he had fallen among stones. "Dead, back in Kentucky, ever so long ago," he murmured, softly. "Didn't stay to see you get wicked." Then he grew stern again. "You've showed yourself up, and you can't tell land from water. You're going to let the boys take you straight. I don't trust you."

He started the mules, and caught hold of his horse's tail, and they set out in single file, held steady by their instinct, stumbling ahead for the water they knew among the mountains. Mules led, and the shouting man brought up the rear, clutching the white tail like a rudder, his feet sliding along through the stones. The country grew higher and rougher, and the peaks blazed in the hot sky; slate and sand and cactus below, gaping cracks and funneled erosions above, rocks like monuments slanting up to the top pinnacles; supreme Arizona, stark and dead in space, like an extinct planet, flooded blind with eternal brightness. The perpetual dominating peaks caught Genesmere's attention.

"Toll on!" he cried to them. "Toll on, you tall mountains. What do you care? Summer and winter, night and day, I've known you, and I've heard you all along. A man can't look but he sees you walling God's country from him, ringing away with your knell."

He must have been lying down during some time, for now he saw the full moon again, and his animals near him, and a fire blazing that himself had evidently built. The coffeepot sat on it, red-hot and split open. He felt almost no suffering at all, but stronger than ever in his life, and he heard something somewhere screaming "Water! Water! Water!" fast and unceasing, like an alarm clock. A rattling of stones made him turn, and there stood a few staring cattle. Instantly he sprang to his feet, and the screaming stopped. "Round 'em up, Russ Genesmere! It's getting late!" he yelled, and ran among the cattle, whirling his rope. They dodged weakly this way and that, and next he was on the white horse urging him after the cows, who ran in a circle. One struck the end of a log that stuck out from the fire, splintering the flames and embers, and Genesmere followed on the tottering horse through the sparks, swinging his rope and yelling in the full moon: "Round 'em up! Round 'em up! Don't you want to make camp? All the rest of the herd's bedded down along with the ravens."

The white horse fell and threw him by the edge of a round hole, but he did not know it till he opened his eyes and it was light again, and the mountains still tolling. Then like a crash of cymbals the Tinaja beat into his recognition. He knew the slate rock; he saw the broken natural stairs. He plunged down them, arms forward like a diver's, and ground his forehead against the bottom. It was dry. His bloodshot eyes rolled once up round the sheer walls. Yes, it was the Tinaja, and his hands began to tear at the gravel. He flung himself to fresh places, fiercely grubbing with his heels, biting into the sand with his teeth; while above him in the cañon his placid animals lay round the real Tinaja Bonita, having slaked their thirst last night, in time, some thirty yards from where he now lay bleeding and fighting the dust in the dry twin hole.

He heard voices, and put his hands up to something round his head. He was now lying out in the light, with a cold bandage round his forehead, and a moist rag on his lips.

"Water!" He could just make the whisper.

But Lolita made a sign of silence.

"Water!" he gasped.

She shook her head, smiling, and moistened the rag. That must be all just now.

His eye sought and traveled, and stopped short, dilating; and Lolita screamed at his leap for the living well.

"Not yet! Not yet!" she said in terror, grappling with him. "Help! Luis!"

So this was their plot, the demon told him—to keep him from water! In a frenzy of strength he seized Lolita. "Proved! Proved!" he shouted, and struck his knife into her. She fell at once to the earth and lay calm, eyes wide open, breathing in the bright sun. He rushed to the water and plunged, swallowing and rolling.

Luis ran up from the cows he was gathering, and when he saw what was done, sank by Lolita to support her. She pointed to the pool.

"He is killing himself!" she managed to say, and her head went lower.

"And I'll help you die, caberon! I'll tear your tongue. I'll—"

But Lolita, hearing Luis' terrible words, had raised a forbidding hand. She signed to leave her and bring Genesmere to her.

The distracted Luis went down the stone stairs to kill the American in spite of her, but the man's appearance stopped him. You could not raise a hand against one come to this. The water-drinking was done, and Genesmere lay fainting, head and helpless arms on the lowest stone, body in the water. The Black Cross stood dry above. Luis heard Lolita's voice, and dragged Genesmere to the top as quickly as he could. She, seeing her lover, cried his name once and died; and Luis cast himself on the earth.

"Fool! Fool!" he repeated, catching at the ground, where he lay for some while until a hand touched him. It was Genesmere.

"I'm seeing things pretty near straight now," the man said. "Come close. I can't talk well. Was—was that talk of yours, and singing—was that bluff?"

"God forgive me!" said poor Luis.

"You mean forgive me," said Genesmere. He lay looking at Lolita. "Close her eyes," he said. And Luis did so. Genesmere was plucking at his clothes, and the Mexican helped him draw out a handkerchief, which the lover unfolded like a treasure. "She used to look like this," he began. He felt and stopped. "Why, it's gone!" he said. He lay evidently seeking to remember where the picture had gone, and his eyes went to the hills whence no help came. Presently Luis heard him speaking, and, leaning to hear, made out that he was murmuring his own name, Russ, in the way Lolita had been used to say it. The boy sat speechless, and no thought stirred in his despair as he watched. The American moved over, and put his arms round Lolita, Luis knowing that he must not offer to help him do this. He remained so long that the boy, who would never be a boy again, bent over to see. But it was only another fainting-fit. Luis waited; now and then the animals moved among the rocks. The sun crossed the sky, bringing the many-colored evening, and Arizona was no longer terrible, but once more infinitely sad. Luis started, for the American was looking at him and beckoning.

"She's not here," Genesmere said, distinctly.

Luis could not follow.

"Not here, I tell you." The lover touched his sweetheart. "This is not her. My punishment is nothing," he went on, his face growing beautiful. "See there!"

Luis looked where he pointed.

"Don't you see her? Don't you see her fixing that camp for me? We're going to camp together now."

But these were visions alien to Luis, and he stared helpless, anxious to do anything that the man might desire. Genesmere's face darkened wistfully.

"Am I not making camp?" he said.

Luis nodded to please him, without at all comprehending.

"You don't see her." Reason was warring with the departing spirit until the end. "Well, maybe you're right. I never was sure. But I'm mortal tired of traveling alone. I hope—"

That was the end, and Russ Genesmere lay still beside his sweetheart. It was a black evening at the cabin, and a black day when Luis and old Ramon raised and fenced the wooden head-stone, with its two forlorn names.

A PILGRIM ON THE GILA

MIDWAY FROM GRANT TO THOMAS COMES PAYMASTER'S HILL, NOT much after Cedar Springs and not long before you sight the valley where the Gila flows. This lonely piece of road must lie three thousand miles from Washington; but in the holiday journey that I made they are near together among the adventures of mind and body that overtook me. For as I turned southward our capital was my first stopping place, and it was here I gathered the expectations of Arizona with which I continued on my way.

Arizona was the unknown country I had chosen for my holiday, and I found them describing it in our National House of Representatives, where I had strolled for sightseeing but stayed to listen. The Democrats were hot to make the territory a state, while the Republicans objected that the place had about it still too much of the raw frontier. The talk and replies of each party were not long in shaking off restraint, and in the sharp exchange of satire the Republicans were reminded that they had not thought Idaho and Wyoming unripe at a season when those Territories were rumored to be Republican. Arizona might be Democratic, but neither cattle wars nor mine revolutions flourished there. Good order and prosperity prevailed. A member from Pennsylvania presently lost his temper, declaring that gigantic generalities about milk and honey and enlightenment would not avail to change his opinion. Arizona was well on to three times the size of New York—had a hundred and thirteen thousand square miles. Square miles of what? The desert of Sahara was twice as big as Arizona, and one of the largest misfortunes on the face of the earth. Arizona had sixty thousand inhabitants, not quite so many as the town of Troy. And what sort of people? He understood that cactus was Arizona's chief crop, stage-robbing her most active industry, and the Apache her leading citizen.

And then the Boy Orator of the Rio Grande took his good chance. I forgot his sallow face and black, unpleasant hair, and even his single gesture—that straining lift of one hand above the shoulder during the suspense of a sentence and that cracking it down into the other at the full stop, endless as a pile-driver. His facts wiped any trick of manner from my notice. Indians? Stage-robbers? Cactus? Yes. He would add famine, drought, impotent law, daily murder; he could add much more, but it was all told in Mr. Pumpelly's book, true as life, thirty years ago—doubtless the latest news in Pennsylvania! Had this report discouraged the gentleman from visiting Arizona? Why, he could go there today in a Pullman car by two great roads and eat his three meals in security. But eastern statesmen were too often content with knowing their particular corner of our map while a continent of ignorance lay in their minds.

At this stroke applause sounded beside me, and, turning, I had my first sight of the yellow duster. The bulky man that wore it shrewdly and smilingly watched the orator, who now dwelt upon the rapid benefits of the railways, the excellent men and things they brought to Arizona, the leap into civilization that the territory had taken. "Let Pennsylvania see those blossoming fields for herself," said he, "those boundless contiguities of shade." And a sort of cluck went off down inside my neighbor's throat, while the speaker with rising heat gave us the tonnage of plums exported from the territory during the past fiscal year. Wool followed.

"Sock it to 'em, Limber Jim!" murmured the man in the duster, and executed a sort of step. He was plainly a personal acquaintance of the speaker's.

Figures never stick by me, nor can I quote accurately the catalogue of statistic abundance now recited in the House of Representatives;

but as wheat, corn, peaches, apricots, oranges, raisins, spices, the rose and the jasmine flowered in the Boy Orator's eloquence, the genial antics of my neighbor increased until he broke into delighted mutterings, such as "He's a stud-horse," and "Put the kybosh on 'em," and many more that have escaped my memory. But the Boy Orator's peroration I am glad to remember, for his fervid convictions lifted him into the domain of metaphor and cadence; and though to be sure I made due allowance for enthusiasm, his picture of Arizona remained vivid with me, and I should have voted to make the territory a state that very day.

"With her snow-clad summits, with the balm of her Southern vineyards, she loudly calls for a sister's rights. Not the isles of Greece, nor any cycle of Cathay, can compete with her horticultural resources, her Salt River, her Colorado, her San Pedro, her Gila, her hundred irrigated valleys, each one surpassing the shaded Paradise of the Nile, where thousands of noble men and elegantly educated ladies have already located, and to which thousands more, like patient monuments, are waiting breathless to throng when the franchise is proclaimed. And if my death could buy that franchise, I would joyfully boast such martyrdom."

The orator cracked his hands together in this supreme moment, and the bulky gentleman in the duster drove an elbow against my side, whispering to me at the same time behind his hand, in a hoarse confidence: "Deserted Jericho! California only holds the record on stoves now."

"I'm afraid I do not catch your allusion," I began. But at my voice he turned sharply, and, giving me one short, ugly stare, was looking about him, evidently at some loss, when a man at his farther side pulled at his duster, and I then saw that he had all along been taking me for a younger companion he had come in with, and with whom he now went away. In the jostle we had shifted places while his eyes were upon the various speakers, and to him I seemed an eavesdropper. Both he and his friend had a curious appearance, and they looked behind them, meeting my gaze as I watched them going; and then they made to each other some laughing comment, of which I felt myself to be the inspiration. I was standing absently on the same spot, still in a mild puzzle over California and the record on stoves. Certainly I had overheard none of their secrets, if they had any; I could not even guess what might be their true opinion about admitting Arizona to our Union.

With this last memory of our capitol and the statesmen we have collected there to govern us, I entered upon my holiday, glad that it was to be passed in such a region of enchantment. For peaches it would be too early, and with roses and jasmine I did not importantly concern myself, thinking of them only as a pleasant sight by the way. But on my gradual journey through Lexington, Bowling Green, Little Rock, and Forth Worth I dwelt upon the shade of the valleys, and the pasture hills dotted with the sheep of whose wool the Boy Orator had spoken; and I wished that our cold Northwest could have been given such a bountiful climate. Upon the final morning of railroad I looked out of the window at an earth which during the night had collapsed into a vacuum, as I had so often seen happen before upon more Northern parallels. The evenness of this huge nothing was cut by our track's interminable scar, and broken to the eye by the towns which now and again rose and littered the horizon like boxes dumped by emigrants. We were still in Texas, not distant from the Rio Grande, and I looked at the boxes drifting by, and wondered from which of them the Boy Orator had been let loose. Twice or three times upon this day of sand I saw green spots shining sudden and bright and biblical in the wilderness. Their isolated loveliness was herald of the valley land I was nearing each hour. The wandering Mexicans, too, bright in rags and swarthy in nakedness, put me somehow in mind of the Old Testament.

In the evening I sat at whiskey with my first acquaintance, a Mr. Mowry, one of several Arizona citizens whom my military friend at San Carlos had written me to look out for on my way to visit him. My train had trundled on to the Pacific, and I sat in a house once more—a saloon on the platform, with an open door through which the night air came pleasantly. This was now the long-expected territory, and time for roses and jasmine to begin. Early in our talk I naturally spoke to Mr. Mowry of Arizona's resources and her chance of becoming a state.

"We'd have got there by now," said he, "only Luke Jenks ain't half that interested in Arizona as he is in Luke Jenks."

I reminded Mr. Mowry that I was a stranger here and unacquainted with the prominent people.

"Well, Luke's as near a hog as you kin be and wear pants. Be with you in a minute," added Mr. Mowry, and shambled from the room. This was because a shot had been fired in a house across the railroad tracks. "I run two places," he explained, returning quite soon from the house and taking up the thread of his whiskey where he had dropped it. "Two outfits. This side for toorists. Th' other pays better. I come here in 'sixty-two."

"I trust no one has been—hurt?" said I, inclining my head towards the farther side of the railroad.

"Hurt?" My question for the moment conveyed nothing to him, and he repeated the word, blinking with red eyes at me over the rim of his lifted glass. "No, nobody's hurt. I've been here a long while, and seen them as was hurt, though." Here he nodded at me depreciatingly, and I felt how short was the time that I had been here. "Th' other side pays better," he resumed, "as toorists mostly go to bed early. Six bits is about the figger you can reckon they'll spend, if you know anything." He nodded again, more solemn over his whiskey. "That kind's no help to business. I've been in this territory from the start, and Arizona ain't what it was. Them mountains are named from me." And he pointed out of the door. "Mowry's Peak. On the map." With this last august statement his mind seemed to fade from the conversation, and he struck a succession of matches along the table and various parts of his person.

"Has Mr. Jenks been in the territory long?" I suggested, feeling the silence weigh upon me.

"Luke? He's a hog. Him the people's choice! But the people of Arizona ain't what they was. Are you interested in silver?"

"Yes," I answered, meaning the political question. But before I could say what I meant he had revived into a vigor of attitude and a wakefulness of eye of which I had not hitherto supposed him capable.

"You come here," said he; and, catching my arm, he took me out of the door and along the track in the night, and round the corner of the railroad hotel into view of more mountains that lay to the south. "You stay here tomorrow," he pursued, swiftly, "and I'll hitch up and drive you over there. I'll show you some rock behind Helen's Dome that 'll beat any you've struck in the whole course of your life. It's on the wood reservation, and when the government abandons the post, as they're going to do—"

There is no need for my entering at length into his urgence, or the plans he put to me for our becoming partners, or for my buying him out and employing him on a salary, or buying him out and employing some other, or no one, according as I chose—the whole bright array of costumes in which he presented to me the chance of making my fortune at a stroke. I think that from my answers he gathered presently a discouraging but perfectly false impression. My eastern hat and inexperienced face (I was certainly young enough to have been his grandchild) had a little misled him; and although he did not in the least believe the simple truth I told him, that I had come to Arizona on no sort of business, but for the pleasure of seeing the country, he now overrated my brains as greatly as he had in the beginning despised them, quite persuaded I was playing some game deeper than common, and either owned already or had my eye upon other silver mines.

"Pleasure of seeing the country, ye say?" His small wet eyes blinked as he stood on the railroad track bareheaded, considering me from head to foot. "All right. Did ye say ye're going to Globe?"

"No. To San Carlos to visit an army officer."

"Carlos is on the straight road to Globe," said Mr. Mowry, vindictively. "But ye might as well drop any idea of Globe, if ye should get one. If it's copper ye're after, there's parties in ahead of you."

Desiring, if possible, to shift his mind from its present unfavorable turn, I asked him if Mr. Adams did not live between here and Solomonsville, my route to Carlos. Mr. Adams was another character of whom my host had written me, and at my mention of his name the face of Mr. Mowry immediately soured into the same expression it had taken when he spoke of the degraded Jenks.

"So you're acquainted with him! He's got mines. I've seen 'em. If you represent any eastern parties, tell 'em not to drop their dollars down old Adams' hole in the ground. He ain't the inexperienced juniper he looks. Him and me's been acquainted these thirty years. People claim it was Cyclone Bill held up the Ehrenberg stage. Well, I guess I'll be seeing how the boys are getting along."

With that he moved away. A loud disturbance of chairs and broken glass had set up in the house across the railroad, and I watched the proprietor shamble from me with his deliberate gait towards the establishment that paid him best. He had left me possessor of much incomplete knowledge, and I waited for him, pacing the platform; but he did not return, and as I judged it inexpedient to follow him, I went to my bed on the tourist side of the track.

In the morning the stage went early, and as our road seemed to promise but little variety—I could see nothing but an empty plain—I was glad to find my single fellow passenger a man inclined to talk. I did not like his mustache, which was too large for his face, nor his too careful civility and arrangement of words; but he was genial to excess, and thoughtful of my comfort.

"I beg you will not allow my valise to incommode you," was one of his first remarks; and I liked this consideration better than any Mr. Mowry had shown me. "I fear you will detect much initial primitiveness in our methods of transportation," he said.

This again called for gracious assurances on my part, and for a while our polite phrases balanced to corners until I was mentally winded keeping up such a pace of manners. The train had just brought him from Tucson, he told me, and would I indulge? On this we shared and complimented each other's whiskey.

"From your flask I take it that you are a Gentile," said he, smiling.

"If you mean tenderfoot," said I, "let me confess at once that flask and owner are from the East, and brand-new in Arizona."

"I mean you're not a Mormon. Most strangers to me up this way are. But they carry their liquor in a plain flat bottle like this."

"Are you a—a—" Embarrassment took me as it would were I to check myself on the verge of asking a courteously disposed stranger if he had ever embezzled.

"Oh, I'm no Mormon," my new friend said, with a chuckle, and I was glad to hear him come down to reasonable English. "But Gentiles are in the minority in this valley."

"I didn't know we'd got to the valleys yet," said I, eagerly, connecting Mormons with fertility and jasmine. And I lifted the flaps of the stage, first one side and then the other, and saw the desert everywhere flat, treeless, and staring like an eye without a lid.

"This is the San Simon Valley we've been in all the time," he replied. "It goes from Mexico to the Gila, about a hundred and fifty miles."

"Like this?"

"South it's rockier. Better put the flap down."

"I don't see where people live," I said, as two smoky spouts of sand jetted from the tires and strewed over our shoes and pervaded our nostrils. "There's nothing—yes, there's one bush coming." I fastened the flaps.

"That's Seven-Mile Mesquite. They held up the stage at this point last October. But they made a mistake in the day. The money had gone down the afternoon before, and they only got about a hundred."

"I suppose it was Mormons who robbed the stage?"

"Don't talk quite so loud," the stranger said, laughing. "The driver's one of them."

"A Mormon or a robber?"

"Well, we only know he's a Mormon."

"He doesn't look twenty. Has he many wives yet?"

"Oh, they keep that thing very quiet in these days, if they do it at all. The government made things too hot altogether. The bishop here knows what hiding for polygamy means."

"Bishop who?"

"Meakum," I thought he answered me, but was not sure in the rattle of the stage, and twice made him repeat it, putting my hand to my ear at last. "Meakum! Meakum!" he shouted.

"Yes, sir," said the driver.

"Have some whiskey?" said my friend, promptly; and when that was over and the flat bottle passed back, he explained in a lower voice, "A son of the bishop's."

"Indeed!" I exclaimed.

"So was the young fellow who put in the mailbags, and that yellow-headed duck in the store this morning." My companion, in the pleasure of teaching new things to a stranger, stretched his legs on the front seat, lifted my coat out of his way, and left all formality of speech and deportment. "And so's the driver you'll have tomorrow if you're going beyond Thomas, and the stock-tender at the sub-agency where you'll breakfast. He's a yellow-head too. The old man's postmaster, and owns this stage line. One of his boys has the mail contract. The old man runs the hotel at Solomonsville and two stores at Bowie and Globe, and the store and mill at Thacher. He supplies the military posts in this district with hay and wood, and a lot of things on and off through the year. Can't write his own name. Signs government contracts with his mark. He's sixty-four, and he's had eight wives. Last summer he married number nine—rest all dead, he says, and I guess that's so. He has fifty-seven recorded children, not counting the twins born last week. Any yellow-heads you'll see in the valley 'll answer to the name of Meakum as a rule, and the other type's curly black like this little driver specimen."

"How interesting there should be only two varieties of Meakum!" said I.

"Yes, it's interesting. Of course the whole fifty-seven don't class up yellow or black curly, but if you could take account of stock you'd find the big half of 'em do. Mothers don't seem to have influenced the type appreciably. His eight families, successive and simultaneous, cover a period of forty-three years, and yellow and black keeps turning up right along. Scientifically, the suppression of Mormonism is a loss to the student of heredity. Some of the children are dead. Get killed now and then, and die too—die from sickness. But you'll easily notice Meakums as you go up the valley. Old man sees all get good jobs as soon as they're old enough. Places 'em on the railroad, places 'em in town, all over the lot. Some don't stay; you couldn't expect the whole fifty-seven to be steady; but he starts 'em all fair. We have six in Tucson now, or five, maybe. Old man's a good father."

"They're not all boys?"

"Certainly not; but more than half are."

"And you say he can't write?"

"Or read, except print, and he has to spell out that."

"But, my goodness, he's postmaster!"

"What's that got to do with it? Young Meakums all read like anything. He don't do any drudgery."

"Well, you wouldn't catch me signing any contracts I couldn't read."

"Do you think you'd catch anybody reading a contract wrong to old Meakum? Oh, momma! Why, he's king round here. Fixes the county elections and the price of tomatoes. Do you suppose any Tucson jury 'll convict any of his Mormons if he says nay? No, sir! It's been tried. Why, that man ought to be in Congress."

"If he's like that I don't consider him desirable," said I.

"Yes, he is desirable," said my friend, roughly. "Smart, can't be fooled, and looks after his people's interests. I'd like to know if that don't fill the bill?"

"If he defeats justice—"

"Oh, rats!" This interruption made me regret his earlier manner, and I was sorry the polish had rubbed through so quickly and brought us to a too precipitate familiarity. "We're western out here," he continued, "and we're practical. When we want a thing, we go after it. Bishop Meakum worked his way down here from Utah through desert and starvation, mostly afoot, for a thousand miles, and his flock today is about the only class in the territory that knows what prosperity feels like, and his laws are about the only laws folks don't care to break. He's got a brain. If he weren't against Arizona's being admitted—"

"He should know better than that," said I, wishing to be friendly. "With your fruit exports and high grade of citizens you'll soon be another California."

He gave me an odd look.

"I am surprised," I proceeded, amiably, "to hear you speak of Mormons only as prosperous. They think better of you in Washington."

"Now, see here," said he, "I've been pleasant to you and I've enjoyed this ride. But I like plain talk."

"What's the matter?" I asked.

"And I don't care for eastern sarcasm."

"There was no intention—"

"I don't take offense where offense is not intended. As for high-grade citizens, we don't claim to know as much as—I suppose it's New York you come from? Gold-bugs and mugwumps—"

"If you can spare the time," said I, "and kindly explain what has disturbed you in my remarks, we'll each be likely to find the rest of these forty miles more supportable."

"I guess I can stand it," said he, swallowing a drink. He folded his arms and resettled his legs; and the noisome hatefulness of his laugh filled me with regret for the wet-eyed Mowry. I would now gladly have taken any amount of Mowry in exchange for this; and it struck me afresh how uncertainly one always reckons with those who suspect their own standing.

"Till Solomonsville," said I, "let us veil our estimation of each other. Once out of this stage and the world will be large enough for both of us." I was wrong there; but presentiments do not come to me often. So I, too, drank some of my own whiskey, lighted a cigar, and observed with pleasure that my words had enraged him.

Before either of us had devised our next remark, the stage pulled up to change horses at the first and last water in forty miles. This station was kept by Mr. Adams, and I jumped out to see the man Mr. Mowry had warned me was not an inexperienced juniper. His appearance would have drawn few but missionaries to him, and I should think would have been warning enough to any but an over-trustful child of six.

"Are you the geologist?" he said at once, coughing heavily; and when I told him I was simply enjoying a holiday, he looked at me sharply and spat against the corner of the stable. "There's one of them fellers expected," he continued, in a tone as if I need not attempt to deny that, and I felt his eye watching for signs of geology about me. I told him that I imagined the geologist must do an active business in Arizona.

"I don't hire 'em!" he exclaimed. "They can't tell me nothing about mineral."

"I suppose you have been here a long while, Mr. Adams?"

"There's just three living that come in ahead of—" The cough split his last word in pieces.

"Mr. Mowry was saying last night—"

"You've seen that old scamp, have you? Buy his mine behind Helen's Dome?"

My mirth at this turned him instantly confidential, and rooted his conviction that I was a geologist. "That's right!" said he, tapping my arm. "Don't you let 'em fool you. I guess you know your business. Now, if you want to look at good paying rock, thousands in sight, in sight, mind you—"

"Are you coming along with us?" called the little Meakum driver, and I turned and saw the new team was harnessed and he ready on his box, with the reins in his hands. So I was obliged to hasten from the disappointed Adams and climb back in my seat. The last I saw of him he was standing quite still in the welter of stable muck, stooping to his cough, the desert sun beating on his old body, and the desert wind slowly turning the windmill above the shadeless mud hovel in which he lived alone.

"Poor old devil!" said I to my enemy, half forgetting our terms in my contemplation of Adams. "Is he a Mormon?"

My enemy's temper seemed a little improved. "He's tried most everything except jail," he answered, his voice still harsh. "You needn't invest your sentiment there. He used to hang out at Twenty Mile in Old Camp Grant days, and he'd slit your throat for fifty cents."

But my sentiment was invested somehow. The years of the old-timers were ending so gray. Their heyday, and carousals, and happy-go-luckiness all gone, and in the remaining hours—what? Empty youth is such a grand easy thing, and empty age so grim!

"Has Mowry tried everything, too?" I asked.

"Including jail," said my companion; and gave me many entertaining incidents of Mowry's career with an ill-smelling saloon cleverness that put him once more into favorable humor with me, while I retained my opinion of him. "And that uneducated sot," he concluded, "that hobo with his record of cattle-stealing and claim-jumping, and his acquittal from jail through railroad influence, actually undertook to run against me last elections. My name is Jenks; Luke Jenks, territorial delegate from Arizona." He handed me his card.

"I'm just from Washington," said I.

"Well, I've not been there this session. Important law business has detained me here. Yes, they backed Mowry in that election. The old spittoon had quite a following, but he hadn't the cash. That gives you some idea of the low standards I have to combat. But I hadn't to spend much. This territory's so poor they come cheap. Seventy-five cents a head for all the votes I wanted in Bisbee, Nogales, and Yuma; and up here the bishop was my good friend. Holding office booms my business some, and that's why I took it, of course. But I've had low standards to fight."

The territorial delegate now talked freely of Arizona's frontier life. "It's all dead," he said, forgetting in his fluency what he had told me about Seven-Mile Mesquite and last October. "We have a community as high toned as any in the land. Our monumental activity—" And here he went off like a cuckoo clock, or the Boy Orator, reciting the glories of Phœnix and Salt River, and the future of silver, in that special dialect of platitudes which is spoken by our more talkative statesmen, and is not quite Latin, quite grammar, or quite falsehood. "We're not all Mowrys and Adamses," said he, landing from his flight.

"In a population of fifty-nine thousand," said I, heartily, "a stranger is bound to meet decent people if he keeps on."

Again he misinterpreted me, but this time the other way, bowing like one who acknowledges a compliment; and we came to Solomonsville in such peace that he would have been astonished at my private thoughts. For I had met no undisguised vagabond nor out-and-out tramp whom I did not prefer to Luke Jenks, vote-buyer and politician. With his catch-penny plausibility, his thin-spread good-fellowship, and his New York clothes, he mistook himself for a respectable man, and I was glad to be done with him.

I could have reached Thomas that evening, but after our noon dinner let the stage go on, and delayed a night for the sake of seeing the bishop hold service next day, which was Sunday, some few miles down the valley. I was curious to learn the Mormon ritual and what might be the doctrines that such a man as the bishop would expound. It dashed me a little to find this would cost me forty-eight hours of Solomonsville, no Sunday stage running. But one friendly English-speaking family—the town was chiefly Mexican—made some of my hours pleasant, and others I spent in walking. Though I went early to bed I slept so late that the ritual was well advanced when I reached the Mormon gathering. From where I was obliged to stand I could only hear the preacher, already in the middle of his discourse.

"Don't empty your swill in the door-yard, but feed it to your hogs," he was saying; and anyone who knows how plainly a man is revealed in his voice could have felt instantly, as I did, that here was undoubtedly a leader of men. "Rotten meat, rotten corn, spoiled milk, the truck that thoughtless folks throw away, should be used. Their usefulness has not ceased because they're rotten. That's the error of the ignorant, who know not that nothing is meant to be wasted in this world. The ignorant stay poor because they break the law of the Lord. Waste not, want not. The children of the Gentiles play in the door-yard and grow sickly and die. The mother working in the house has a pale face and poison in her blood. She cannot be a strong wife. She cannot bear strong sons to the man. He stays healthy because he toils in the field. He does not breathe the tainted air rising from the swill in the door-yard. Swill is bad for us, but it is good for swine. Waste it by the threshold it becomes deadly, and a curse falls upon the house. The mother and children are sick because she has broken a law of the Lord. Do not let me see this sin when I come among you in the valley. Fifty yards behind each house, with clean air between, let me see the well-fed swine receiving each day, as was intended, the garbage left by man. And let me see flowers in the door-yard, and stout, blooming children. We will sing the twenty-ninth hymn."

The scales had many hours ago dropped from my eyes, and I saw Arizona clear, and felt no repining for roses and jasmine. They had been a politician's way of foisting one more silver state upon our Senate, and I willingly renounced them for the real thing I was getting; for my holiday already far outspangled the motliest dream that ever visited me, and I settled down to it as we settle down in our theater chairs, well pleased with the flying pantomime. And when, after the hymn and a blessing—the hymn was poor stuff about wanting to be a Mormon and with the Mormons stand—I saw the bishop get into a wagon, put on a yellow duster, and drive quickly away, no surprise struck me at all. I merely said to myself: Certainly. How dull not to have foreseen that! And I knew that we should speak together soon, and he would tell me why California only held the record on stoves.

But oh, my friends, what a country we live in, and what an age, that the same stars and stripes should simultaneously wave over this and over Delmonico's! This too I kept thinking as I killed more hours in walking the neighborhood of Solomonsville, an object of more false hope to natives whom I did not then observe. I avoided Jenks, who had business clients in the town. I went among the ditches and the fields thus turned green by the channeled Gila; and though it was scarce a paradise surpassing the Nile, it was grassy and full of sweet smells until after a few miles each way, when the desert suddenly met the pleasant verdure full in the face and corroded it to death like vitriol. The sermon came back to me as I passed the little Mormon homes, and the bishop rose and rose in my esteem, though not as one of the children of light. That sagacious patriarch told his flock the things of weekday wisdom down to their level, the cleanly things next to godliness, to keep them from the million squalors that stain our Gentile poor; and if he did not sound much like the Gospel, he and Deuteronomy were alike as two peas. With him and Moses thus in my thoughts, I came back after sunset, and was gratified to be late for supper. Jenks had left the dining room, and I ate in my own company, which had become lively and full of intelligent impressions. These I sat recording later in my journal, when a hesitating knock came at my bedroom, and two young men in cowboy costume entered like shy children, endeavoring to step without creaking.

"Meakums!" my delighted mind exclaimed, inwardly; but the yellow one introduced the black curly one as Mr. Follet, who, in turn, made his friend Mr. Cunningham known to me, and at my cordial suggestion they sat down with increasing awkwardness, first leaving their hats outside the door.

"We seen you walking around," said one.

"Lookin' the country over," said the other.

"Fine weather for traveling," said the first.

"Dusty though," said the second.

Perceiving them to need my help in coming to their point, I said, "And now about your silver mine."

"You've called the turn on us!" exclaimed yellow, and black curly slapped his knee. Both of them sat looking at me, laughing enthusiastically, and I gathered they had been having whiskey this Sunday night. I confess that I offered them some more, and when they realized my mildness they told me with length and confidence about the claims they had staked out on Mount Turnbull. "And there's lots of lead, too," said yellow.

"I do not smelt," said I, "or deal in any way with ore. I have come here without the intention of buying anything."

"You ain't the paymaster?" burst out black curly, wrinkling his forehead like a pleasant dog.

Yellow touched his foot.

"Course he ain't!" said curly, with a swerve of his eye. "He ain't due. What a while it always is waitin'!"

Now the paymaster was nothing to me, nor whom he paid. For all I knew, my visitors were on his roll; and why yellow should shy at the mention of him and closely watch his tipsy mate I did not try to guess. Like everyone I had met so far in Arizona, these two evidently doubted I was here for my pleasure merely; but it was with entire good-humor that they remarked a man had the right to mind his own business; and so, with a little more whiskey, we made a friendly parting. They recommended me to travel with a pistol in this country, and I explained that I should do myself more harm than good with a weapon that anyone handled more rapidly than I, with my inexperience.

"Good night, Mr. Meakum," I said.

"Follet," corrected black curly.

"Cunningham," said yellow, and they picked up their hats in the hall and withdrew.

I think now those were their names—the time was coming when I should hear them take oath on it—yet I do not know. I heard many curious oaths taken.

I was glad to see black curly in the stage next day, not alone for his company, but to give him a right notion of what ready money I had about me. Thinking him over, and his absence of visible means of support, and his interest in me, I took opportunity to mention, quite by the way, that five or six dollars was all that I ever carried on my person, the rest being in New York drafts, worthless in any hands but mine. And I looked at the time once or twice for him to perceive the cheapness of my nickel watch. That the bishop was not his father I had indirect evidence when we stopped at Thacher to change horses and drop a mail-sack, and the Mormon divine suddenly lifted the flap and inspected us. He nodded to me and gave Follet a message.

"Tell your brother" (wouldn't a father have said Tom or Dick?) "that I've given him chances enough and he don't take 'em. He don't feed my horses, and my passengers complain he don't feed them— though that's not so serious!" said he to me, with a jovial wink. "But I won't have my stock starved. You'll skip the station and go through to Thomas with this pair," he added to the driver in his voice of lusty command. "You'll get supper at Thomas. Everything's moved on there from today. That's the rule now." Then he returned to black curly, who, like the driver, had remained cowed and respectful throughout the short harangue. "Your brother could have treated me square and made money by that station. Tell him that, and to see me by Thursday. If he's thinking of peddling vegetables this season I'll let him sell to Fort Bowie. Safford takes Carlos, and I won't have two compete in the same market, or we'll be sinking low as eastern prices," said he to me, with another wink. "Drive on now. You're late."

He shut the flap, and we were off quickly—too quickly. In the next few moments I could feel that something all wrong went on; there was a jingle and snapping of harness, and such a voice from the bishop behind us that I looked out to see him. We had stopped, and he was running after us at a wonderful pace for a man of sixty-four.

"If you don't drive better than that," said the grizzled athlete, arriving cool and competent, "you'll saw wood for another year. Look how you've got them trembling."

It was a young pair, and they stood and steamed while the broken gear was mended.

"What did California hold the record in before the Boy Orator broke it?" said I, getting out.

He shot at me the same sinister look I had seen in the capitol, the look he must always wear, I suppose, when taken aback. Then he laughed broadly and heartily, a strong pleasant laugh that nearly made me like him. "So you're that fellow! Ho, ho! Away down here now. Oh, ho, ho! What's your business?"

"You wouldn't believe if I told you," said I, to his sudden sharp question.

"Me? Why, I believe everything I'm told. What's your name?"

"Will you believe I haven't come to buy anybody's silver mine?"

"Silver! I don't keep it. Unloaded ten years ago before the rabbit died."

"Then you're the first anti-silver man I've met."

"I'm anti anything I can't sell, young man. Here's all there is to silver: Once upon a time it was hard to get, and we had to have it. Now it's easy. When it gets as common as dirt it'll be as cheap as dirt. Same as watermelons when it's a big crop. D'you follow me? That's silver for you, and I don't want it. So you've come away down here. Well, well! What did you say your name was?"

I told him.

"Politician?"

"God forbid!"

"Oh, ho, ho! Well, yes. I took a look at those buzzards there in Washington. Our Senate and Representatives. They were screeching a heap. All about ratios. You'll be sawing wood yet!" he shouted to the driver, and strode up to help him back a horse. "Now ratio is a good-sounding word too, and I guess that's why they chew on it so constant. Better line of language that they get at home. I'll tell you about Congress. Here's all there is to it: You can divide them birds in two lots. Those who know better and those who don't. D'you follow me?"

"And which kind is the Boy Orator?"

"Limber Jim? Oh, he knows better. I know Jim. You see, we used to have a saying in Salt Lake that California had the smallest stoves and the biggest liars in the world. Now Jim—well, there's an old saying busted. But you'll see Arizona 'll go back on the Democrats. If they put wool on the free list she'll stay Republican, and they won't want her admitted, which suits me first-rate. My people here are better off as they stand."

"But your friend Mr. Jenks favors admission!" I exclaimed.

"Luke? He's been talking to you, has he? Well now, Luke. Here's all there is to him: Natural gas. That's why I support him, you see. If we sent a real smart man to Washington he might get us made a state. Ho, ho! But Luke stays here most of the time, and he's no good anyway. Oh, ho, ho! So you're buying no mines this season?"

Once more I found myself narrating the insignificance of my visit to Arizona—the bishop must have been a hard inquisitor for even the deeply skillful to elude—and for the first time my word was believed. He quickly took my measure, saw that I had nothing to hide, and after telling me I could find good hunting and scenery in the mountains north, paid me no further attention, but masterfully laid some final commands on the intimidated driver. Then I bade goodbye to the bishop, and watched that old locomotive moving vigorously back along the road to his manifold business.

The driver was ill pleased to go hungry for his supper until Thomas, but he did not dare complain much over the new rule, even to black curly and me. This and one other thing impressed me. Some miles farther on we had passed out of the dust for a while, and rolled up the flaps.

"She's waiting for you," said the driver to black curly, and that many-sided youth instantly dived to the bottom of the stage, his boots and pistol among my legs.

"Throw your coat over me," he urged.

I concealed him with that and a mail-sack, and stretched my head out to see what lioness stood in his path. But it was only a homelike little cabin, and at the door a woman, comely and mature, eying the stage expectantly. Possibly wife, I thought, more likely mother, and I asked, "Is Mrs. Follet strict?" choosing a name to fit either.

The driver choked and chirruped, but no sound came from under the mail sack until we had passed the good day to the momentous female, whose response was harsh with displeasure as she wheeled into her door. A sulky voice then said, "Tell me when she's gone, Bill." But we were a safe two hundred yards on the road before he would lift his head, and his spirits were darkened during the remainder of the journey.

"Come and live East," said I, inviting him to some whiskey at the same time. "Back there they don't begin sitting up for you so early in the evening."

This did not enliven him, although upon our driver it seemed to bring another fit as much beyond the proportion of my joke as his first had been. "She tires a man's spirit," said black curly, and with this rueful utterance he abandoned the subject; so that when we reached Thomas in the dim night my curiosity was strong, and I paid little heed to this new place where I had come or to my supper. Black curly had taken himself off, and the driver sat at the table with me, still occasionally snickering in his plate. He would explain nothing that I asked him until the gaunt woman who waited on us left us for the kitchen, when he said, with a nervous, hasty relish, "The Widow Sproud is slick," and departed.

Consoled by no better clew than this I went to bed in a downstairs room, and in my strange rising next day I did not see the driver again. Callings in the air awaked me, and a wandering sound of wheels. The gaunt woman stood with a lamp in my room saying the stage was ready, and disappeared. I sprang up blindly, and again the callings passed in the blackness outside—long cries, inarticulate to me. Wheels heavily rolled to my door, and a whip was struck against it, and there loomed the stage, and I made out the calling. It was the three drivers, about to separate before the dawn on their three diverging ways, and they were wailing their departure through the town that travelers might hear, in whatever place they lay sleeping. "Boo-wie! All aboard!" came from somewhere, dreary and wavering, met at farther distance by the floating antiphonal, "Aboa-rd, aboa-rd for Grant!" and in the chill black air my driver lifted his portion of the strain, chanting, "Car-los! Car-los!" One last time he circled in the nearer darkness with his stage to let me dress. Mostly unbuttoned, and with not even a half minute to splash cold water in my eyes, I clambered solitary into the vehicle and sat among the leather mailbags, some boxes, and a sack of grain, having four hours yet till breakfast for my contemplation. I heard the faint reveille at Camp Thomas, but to me it was a call for more bed, and I pushed and pulled the grain-sack until I was able to distribute myself and in a manner doze, shivering in my overcoat. Not the rising of the sun upon this blight of sand, nor the appearance of a cattle herd, and both black curly and yellow driving it among its dust clouds, warmed my frozen attention as I lay in a sort of spell. I saw with apathy the mountains, extraordinary in the crystal prism of the air, and soon after the strangest scene I have ever looked on by the light of day. For as we went along the driver would give a cry, and when an answering cry came from the thorn-bush we stopped, and a naked Indian would appear, running, to receive a little parcel of salt or sugar or tobacco he had yesterday given the driver some humble coin to buy for him in Thomas. With changeless pagan eyes staring a moment at me on my sack of grain, and a grunt when his purchase was set in his hands, each black-haired desert figure turned away, the bare feet moving silent, and the copper body, stark naked except the breech-clout, receding to dimness in the thorn-bush. But I lay in-curious at this new vision of what our wide continent holds in fee under the single title United States, until breakfast came. This helped me, and I livened somewhat at finding the driver and the breakfast man were both genuine Meakums, as Jenks had told me they would be.

It surprised me to discover now that I was looked for along the Gila, and my name approximately known, and when I asked if my friend Captain Stirling had spoken of my coming, it was evidently not he, but the news was in the air. This was a prominence I had never attained in any previous part of the world, and I said to the driver that I supposed my having no business made me a curiosity. That might have something to do with it, he answered (he seemed to have a literal mind), but some had thought I was the paymaster,

"Folks up here," he explained, "are liable to know who's coming."

"If I lived here," said I, "I should be anxious for the paymaster to come early and often."

"Well, it does the country good. The soldiers spend it all right here, and us civilians profit some by it."

Having got him into conversation, I began to introduce the subject of black curly, hoping to lead up to the Widow Sproud; but before I had compassed this we reached San Carlos, where a blow awaited me. Stirling, my host, had been detailed on a scout this morning! I was stranded here, a stranger, where I had come thousands of miles to see an old friend. His regret and messages to make myself at home, and the quartermaster's hearty will to help me to do so could not cure my blankness. He might be absent two weeks or more. I looked round at Carlos and its staring sand. Then I resolved to go at once to my other friends now stationed at Fort Grant. For I had begun to feel myself at an immense distance from any who would care what happened to me

"Each Black-haired Desert Figure"

for good or ill, and I longed to see some face I had known before. So in gloom I retraced some unattractive steps. This same afternoon I staged back along the sordid, incompetent Gila River, and to kill time pushed my Sproud inquiry, at length with success. To check the inevitably slipshod morals of a frontier commonwealth, Arizona has a statute that in reality only sets in writing a presumption of the common law, the ancient presumption of marriage, which is that when a man and woman go to housekeeping for a certain length of time, they shall be deemed legally married. In Arizona this period is set at twelve months, and ten had run against Mrs. Sproud and young Follet. He was showing signs of leaving her. The driver did not think her much entitled to sympathy, and certainly she showed later that she could devise revenge. As I thought over these things we came again to the cattle herd, where my reappearance astonished yellow and black curly. Nor did the variance between my movements and my reported plans seem wholly explained to them by Stirling's absence, and at the station where I had breakfasted I saw them question the driver about me. This interest in my affairs heightened my desire to reach Fort Grant; and when next day I came to it after another waking to the chanted antiphonals and another faint reveille from Camp Thomas in the waning dark, extreme comfort spread through me. I sat in the club with the officers, and they taught me a new game of cards called Solo, and filled my glass. Here were lieutenants, captains, a major, and a colonel, American citizens with a love of their country and a standard of honor; here floated our bright flag serene against the lofty blue, and the mellow horns sounded at guard-mounting, bringing moisture to the eyes. The day was punctuated with the bright trumpet, people went and came in the simple dignity of duty, and once again I talked with good men and women. God bless our soldier people! I said it often.

They somewhat derided my uneasiness in the Gila Valley, and found my surmisings sensational. Yet still they agreed much ready money was an unwise thing on a stage journey, although their profession (I suppose) led them to take being "held up" less seriously than I with my peaceful traditions of elevators and the downtown lunch. In the wide Sulphur Springs valley where I rode at large, but never so long or so far that Fort Grant lay not in sight across that miracle of air, it displeased me to come one morning upon yellow and black curly jogging along beneath the government telegraph line.

"You cover a wide range," said I.

"Cowboys have to," they answered. "So you've not quit us yet?"

"I'm thinking of taking a hunt and fish towards Fort Apache."

"We're your men, then. You'll find us at Thomas any time. We're gathering stock up these draws, but that 'll be through this week."

They spurred their horses and vanished among the steep little hills that run up to Mount Graham. But indeed they should be no men of mine! Stirling had written me his scout was ended, and San Carlos worth a longer visit than I had made there, promising me an escort should I desire to camp in the mountains. An escort it should be, and no yellow or black curly, over-curious about my private matters! This fell in excellently with the coming paymaster's movements. Major Pidcock was even now on his way to Fort Grant from Fort Bowie; and when he went to Thomas and Carlos I would go, too, in his ambulance: and I sighed with pleasure at escaping that stage again.

Major Pidcock arrived in a yellow duster, but in other respects differed from the bishop, though in his body a bulky man. We were introduced to each other at the club.

"I am glad, sir, to meet you at last," I said to him. "The whole Gila Valley has been taking me for you."

"Oh—ah!" said Pidcock, vaguely, and pulling at some fat papers in his coat; "indeed. I understand that is a very ignorant population. Colonel Vincent, a word with you. The Department Commander requests me—" And here he went off into some official talk with the Colonel.

I turned among the other officers, who were standing by an open locker having whiskey, and Major Evlie put his hand on my shoulder. "He doesn't mean anything," he whispered, while the rest looked knowingly at me. Presently the Colonel explained to Pidcock that he would have me to keep him company to Carlos.

"Oh—ah, Colonel. Of course we don't take civilians not employed by the government, as a rule. But exceptions—ah—can be made," he said to me. "I will ask you to be ready immediately after breakfast tomorrow." And with that he bowed to us all and sailed forth across the parade-ground.

The Colonel's face was red, and he swore in his quiet voice; but the lips of the lieutenants by the open locker quivered fitfully in the silence.

"Don't mind Pidcock," Evlie remarked. "He's a paymaster." And at this the line officers became disorderly, and two lieutenants danced together; so that, without catching Evlie's evidently military joke, I felt pacified.

"And I've got to have him to dinner," sighed the Colonel, and wandered away.

"You'll get on with him, man—you'll get on with him in the ambulance," said my friend Paisley. "Flatter him, man. Just ask him about his great strategic stroke at Cayuse Station that got him his promotion to the pay department."

Well, we made our start after breakfast, Major Pidcock and I, and another passenger too, who sat with the driver—a black cook going to the commanding officer's at Thomas. She was an old plantation mammy, with a kind but bewildered face, and I am sorry that the noise of our driving lost me much of her conversation; for whenever we slowed, and once when I walked up a hill, I found her remarks to be steeped in a flighty charm.

"Fo' Lawd's sake!" said she. "Wat's dat?" And when the driver told her that it was a jackrabbit, "You go 'long!" she cried, outraged. "I'se seed rabbits earlier 'n de mawnin' dan yo'self." She watched the animal with all her might, muttering, "Law, see him squot," and "Hole on, hole on!" and "Yasser, he done gone fo' sho. My grashus, you lemme have a scatter shoot-gun an' a spike-tail smell dog, an' I'll git one of dey narrah-gauge mules."

"I shall not notice it," said Major Pidcock to me, with dignity. "But they should have sent such a creature by the stage. It's unsuitable, wholly."

"Unquestionably," said I, straining to catch the old lady's song on the box:

> "Don't you fo'git I's a-comin' behind you—
>   Lam slam de lunch ham."

"This is insufferable," said Pidcock. "I shall put her off at Cedar Springs."

I suppose the drive was long to him, but to me it was not. Noon and Cedar Springs prematurely ended the first half of this day most memorable in the whole medley of my excursion, and we got down to dine. Two travelers bound for Thomas by our same road were just setting out, but they firmly declined to transport our cook, and Pidcock moodily saw them depart in their wagon, leaving him burdened still; for this was the day the stage made its down trip from Thomas. Never before had I seen water paid for. When the major, with windy importance, came to settle his bill, our dozen or fourteen escort horses and mules made an item, the price of watering two head being two bits, quite separate from the feed; and I learned that water was thus precious over most of the territory.

Our cook remounted the box in high feather, and began at once to comment upon Arizona. "Dere ain't no winter, nor no spring, nor no rain de hole year roun'. My! What a country fo' to gib de chick'ns courage! Dey hens must jus' sit an' lay an' lay. But de po' ducks done have a mean time.

"O—Lawd!
    Sinner is in my way, Daniel."

"I would not permit a cook like that inside my house," said Major Pidcock.

"She may not be dangerous," I suggested.

"Land! Is dey folks gwineter shoot me?" Naturally I looked, and so did the major; but it was two of our own mounted escort that she saw out to the right of us among the hills. "Tell dem nigger jockeys I got no money. Why do dey triflin' chillun ride in de kerridge?" She did not mean ourselves, but the men with their carbines in the escort wagon in front of us. I looked out at them, and their mouths were wide open for joy at her. It was not a stately progress for twenty-eight thousand dollars in gold and a paymaster to be making. Major Pidcock unbottoned his duster and reclined to sleep, and presently I also felt the after-dinner sloth shutting my eyes pleasantly to this black road.

"Heave it, chillun! Can't you heave?" I heard our cook say, and felt us stop.

"What's that?" I asked, drowsily.

"Seems to be a rock fallen down," the major answered. "Start it, men; roll it!"

I roused myself. We were between rocks and banks on the brow of a hill, down which the narrow road descended with a slight turn. I could see the escort wagon halted ahead of us, and beyond it the men stooping at a large stone, around which there was no possible room to drive. This stone had fallen, I reflected, since those travelers for Thomas—

There was a shot, and a mule rolled over.

I shall never forget that. It was like the theater for one paralyzed second! The black soldiers, the mule, the hill, all a clear picture seen through an opera-glass, stock-still, and nothing to do with me—for a congealed second. And, dear me, what a time we had then!

Crackings volleyed around us, puffs of smoke jetted blue from rock ramparts which I had looked at and thought natural—or, rather, not thought of at all—earth and gravel spattered up from the ground, the bawling negress spilled off her box and ran in spirals, screaming, "Oh, bless my soul, bless my soul!" and I saw a yellow duster flap out of the ambulance. "Lawd grashus, he's a-leavin' us!" screeched the cook, and she changed her spirals for a beeline after him. I should never have run but for this example, for I have not naturally the presence of mind, and in other accidents through which I have passed there has never been promptness about me; the reasoning and all has come when it was over, unless it went on pretty long, when I have been sometimes able to leap to a conclusion. But yes, I ran now, straight under a screen of rocks, over the top of which rose the heads of yellow and black curly. The sight of them sent rushing over me the first agreeable sensation I had felt—shapeless rage—and I found myself shouting at them, "Scoundrels! Scoundrels!" while shooting continued briskly around me. I think my performance would have sincerely entertained them could they have spared the time for it; and as it was, they were regarding me with obvious benevolence, when Mr. Adams looked evilly at me across the stones, and black curly seized the old devil's rifle in time to do me a good turn. Mr. Adams' bullet struck short of me ten feet, throwing the earth in my face. Since then I have felt no sympathy for that tobacco-running pioneer. He listened, coughing, to what black curly said as he pointed to me, and I see now that I have never done a wiser thing than to go unarmed in that country. Curly was telling Mr. Adams that I was harmless. Indeed, that was true! In the bottom of this cup, target for a circled rim of rifles, separated from the widely scattered major and his men, aware of nothing in particular, and seeing nothing in particular but smoke and rocks and faces peering everywhere, I walked to a stone and sat upon it, hypnotized again into a spectator. From this undisturbed vantage I saw shape itself the theft of the gold—the first theft, that is; for it befell me later to witness a ceremony by which these eagles of Uncle Sam again changed hands in a manner that stealing is as good a name for as any.

They had got two mules killed, so that there could be no driving away in a hurry, and I saw that killing men was not a part of their war, unless required as a means to their end. Major Pidcock had spared them this necessity; I could see him nowhere; and with him to imitate I need not pause to account for the members of our dismounted escort. Two soldiers, indeed, lay on the ground, the sergeant and another, who had evidently fired a few resisting shots; but let me say at once that these poor fellows recovered, and I saw them often again through this adventure that bound us together, else I could not find so much hilarity in my retrospect. Escort wagon and ambulance stood empty and foolish on the road, and there lay the ingenious stone all by itself, and the carbines all by themselves foolish in the wagon, where the innocent soldiers had left them on getting out to move the stone. Smoke loitered thin and blue over this now exceedingly quiet scene, and I smelt it where I sat. How secure the robbers had felt themselves, and how reckless of identification! Midday, a public road within hearing of a ranch, an escort of a dozen regulars, no masks, and the stroke perpetrated at the top of a descent, contrary to all laws of road agency. They swarmed into sight from their ramparts. I cannot tell what number, but several I had never seen before and never saw again; and Mr. Adams and yellow and black curly looked so natural that I wondered if Jenks and the bishop would come climbing down too. But no more old friends turned up that day. Some went to the ambulance swift and silent, while others most needlessly stood guard.

Nothing was in sight but my seated inoffensive form, and the only sound was, somewhere among the rocks, the voice of the incessant negress speeding through her prayers. I saw them at the ambulance, surrounding, passing, lifting, stepping in and out, ferreting, then moving slowly up with their booty round the hill's brow. Then silence; then hoofs; then silence again, except the outpouring negress, scriptural, melodious, symbolic:

> "Oh—Lawd!
> Sinner is in my way, Daniel."

All this while I sat on the stone. "They have done us brown," I said aloud, and hearing my voice waked me from whatever state I had been in. My senses bounded, and I ran to the hurt soldiers. One was very sick. I should not have known what to do for them, but people began to arrive, brought from several quarters by the fusillade—two in a wagon from Cedar Springs, two or three on horses from the herds they were with in the hills, and a very old man from somewhere, who offered no assistance to anyone, but immediately seated himself and began explaining what we all should have done. The negress came out of her rocks, exclamatory with pity over the wounded, and, I am bound to say, of more help to them than any of us, kind and motherly in the midst of her ceaseless discourse. Next arrived Major Pidcock in his duster, and took charge of everything.

"Let yer men quit the'r guns, did ye, General?" piped the very old man. "Escort oughtn't never to quit the'r guns. I seen that at Molino del Rey. And ye should have knowed that there stone didn't crawl out in the road like a turtus to git the sunshine."

"Where were you?" thundered the major to the mounted escort, who now appeared, half an hour after the event, from our flanks, which they had been protecting at an immense distance. "Don't you know your duty's to be on hand when you hear firing?"

"Law, honey!" said the cook, with a guffaw. "Lemme git my han's over my mouf."

"See them walls they fooled yer with!" continued the old man, pointing with his stick. "I could have told yer them wasn't natural.

Them doesn't show like country rock"; by which I found that he meant their faces were new-exposed and not weather-beaten.

"No doubt you could have saved us, my friend," said the major, puffing blandly.

But one cannot readily impress ninety summers. "Yes, I could have told yer that," assented the sage, with senile complacence. "My wife could have told yer that. Any smart girl could have told yer that."

"I shall send a despatch for reinforcements," announced Pidcock. "Tap the telegraph wire," he ordered.

"I have to repawt to the major," said a soldier, saluting, "dat de line is cut."

At this I was taken with indecent laughter, and turned away, while ninety summers observed, "Of course them boys would cut the wire if they knew their business."

Swearing capably, the major now accounted clearly to us for the whole occurrence, striding up and down, while we lifted the hurt men into the ranch wagon, and arranged for their care at Cedar Springs. The escort wagon hurried on to Thomas for a doctor. The ambulance was, of course, crippled of half its team, and the dead mules were cleared from their harness and got to the road-side. Having satisfactorily delivered himself of his explanation, the major now organized a party for following the trail of the robbers, to learn into what region they had betaken themselves. Incredible as it may seem, after my late unenterprising conduct, I asked one of the riders to lend me his horse, which he did, remarking that he should not need it for an hour, and that he was willing to risk my staying absent longer than that.

So we rode away. The trail was clear, and we had but little trouble to follow it. It took us off to the right through a mounded labyrinth of hillocks, puny and gray like ash-heaps, where we rose and fell in the trough of the sullen landscape. I told Pidcock of my certainty about three of the robbers, but he seemed to care nothing for this, and was something less than civil at what he called my suggestions.

"When I have ascertained their route," he said, "it will be time enough to talk of their identity."

In this way we went for a mile or so, the trail leading us onward, frank and straight, to the top of a somewhat higher hill, where it suddenly expired off the earth. No breath vanishes cleaner from glass, and it brought us to a dead halt. We retraced the tracks to make sure we had not lost them before, but there was no mistake, and again we halted dead at the vanishing-point. Here were signs that something out of the common had happened. Men's feet and horseshoe prints, aimless and superimposed, marked a trodden frame of ground, inside which was nothing, and beyond which nothing lay but those faint tracks of wandering cattle and horses that scatter everywhere in this country. Not one defined series, not even a single shod horse, had gone over this hill, and we spent some minutes vainly scouring in circles wider and wider. Often I returned to stare at the trodden, imperturbable frame of ground, and caught myself inspecting first the upper air, and next the earth, and speculating if the hill were hollow; and mystery began to film over the hitherto sharp figures of black curly and yellow, while the lonely country around grew so unpleasant to my nerves that I was glad when Pidcock decided that he must give up for today. We found the little group of people beginning to disperse at the ambulance.

"Fooled yer ag'in, did they?" said the old man. "Played the blanket trick on yer, I expect. Guess yer gold's got pretty far by now." With this parting, and propped upon his stick, he went as he had come. Not even at any time of his youth, I think, could he have been companionable, and old age had certainly filled him with the impartial malevolence of the devil. I rejoice to say that he presided at none of our further misadventures.

Short twenty-eight thousand dollars and two mules, we set out anew, the major, the cook, and I, along the Thomas road, with the sun drawing closer down upon the long steel saw that the peaks to our westward made. The site of my shock lay behind me—I knew now well enough that it had been a shock, and that for a long while to come I should be able to feel the earth spatter from Mr. Adams' bullet against my ear and sleeve whenever I might choose to conjure that moment up again—and the present comfort in feeling my distance from that stone in the road increase continually put me in more cheerful spirits. With the quick rolling of the wheels many subjects for talk came into my mind, and had I been seated on the box beside the cook we should have found much in common. Ever since her real tenderness to those wounded men I had wished to ask the poor old creature how she came in this weary country, so far from the pleasant fields of cotton and home. Her hair was gray, and she had seen much, else she had never been so kind and skillful at bandaging. And I am quite sure that somewhere in the chambers of her incoherent mind and simple heart abided the sweet ancient fear of God and love of her fellow-men— virtues I had met but little in Arizona.

"De hole family, scusin' two," she was saying, "dey bust loose and tuck to de woods." And then she moralized upon the two who stayed behind and were shot. "But de Gennul he 'low dat wuz mighty pore reasonin'."

I should have been glad to exchange views with her, for Major Pidcock was dull company. This prudent officer was not growing distant from his disaster, and as night began to come, and we neared Thomas, I suppose the thought that our ambulance was driving him perhaps to a court-martial was enough to submerge the man in gloom. To me and my news about the robbers he was a little more considerate, although he still made nothing of the fact that some of them lived in the Gila Valley, and were of the patriarchal tribe of Meakum.

"Scoundrels like that," he muttered, lugubriously, "know every trail in the country, and belong nowhere. Mexico is not a long ride from here. They can get a steamer at Guaymas and take their choice of ports down to Valparaiso. Yes, they'll probably spend that money in South America. Oh, confound that woman!"

For the now entirely cheerful negress was singing:

"Dar's de gal, dar's my Susanna.
How by gum you know?
Know her by de red bandanna,
An' de shoestring hangin' on de flo'—
Dad blam her!
An' de shoestring hangin'—

"Goodness grashus! What *you* gwineter do?"

At this sudden cry and the stopping of the ambulance I thought more people were come for our gold, and my spirit resigned itself. Sit still was all I should do now, and look for the bright day when I should leave Arizona forever. But it was only Mrs. Sproud. I had clean forgotten her, and did not at once take in to what an important turn the affairs of some of us had come. She stepped out of the darkness, and put her hand on the door of the ambulance.

"I suppose you're the Paymaster?" Her voice was soft and easy, but had an ample volume. As Pidcock was replying with some dignity that she was correct, she caught sight of me. "Who is this man?" she interrupted him.

"My clerk," said Pidcock; and this is the promptest thing I can remember of the major, always excepting his conduct when the firing began on the hill. "You're asking a good many questions, madam," he added.

"I want to know who I'm talking to," said she, quietly. "I think I've seen property of yours this evening."

"You had better get in, madam; better get in."

"This is the Paymaster's team from Fort Grant?" said Mrs. Sproud to the driver.

"Yes, yes, madam. Major Pidcock—I am Major Pidcock, Paymaster to the United States Army in the Department of Colorado. I suppose I understand you."

"Seven canvas sacks," said Mrs. Sproud, standing in the road.

"Get in, madam. You can't tell who may be within hearing. You will find it to your advantage to keep nothing—"

Mrs. Sproud laughed luxuriously, and I began to discern why black curly might at times have been loath to face her.

"I merely meant, madam—I desired to make it clear that—a—"

"I think I know what you meant. But I have no call to fear the law. It will save you trouble to believe that before we go any further."

"Certainly, madam. Quite right." The man was sweating. What with court-martial and Mrs. Sproud, his withers were wrung. "You are entirely sure, of course, madam—"

"I am entirely sure I know what I am about. That seems to be more than some do that are interested in this gold—the folks, for instance, that have hid it in my haystack."

"Haystack! Then they're not gone to Mexico!"

"Mexico, sir? They live right here in this valley. Now I'll get in, and when I ask you, you will please to set me down." She seated herself opposite us and struck a match. "Now we know what we all look like," said she, holding the light up, massive and handsome. "This young man is the clerk, and we needn't mind him. I have done nothing to fear the law, but what I am doing now will make me a traveler again. I have no friends here. I was acquainted with a young man." She spoke in the serenest tone, but let fall the match more quickly than its burning made needful. "He was welcome in my home. He let them cook this up in my house and never told me. I live a good ways out on the road, and it was a safe place, but I didn't think why so many met him, and why they sat around my stable. Once in a while this week they've been joking about winning the soldiers' pay—they often win that—but I thought it was just cowboy games, till I heard horses coming quick at sundown this afternoon, and I hid. Will hunted around and said—and said I was on the stage coming from Solomonsville, and so they had half an hour yet. He thought so. And, you see, nobody lives in the cabin but—but me." Mrs. Sproud paused a moment here, and I noticed her breathing. Then she resumed: "So I heard them talk some; and when they all left, pretty soon, I went to the haystack, and it was so. Then the stage came along and I rode to Thomas."

"You left the gold there!" groaned the wretched major, and leaned out of the ambulance.

"I'm not caring to touch what's none of mine. Wait, sir, please; I get out here. Here are the names I'm sure of. Stop the driver, or I'll jump." She put a paper in the major's hand. "It is Mrs. Sproud's haystack," she added.

"Will you—this will never—can I find you tomorrow?" he said, helplessly, holding the paper out at her.

"I have told you all I know," said Mrs. Sproud, and was gone at once.

Major Pidcock leaned back for some moments as we drove. Then he began folding his paper with care. "I have not done with that person," said he, attempting to restore his crippled importance. "She will find that she must explain herself."

Our wheels whirled in the sand and we came quickly to Thomas, to a crowd of waiting officers and ladies; and each of us had an audience that night—the cook, I feel sure, while I myself was of an importance second only to the major's. But he was at once closeted with the commanding officer, and I did not learn their counsels, hearing only at breakfast that the first step was taken. The detail sent out had returned from the haystack, bringing gold indeed—one-half sackful. The other six were gone, and so was Mrs. Sproud. It was useless to surmise, as we, however, did that whole forenoon, what any of this might mean; but in the afternoon came a sign. A citizen of the Gila Valley had been paying his many debts at the saloon and through the neighborhood in gold. In one well known for the past two years to be without a penny it was the wrong moment to choose for honest affluence, and this citizen was the first arrest. This further instance of how secure the robbers felt themselves to be outdid anything that had happened yet, and I marveled until following events took from me the power of astonishment. The men named on Mrs. Sproud's paper were fewer than I think fired upon us in the attack, but every one of them was here in the valley, going about his business. Most were with the same herd of cattle that I had seen driven by yellow and black curly near the sub-agency, and they two were there. The solvent debtor, I should say, was not arrested this morning. Plans that I, of course, had no part in delayed matters, I suppose for the sake of certainty. Black curly and his friends were watched, and found to be spending no gold yet; and since they did not show sign of leaving the region, but continued with their cattle, I imagine every effort was being made to light upon their hidden treasure. But their time came, and soon after it mine. Stirling, my friend, to whom I had finally gone at Carlos, opened the wire door of his quarters where I sat one morning, and with a heartless smile introduced me to a gentleman from Tucson.

"You'll have a chance to serve your country," said Stirling.

I was subpœnaed!

"Certainly not!" I said, with indignation. "I'm going East. I don't live here. You have witnesses enough without me. We all saw the same thing."

"Witnesses never see the same thing," observed the man from Tucson. "It's the government that's after you. But you'll not have to wait. Our case is first on the list."

"You can take my deposition," I began; but what need to dwell upon this interview? "When I come to visit you again," I said to Stirling, "let me know." And that pink-faced, gray-haired captain still shouted heartlessly.

"You're an egotist," said he. "Think of the scrape poor old Pidcock has got himself into."

"The government needs all the witnesses it can get," said the man from Tucson. "Luke Jenks is smart in some ways."

"Luke Jenks?" I sat up in my canvas extension-chair.

"Territorial delegate; firm of Parley and Jenks, Tucson. He's in it."

"By heavens!" I cried, in unmixed delight. "But I didn't see him when they were shooting at us."

The man from Tucson stared at me curiously. "He is counsel for the prisoners," he explained.

"The delegate to Washington defends these thieves who robbed the United States?" I repeated.

"Says he'll get them off. He's going to stay home from Washington and put it through in shape."

It was here that my powers of astonishment went into their last decline, and I withheld my opinion upon the character of Mr. Jenks as a public man. I settled comfortably in my canvas chair.

"The prisoners are citizens of small means, I judge," said I. "What fee can they pay for such a service?"

"Ah!" said Stirling.

"That's about it, I guess," said the man from Tucson. "Luke is mighty smart in his law business. Well, gents, good day to you. I must be getting after the rest of my witnesses."

"Have you seen Mrs. Sproud?" I asked him.

"She's quit the country. We can't trace her. Guess she was scared."

"But that gold!" I exclaimed, when Sterling and I were alone. "What in the world have they done with those six other bags?"

"Ah!" said he, as before. "Do you want to bet on that point? Dollars to doughnuts Uncle Sam never sees a cent of that money again. I'll stake my next quarter's pay—"

"Pooh!" said I. "That's poor odds against doughnuts if Pidcock has the paying of it." And I took my turn at laughing at the humorous Stirling.

"That Mrs. Sproud is a sensible woman to have gone," said he, reflectively. "They would know she had betrayed them, and she wouldn't be safe in the valley. Witnesses who know too much sometimes are found dead in this country—but you'll have government protection."

"Thank you kindly," said I. "That's what I had on the hill."

But Stirling took his turn at me again with freshened mirth.

Well, I think that we witnesses were worth government protection. At seasons of especial brightness and holiday, such as Christmas and Easter, the theaters of the variety order have a phrase which they sometimes print in capitals upon their bills—Combination Extraordinary; and when you consider Major Pidcock and his pride, and the old plantation cook, and my reserved eastern self, and our coal-black escort of the hill, more than a dozen, including Sergeant Brown and the private, both now happily recovered of their wounds, you can see what appearance we made descending together from the mean Southern Pacific train at Tucson, under the gaze of what I take to have been the town's whole population, numbering five thousand.

Stirling, who had come to see us through, began at his persiflage immediately, and congratulated me upon the house I should play to, speaking of box-office receipts and a benefit night. Tucson is more than half a Mexican town, and in its crowd upon the platform I saw the gaudy shawls, the earrings, the steeple straw hats, the old shriveled cigarette-rolling apes, and the dark-eyed girls, and sifted with these the loungers of our own race, boots, overalls, pistols, hotel clerks, express agents, freight hands, waitresses, red-shirts, soldiers from Lowell Barracks, and officers, and in this mass and mess of color and dust and staring, Bishop Meakum, in his yellow duster, by the door of the Hotel San Xavier. But his stare was not, I think now, quite of the same idleness with the rest. He gave me a short nod, yet not unfriendly, as I passed by him to register my name. By the counter I found the wet-eyed Mowry standing.

"How's business on the other side of the track?" I said to him.

"Fair to middlin'. Get them mines ye was after at Globe?"

"You've forgotten I told you they're a property I don't care for, Mr. Mowry. I suppose it's interest in this recent gold discovery that brings you to Tucson." He had no answer for me but a shrewd shirking glance that flattered my sense of acumen, and adding, pleasantly, "So many of your Arizona citizens have forsaken silver for gold just now," I wrote my name in the hotel book, while he looked to remind himself what it was.

"Why, you're not to stay here," said Stirling, coming up, "You're expected at the barracks."

He presented me at once to a knot of officers, each of whom in turn made me known to some additional bystander, until it seemed to me that I shook a new hand sixty times in this disordered minute by the hotel book, and out of the sixty caught one name, which was my own.

These many meetings could not be made perfect without help from the saloon-keeper, who ran his thriving trade conveniently at hand in the office of the San Xavier. Our group remained near him, and I silently resolved to sleep here at the hotel, away from the tempting confusion of army hospitality upon this eve of our trial. We were expected, however, to dine at the post, and that I was ready to do. Indeed, I could scarcely have got myself out of it without rudeness, for the ambulance was waiting us guests at the gate. We went to it along a latticed passage at the edge of a tropical garden, only a few square yards in all, but how pretty! And what an oasis of calm in the midst of this teeming desolation of unrest! It had upon one side the railway station, wooden, sordid, congesting with malodorous packed humanity; on the next the rails themselves and the platform, with steam and bells and baggage trucks rolling and bumping; the hotel stood on the third, a confusion of tongues and trampings; while a wide space of dust, knee-deep, and littered with manœuvring vehicles, hemmed in this silent garden on the fourth side. A slender slow little fountain dropped inaudibly among some palms, a giant cactus, and the broadspread shade of trees I did not know. This was the whole garden, and a tame young antelope was its inhabitant. He lay in the unchanging shade, his large eyes fixed remotely upon the turmoil of this world, and a sleepy charm touched my senses as I looked at his domain. Instead of going to dinner, or going anywhere, I should have liked to recline indefinitely beneath those palms and trail my fingers in the cool fountain. Such enlightened languor, however, could by no happy chance be the lot of an important witness in a western robbery trial, and I dined and wined with the jovial officers, at least talking no business.

With business I was sated. Pidcock and the attorney for the United States—I can remember neither his name nor the proper title of his office, for he was a nobody, and I had forgotten his features each new time that we met—had mapped out the trial to me, preparing and rehearsing me in my testimony until they had pestered me into a hatred of them both. And when word was brought me here, dining at Lowell Barracks, where I had imagined myself safe from justice, that this same attorney was waiting to see me, I rose and I played him a trick. Possibly I should not have done it but for the saloon-keeper in the afternoon and this sustained dining now; but I sent him word I should be with him directly—and I wandered into Tucson by myself!

Faithful to my last strong impression there, I went straight to the tiny hotel garden, and in that darkness lay down in a delicious and torpid triumph. The attorney was most likely waiting still. No one on earth knew where I was. Pidcock could not trace me now. I could see the stars through the palms and the strange trees, the fountain made a little sound, somewhere now and then I could hear the antelope, and, cloaked in this black serenity, I lay smiling. Once an engine passed heavily, leaving the station utterly quiet again, and the next I knew it was the antelope's rough tongue that waked me, and I found him nibbling and licking my hand. People were sitting in the latticed passage, and from the light in the office came Mr. Mowry, untying a canvas sack that he held. At this sight my truancy to discretion was over, and no head could be more wakeful or clear than mine instantly became.

"How much d'yer want this time, Mr. Jenks?" inquired Mowry.

I could not hear the statesman's reply, but thought, while the sound of clinking came to me, how a common cause will often serve to reconcile the most bitter opponents. I did not dare go nearer to catch all their talk, and I debated a little upon my security even as it was, until my own name suddenly reached me.

"Him?" said Mowry. "That there tailor-made boy? They've got him sleepin' at the barracks."

"Nobody but our crowd's boarding here," said someone.

"They think we're laying for their witnesses," said the voice of Jenks. And among the various mingled laughs rose distinct a big one that I knew.

"Oh, ho, ho! Well, yes. Tell you about witnesses. Here's all there is to them: spot cash to their figure, and kissing the Book. You've done no work but what I told you?" he added, sharply.

"We haven't needed to worry about witnesses in any shape, Bishop."

"That's good. That's economy. That little eastern toorist is harmless."

"Leave him talk, Bishop. Leave 'em all tell their story."

"It's going to cost the whole stake, though," said Jenks.

"Deserted Jericho!" remarked old Meakum.

"I don't try cases for nothing, bishop. The deal's covered. My clients have publicly made over to me their horses and saddles."

"Oh, ho, ho!" went the bishop. But this last word about the horses was the only part of the talk I could not put a plain meaning upon.

Mr. Mowry I now saw reenter the lighted door of the office, with his canvas sack in his hand. "This 'll be right here in the safe," said he.

"All right," answered Jenks. "I'll not be likely to call on you anymore for a day or so."

"Hello!" said the office clerk, appearing in his shirtsleeves. "You fellows have made me forget the antelope." He took down a lantern, and I rose to my feet.

"Give us a drink before you feed him," said Jenks. Then I saw the whole of them crowd into the door for their nightcap, and that was all I waited for.

I climbed the garden fence. My thoughts led me at random through quantities of soft dust, and over the rails, I think, several times, until I stood between empty and silent freight trains, and there sat down. Harmless! It seemed to me they would rate me differently in the morning. So for a while my mind was adrift in the turbulent cross-currents of my discovery; but it was with a smooth, innocent surface that I entered the hotel office and enjoyed the look of the clerk when he roused and heard me, who, according to their calculations, should have been in slumber at the barracks, asking to be shown my room here. I was tempted to inquire if he had fed the antelope—such was the pride of my elation—and I think he must have been running over questions to put me; but the two of us marched up the stairs with a lamp and a key, speaking amiably of the weather for this time of year, and he unlocked my door with a politeness and hoped I would sleep well with a consideration that I have rarely met in the hotel clerk. I did not sleep well. Yet it seemed not to matter. By eight I had breakfast, and found the attorney—Rocklin I shall name him, and that will have to answer—and told him how we had become masters of the situation.

He made me repeat it all over, jotting memoranda this second time; and when my story was done, he sat frowning at his notes, with a cigar between his teeth.

"This ain't much," he said. "Luckily I don't need anything more. I've got a dead open-and-shut case without it."

"Why don't you make it deader, then?" said I. "Don't you see what it all means?"

"Well, what does it all mean?"

Either the man was still nettled at my treatment of him last evening, or had no liking for amateur opinions and help; otherwise I see no reason for the disparagement with which he regarded me while I interpreted what I had overheard, piece by piece, except the horse and saddle remark.

"Since that don't seem clear, I'll explain it to you," he said, "and then you'll know it all. Except their horses and saddles, the accused haven't a red cent to their names—not an honest one, that is. So it looks well for them to be spending all they've apparently got in the world to pay counsel fees. Now I have this case worked up," he pursued, complacently, "so that any such ambiguous stuff as yours is no good to me at all—would be harmful, in fact. It's not good policy, my friend, to assail the character of opposing counsel. And Bishop Meakum! Are you aware of his power and standing in this section? Do you think you're going to ring him in?"

"Great goodness!" I cried. "Let me testify, and then let the safe be opened."

Rocklin looked at me a moment, the cigar wagging between his teeth, and then he lightly tossed his notes in the wastepaper basket.

"Open your safe," said he, "and what then? Up steps old Mowry and says, 'I'll thank you to let my property alone.' Where's your proof? What word did any of them drop that won't bear other constructions? Mowry's well known to have money, and he has a right to give it to Jenks."

"If the gold could be identified?" I suggested.

"That's been all attended to," he answered, with increasing complacence. "I'm obliged to you for your information, and in a less sure case I might risk using it, but—why, see here; we've got 'em hands down!" And he clapped me on the knee. "If I had met you last evening I was going to tell you our campaign. Pidcock 'll come first, of course, and his testimony 'll cover pretty much the whole ground. Then, you see, the rest of you I'll use mainly in support. Sergeant Brown—he's very strong, and the black woman, and you—I'll probably call you third or fourth. So you'll be on hand sure now?"

Certainly I had no thought of being anywhere else. The imminence of our trial was now heralded by the cook's coming to Rocklin's office punctual to his direction, and after her Pidcock almost immediately. It was not many minutes before the more important ones of us had gathered, and we proceeded to court, once again a Combination Extraordinary—a spectacle for Tucson. So much stir and prosperity had not blossomed in the town for many years, its chief source of life being the money that Lowell Barracks brought to it. But now its lodgings were crowded and its saloons and Mexican dens of entertainment waked to activity. From a dozing sunburnt village of adobe walls and almond trees it was become something like those places built in a single western day of riot extravagance, where corner lots are clamored for and men pay a dollar to be shaved.

Jenks was before us in the room with his clients. He was practicing what I always think of as his celluloid smile, whispering, and all-hail with everybody. One of the prisoners had just such another mustache as his own, too large for his face; and this had led me since to notice a type of too large mustaches through our country in all ranks, but of similar men, who generally have either stolen something or lacked the opportunity. Catching sight of me, Jenks came at once, friendly as you please, shaking my passive hand, and laughing that we should meet again under such circumstances.

"When we're through this nuisance," said he, "you must take dinner with me. Just now, you understand, it wouldn't look well to see me hobnobbing with a government witness. See you again!" And he was off to someone else.

I am confident this man could not see himself as others—some others, at least—saw him. To him his whole performance was natural and professional, and my view that he was more infamous by far than the thieves would have sincerely amazed him. Indeed, for one prisoner I felt very sorry. Young black curly was sitting there, and, in contrast to Mr. Adams, down whose beard the tobacco forever ran, he seemed downcast and unhardened, I thought. He was getting his deserts through base means. It was not for the sake of justice but from private revenge that Mrs. Sproud had moved; and, after all, had the boy injured her so much as this? Yet how could I help him? They were his deserts. My mood was abruptly changed to diversion when I saw among our jury specimens of both types of Meakum, and prominent among the spectator throng their sire, that canny polygamist, surveying the case with the same forceful attention I had noticed first in the House of Representatives, and ever since that day. But I had a true shock of surprise now. Mrs. Sproud was in court. There could be no mistake. No one seemed to notice her, and I wondered if many in the town knew her face, and with what intent she had returned to this dangerous neighborhood. I was so taken up with watching her and her furtive appearance in the almost concealed position she had chosen that I paid little heed to the government's opening of its case. She had her eyes upon black curly, but he could not see her. Pidcock was in the midst of his pompous recital when the court took its noon intermission. Then I was drawn to seek out black curly as he was conducted to his dinner.

"Good day," said he, as I came beside him.

"I wish I didn't have to go on oath about this," I said.

"Oath away," he answered, doggedly. "What's that got to do with me?"

"Oh, come!" I exclaimed.

"Come where?" He looked at me defiantly.

"When people don't wish to be trailed," I went on, "do I understand they sometimes spread a blanket and lead their horses on it and take off their shoes? I'm merely asking out of a traveler's curiosity."

"I guess you'll have to ask them that's up on such tricks," he answered, grinning.

I met him in the eyes, and a strong liking for him came over me. "I probably owe you my life," I said, huskily. "I know I do. And I hate—you must consider me a poor sort of bird."

"Blamed if I know what you're drivin' at," said black curly. But he wrinkled his forehead in the pleasant way I remembered. "Yer whiskey was good all right," he added, and gave me his hand.

"Look here," said I. "She's come back."

This took the boy unguarded, and he swore with surprise. Then his face grew sombre. "Let her," he remarked; and that was all we said.

At the afternoon sitting I began to notice how popular sympathy was not only quite against the United States, but a sentiment amounting to hatred was shown against all soldiers. The voice of respectability seemed entirely silent; decent citizens were there, but not enough of them. The mildest opinion was that Uncle Sam could afford to lose money better than poor people, and the strongest was that it was a pity the soldiers had not been killed. This seemed inappropriate in a territory desiring admission to our Union. I supposed it something local then, but have since observed it to be a prevailing western antipathy. The unthinking sons of the sagebrush ill tolerate a thing which stands for discipline, good order, and obedience, and the man who lets another command him they despise. I can think of no threat more evil for our democracy, for it is a fine thing diseased and perverted—namely, independence gone drunk.

Pidcock's examination went forward, and the half-sack of gold from the haystack brought a great silence in court. The major's identification of the gold was conducted by Rocklin with stage effect, for it was an undoubted climax; but I caught a most singular smile on the face of Bishop Meakum, and there sat Mrs. Sproud, still solitary and engulfed in the throng, her face flushed and her eyes blazing. And here ended the first day.

In the morning came the major's cross-examination, with the room more crowded than before, but I could not find Mrs. Sproud. Rocklin did not believe I had seen her, and I feared something had happened to her. The bishop had walked to the court with Jenks, talking and laughing upon general subjects, so far as I could hear. The counsel for the prisoners passed lightly over the first part of the evidence, only causing an occasional laugh on the score of the major's military prowess, until he came to the gold.

"You said this sack was one of yours, Major?" he now inquired.

"It is mine, sir."

A large bundle of sacks was brought. "And how about these? Here are ten, fifteen—about forty. I'll get some more if you say so. Are they all yours?"

"Your question strikes me as idle, sir." The court rapped, and Jenks smiled. "They resemble mine," said Pidcock. "But they are not used."

"No; not used." Jenks held up the original, shaking the gold. "Now I'm going to empty your sack for a moment."

"I object," said Rocklin, springing up.

"Oh, it's all counted," laughed Jenks; and the objection was not sustained. Then Jenks poured the gold into a new sack and shook that aloft. "It makes them look confusingly similar, Major. I'll just put my card in your sack."

"I object," said Rocklin, with anger, but with futility. Jenks now poured the gold back into the first, then into a third, and thus into several, tossing them each time on the table, and the clinking pieces sounded clear in the room. Bishop Meakum was watching the operation like a wolf. "Now, Major," said Jenks, "is your gold in the original sack, or which sack is my card in?"

This was the first time that the room broke out loudly; and Pidcock, when the people were rapped to order, said, "The sack's not the thing."

"Of course not. The gold is our point. And of course you had a private mark on it. Tell the jury, please, what the private mark was."

He had none. He spoke about dates, and new coins, he backed and filled, swelled importantly, and ended like a pricked bladder by recanting his identification.

"That is all I have to say for the present," said Jenks.

"Don't complicate the issue by attempting to prove too much, Mr. Rocklin," said the judge.

Rocklin flushed, and called the next witness, whispering sulkily to me, "What can you expect if the court starts out against you?" But the court was by no means against him. The judge was merely disgusted over Rocklin's cardinal folly of identifying coin under such loose conditions.

And now came the testimony of Sergeant Brown. He told so clear a story as to chill the enthusiasm of the room. He pointed to the man with the mustache, black curly, and yellow. "I saw them shooting from the right of the road," he said. Jenks tried but little to shake him, and left him unshaken. He was followed by the other wounded soldier, whose story was nearly the same, except that he identified different prisoners.

"Who did you say shot you?" inquired Jenks. "Which of these two?"

"I didn't say. I don't know."

"Don't know a man when he shoots you in broad daylight?"

"Plenty was shooting at me," said the soldier. And his testimony also remained unshaken.

Then came my own examination, and Jenks did not trouble me at all, but, when I had likewise identified the men I knew, simply bowed smilingly, and had no questions to ask his friend from the East.

Our third morning began with the negress, who said she was married, told a scattered tale, and soon stated that she was single, explaining later that she had two husbands, and one was dead, while the other had disappeared from her ten years ago. Gradually her alarm subsided and she achieved coherence.

"What did this gentleman do at the occurrence?" inquired Jenks, indicating me.

"Dat gemman? He jes flew, sir, an' I don' blame him fo' bein' no wusser skeer'd dan de hole party. Yesser, we all flew scusin' dey two pore chillun; an' we stayed till de 'currence was ceased."

"But the gentleman says he sat on a stone, and saw those men firing."

"Land! I seed him goin' like he was gwineter Fo't Grant. He run up de hill, an' de Gennul he run down like de day of judgment."

"The general ran?"

"Lawd grashus, honey, yo' could have played checkers on dey coat tails of his."

The court rapped gently.

"But the gold must have been heavy to carry away to the horses. Did not the general exert his influence to rally his men?"

"No, sah. De Gennul went down de hill, an' he took his inflooence with him."

"I have no further questions," said Jenks. "When we come to our alibis, gentlemen, I expect to satisfy you that this lady saw more correctly, and when she is unable to recognize my clients it is for a good reason."

"We've not got quite so far yet," Rocklin observed. "We've reached the haystack at present."

"Aren't you going to make her describe her own confusion more?" I began, but stopped, for I saw that the next witness was at hand, and that it was Mrs. Sproud.

"How's this?" I whispered to Rocklin. "How did you get her?"

"She volunteered this morning, just before trial. We're in big luck."

The woman was simply dressed in something dark. Her handsome face was pale, but she held a steady eye upon the jury, speaking clearly and with deliberation. Old Meakum, always in court and watchful, was plainly unprepared for this, and among the prisoners, too, I could discern uneasiness. Whether or no any threat or constraint had kept her invisible during these days, her coming now was a thing for which none of us were ready.

"What do I know?" she repeated after the counsel. "I suppose you have been told what I said I knew."

"We'd like to hear it directly from you, Mrs. Sproud," Rocklin explained.

"Where shall I start?"

"Well, there was a young man who boarded with you, was there not?"

"I object to the witness being led," said Jenks. And Bishop Meakum moved up beside the prisoners' counsel and began talking with him earnestly.

"Nobody is leading me," said Mrs. Sproud, imperiously, and raising her voice a little. She looked about her. "There was a young man who boarded with me. Of course that is so."

Meakum broke off in his confidences with Jenks, and looked sharply at her.

"Do you see your boarder anywhere here?" inquired Rocklin; and from his tone I perceived that he was puzzled by the manner of his witness.

She turned slowly, and slowly scrutinized the prisoners one by one. The head of black curly was bent down, and I saw her eyes rest upon it while she stood in silence. It was as if he felt the summons of her glance, for he raised his head. His face was scarlet, but her paleness did not change.

"He is the one sitting at the end," she said, looking back at the jury. She then told some useless particulars, and brought her narrative to the afternoon when she had heard the galloping. "Then I hid. I hid because this is a rough country."

"When did you recognize that young man's voice?"

"I did not recognize it."

Black curly's feet scraped as he shifted his position.

"Collect yourself, Mrs. Sproud. We'll give you all the time you want. We know ladies are not used to talking in court. Did you not hear this young man talking to his friends?"

"I heard talking," replied the witness, quite collected. "But I could not make out who they were. If I could have been sure it was him and friends, I wouldn't have stayed hid. I'd have had no call to be scared."

Rocklin was dazed, and his next question came in a voice still more changed and irritable.

"Did you see anyone?"

"No one."

"What did you hear them say?"

"They were all talking at once. I couldn't be sure."

"Why did you go to the haystack?"

"Because they said something about my haystack, and I wanted to find out, if I could."

"Did you not write their names on a paper and give it to this gentleman? Remember you are on oath, Mrs. Sproud."

By this time a smile was playing on the features of Jenks, and he and Bishop Meakum talked no longer together, but sat back to watch the woman's extraordinary attempt to undo her work. It was shrewd, very shrewd, in her to volunteer as our witness instead of as theirs. She was ready for the paper question, evidently.

"I wrote—" she began, but Rocklin interrupted.

"On oath, remember!" he repeated, finding himself cross-examining his own witness. "The names you wrote are the names of these prisoners here before the court. They were traced as the direct result of your information. They have been identified by three or four persons. Do you mean to say you did not know who they were?"

"I did not know," said Mrs. Sproud, firmly. "As for the paper, I acted hasty. I was a woman, alone, and none to consult or advise me. I thought I would get in trouble if I did not tell about such goings on, and I just wrote the names of Will—of the boys that came round there all the time, thinking it was most likely them. I didn't see him, and I didn't make out surely it was his voice. I wasn't sure enough to come out and ask what they were up to. I didn't stop to think of the harm I was doing on guesswork."

For the first time the note of remorse conquered in her voice. I saw how desperation at what she had done when she thought her love was cured was now bracing the woman to this audacity.

"Remember," said Rocklin, "the gold was also found as the direct result of your information. It was you who told Major Pidcock in the ambulance about the seven sacks."

"I never said anything about seven sacks."

This falsehood was a master-stroke, for only half a sack had been found. She had not written this down. There was only the word of Pidcock and me to vouch for it, while against us stood her denial, and the actual quantity of gold.

"I have no further questions," said Rocklin.

"But I have," said Jenks. And then he made the most of Mrs. Sproud, although many in the room were laughing, and she herself, I think, felt she had done little but sacrifice her own character without repairing the injury she had done black curly. Jenks made her repeat that she was frightened; not calm enough to be sure of voices, especially many speaking together; that she had seen no one throughout. He even attempted to show that the talk about the haystack might have been purely about hay, and that the half-sack of gold might have been put there at another time—might belong to some honest man this very moment.

"Did you ever know the young man who boarded with you to do a dishonorable thing?" inquired Jenks. "Did you not have the highest opinion of him?"

She had not expected a question like this. It nearly broke the woman down. She put her hand to her breast, and seemed afraid to trust her voice. "I have the highest opinion of him," she said, word painfully following word. "He—he used to know that."

"I have finished," said Jenks.

"Can I go?" asked the witness, and the attorneys bowed. She stood one hesitating moment in the witness-stand, and she looked at the jury and the court; then, as if almost in dread, she let her eyes travel to black curly. But his eyes were sullenly averted. Then Mrs. Sproud slowly made her way through the room, with one of the saddest faces I have ever seen, and the door closed behind her.

We finished our case with all the prisoners identified, and some of them doubly. The defense was scarcely more than a sham. The flimsy alibis were destroyed even by the incompetent, unready Rocklin, and when the charge came blackness fell upon the citizens of Tucson. The judge's cold statements struck them as partisan, and they murmured and looked darkly at him. But the jury, with its Meakums, wore no expression at all during any of his remarks. Their eyes were upon him, but entirely fishlike. He dismissed the cumbersome futilities one by one. "Now three witnesses have between them recognized all the prisoners but one," he continued. "That one, a reputed pauper, paid several hundred dollars of debts in gold the morning after the robbery. The money is said to be the proceeds of a cattle sale. No cattle have ever been known to belong to this man, and the purchaser had never been known to have any income until this trial began. The prisoner's name was on Mrs. Sproud's paper. The statement of one witness that he sat on a stone and saw three other of the prisoners firing has been contradicted by a woman who described herself as having run away at once; it is supported by two men who are admitted by all to have remained, and in consequence been shot. Their statements have been assailed by no one. Their testimony stands on the record unimpeached. They have identified five prisoners. If you believe them—and remember that not a word they said has been questioned—" here the judge emphasized more and more clearly. He concluded with the various alternatives of fact according to which the jury must find its several possible verdicts. When he had finished, the room sat sullen and still, and the twelve went out. I am told that they remained ten minutes away. It seemed one to me.

When they had resumed their seats I noticed the same fishlike oracular eye in most of them unchanged. "Not guilty," said the foreman.

"What!" shouted the judge, startled out of all judicial propriety. "None of 'em?"

"Not guilty," monotonously repeated the foreman.

We were silent amid the din of triumph now raised by Tucson. In the laughter, the handshaking, the shouting, and the jubilant pistol-shots that some particularly free spirit fired in the old Cathedral Square, we went to our dinner; and not even Stirling could joke. "There's a certain natural justice done here in spite of them," he said. "They are not one cent richer for all their looted twenty-eight thousand. They come out free, but penniless."

"How about Jenks and that jury?" said I. And Stirling shrugged his shoulders.

But we had yet some crowning impudence to learn. Later, in the street, the officers and I met the prisoners, their witnesses, and their counsel emerging from a photographer's studio. The territorial delegate had been taken in a group with his acquitted thieves. The bishop had declined to be in this souvenir.

"That's a picture I want," said I. "Only I'll be sorry to see your face there," I added to black curly.

"Indeed!" put in Jenks.

"Yes," said I. "You and he do not belong in the same class. By the way, Mr. Jenks, I suppose you'll return their horses and saddles now?"

Too many were listening for him to lose his temper, and he did a sharp thing. He took this public opportunity for breaking some news to his clients. "I had hoped to," he said; "that is, as many as were not needed to defray necessary costs. But it's been an expensive suit, and

I've found myself obliged to sell them all. It's little enough to pay for clearing your character, boys."

They saw through his perfidy to them, and that he had them checkmated. Any protest from them would be a confession of their theft. Yet it seemed an unsafe piece of villany in Jenks.

"They look disappointed," I remarked. "I shall value the picture very highly."

"If that's eastern sarcasm," said Jenks, "it's beyond me."

"No, Mr. Jenks," I answered. "In your presence sarcasm drops dead. I think you'll prosper in politics."

But there I was wrong. There is some natural justice in these events, though I wish there were more. The jury, it is true, soon seemed oddly prosperous, as Stirling wrote me afterwards. They painted their houses; two of them, who had generally walked before, now had wagons; and in so many of their gardens and small ranches did the plants and fruits increase that, as Stirling put it, they had evidently sowed their dollars. But upon Jenks territorial displeasure did descend. He had stayed away too much from Washington. A pamphlet appeared with the title, "What Luke Jenks Has Done for Arizona." Inside were twenty blank pages, and he failed of re-election.

Furthermore, the government retaliated upon this district by abandoning Camp Thomas and Lowell Barracks, those important sources of revenue for the neighborhood. The brief boom did not help Tucson very long, and left it poorer than ever.

At the station I saw Mrs. Sproud and black curly, neither speaking to the other. It was plain that he had utterly done with her, and that she was too proud even to look at him. She went West, and he as far east as Willcox. Neither one have I ever seen again.

But I have the photograph, and I sometimes wonder what has happened to black curly. Arizona is still a territory; and when I think of the Gila Valley and of the Boy Orator, I recall Bishop Meakum's remark about our statesmen at Washington: "You can divide them birds in two lots—those who know better, and those who don't. D'you follow me?"

ENDNOTES

INTRODUCTION

[1] Owen Wister, "The Evolution of the Cow-Puncher," *Harper's New Monthly Magazine* 91 (September 1895): 603–604.
[2] Owen Wister, *The Virginian: A Horseman of the Plains* (Lincoln: University of Nebraska Press, 1992), 36, 57, 71, 56.
[3] Wister, "Cow-Puncher," 604, 606.
[4] Owen Wister, *Members of the Family* (New York: Macmillan, 1911), 9–11.

THE GENERAL'S BLUFF

[1] Let me no longer pervert General Crook's military tactics. It was a dismounted charge that he ordered on this occasion, as a friend who was present has written me since the first publication of this story.

SUGGESTED READING

ATHEARN, ROBERT G. *The Mythic West in Twentieth-Century America.* Lawrence: University Press of Kansas, 1986.

BOLD, CHRISTINE. *Selling the Wild West: Popular Western Fiction, 1860 to 1960.* Bloomington: Indiana University Press, 1987.

ETULAIN, RICHARD W. *Re-Imagining the Modern American West: A Century of Fiction, History, and Art.* Tucson: University of Arizona Press, 1996.

GRAULICH, MELODY, AND STEPHEN TATUM, EDS. *Reading "The Virginian" in the New West.* Lincoln: University of Nebraska Press, 2003.

LUTZ, TOM. *American Nervousness, 1903: An Anecdotal History.* Ithaca, NY: Cornell University Press, 1991.

SLOTKIN, RICHARD. *Gunfighter Nation: The Myth of the Frontier in Twentieth-Century America.* New York: Atheneum, 1992.

SMITH, SHERRY L. *The View from Officers' Row: Army Perceptions of Western Indians.* Tucson: University of Arizona Press, 1990.

TUTTLE, JENNIFER S. "Rewriting the West Cure: Charlotte Perkins Gilman, Owen Wister, and the Sexual Politics of Neurasthenia." In *The Mixed Legacy of Charlotte Perkins Gilman,* edited by Catherine J. Golden and Joanna Schneider Zangrando, 103–21. Newark: University of Delaware Press, 2000.

UTLEY, ROBERT M. *Frontier Regulars: The United States Army and the Indian, 1866–1891.* New York: Macmillan, 1973.

UTLEY, ROBERT M., AND WILCOMB E. WASHBURN. *Indian Wars.* Boston: Houghton Mifflin, 2002.